RIVER CITY BLUES

Ward Howarth

For Vaughn

It is a father's burden
That he pass to his son
Not only his hopes and dreams
But his vices and afflictions, as well.

During World War II, the armed forces gave birth to a host of military slang terms, many of which were expressed by way of acronyms.

For example, **SNAFU** stands for the sarcastic expression *situation normal, all fouled up*. Similarly, **SUSFU** stands for *situation unchanged, still fouled up* while **FUBAR** stands for *fouled up beyond all recognition*.

SNAFU

December 31, 1943 — January 8, 1944

CHAPTER ONE

BENNIE AND NILES scoped the old building from unmarked wheels across the street. They were huddled up in an alleyway off Cary at 18th, just north of Tobacco Row. The takedown had them operating in First Station's bailiwick unannounced, and they were sure to catch flak for it.

Bennie studied their mark. Low rent apartments and a rusty fire escape sat over Pearl's lunch counter, a first floor dive that doubled as a contraband drop. Bennie scanned the hot sheet for possible finds: counterfeit ration books and stamps, shoes, sugar. Each one commanded top dollar on the black market.

Det. Lt. Jack Reed and his partner, Det. Sgt. Eugene Mills, were parked in their own unmarked just south of the building, diagonally across from Bennie and Niles. Bennie reviewed their plan. On Reed's signal, they would storm in, secure any goods or materials, and detain anyone on the premises for questioning. The use of force was strongly encouraged. Jack's emphasis, but Bennie knew the directive came straight from The Cane, under pressure from more bad press and politico fear-mongering.

Niles stretched out in the passenger seat. Car bound stakeouts made you stiff.

"See anything?" he asked.

"Negative," said Bennie.

Niles huffed. "Boy, I sure hope this delivers. Traffic detail's the pits."

"You put in for a transfer yet?"

"*This* morning. The Cane says it shouldn't take too long. Says they grease the skids at city hall for the V Squad."

V as in Victory, aka The Victory Squad, the department's newest desk, formed in response to a citywide uptick in wartime crime.

"Good," said Bennie. "I need a proper partner. Every week, it's someone new."

"Did you hear they hired someone out of the 'Pen last week?"

"No shit?"

"No shit. Guy did a deuce for burglary. Jack says they hired him for his *expertise*, can you believe that?"

"Hell, it's wartime. I'll believe anything."

Bennie rolled his neck and yawned big. Bad dreams and broken sleep, two nights running. Jungle nightmares on repeat. He caught his reflection in the rearview: tired blue eyes, two-day stubble, his buzz cut running long. He made a mental note: see Walter and get a trim ASAP.

A car drove by and they sat up, alert. No signal came their way. They cracked the windows and relaxed. The scent of tobacco charged the air. Somewhere, in the distance, Bennie heard whispers of *Auld Lang Syne*.

"So," said Niles, "you ever figure out how many Japs you killed?"

A running joke between them. Bennie flashed on Jap bodies and severed limbs. He had engaged a minimum of fifteen close range kills in the jungle. A few of them eyeball to eyeball.

"Enough," said Bennie.

"That many, huh?"

"Shit, I practically won the war."

Light chuckles. A long beat that stretched on and on. No signal from Jack. The two men shuffled in their seats. They were both antsy for it to get going.

"Well, whatever happens tonight," said Niles," I hope it doesn't go long. Cheryl Lee got her points today and found us a couple of lamb chops." He grinned and licked his lips like some cartoon wolf.

Niles was a gas, all six feet and two hundred pounds of him. A traffic cop by day, he was on loan to the Victory Squad for tonight's raid. Color blindness kept him from active service, not that he minded. Niles was a family man through and through, with a wife and two kids. His size paid dividends for the department. In his off hours, Niles doubled as the policemen's resident bruiser, raising dough for the retirees' pension fund by trading fists with some heel on the fire squad.

An engine's purr put them both on edge. A delivery truck coasted to a stop in front of Pearl's. A moment later, the driver stepped out. Soft footsteps carried him to Pearl's front door and inside the joint.

Time stood still. Bennie felt his nerves quiver. Niles shadow-boxed, throwing quick jabs and hooks. Bennie fingered his shoulder clip for reassurance, his loaded .38 a comfort.

They were to wait for Jack's signal before approaching the door: three pulses from an air raid warden's flashlight.

On third light, Jack and Eugene would storm Pearl's back door while Bennie and Niles came in from the street.

Seconds ticked away.

A full minute passed.

Bennie and Niles exchanged looks: *What the hell?*

Then, all at once: a crash/screams/gunshots.

GO.

Bennie and Niles padded around the truck, flanking opposite sides of the street door. Bennie two-handed his gun, tingling. He felt the jungle all around him.

Their backs hit the wall.

Their eyes locked.

Bennie nodded: do it *NOW*.

Niles walloped the door with the butt of his shotgun, breaking it from the hinges. Mayhem inside: more shots and screams. Bennie turned and kicked the door all the way in. Instincts threw him to the floor. He rolled inside and came up drawing on three armed Negroes. One of them turned to fire at Bennie. Niles caught him square in the chest with a round of buckshot. The other two Negroes went cold and dropped their guns.

"Sherwood!"

Bennie quick-scanned the room. There, near the back: Jack and Eugene, hunched on the floor, a pool of blood between them.

"Out the back," Jack shouted, nodding toward the rear.

Bennie caught the fumes of a shadow on its way out. He threw a quick glance back at Niles: the big boxer, his stone-locked arms glued to the shotgun, his face flooded with this *look*. The one you got from taking another man's life.

Jack yelled, "Sherwood!"

Bennie leapt to his feet and darted out the back door. His night vision kicked in. *There*, across the alley, that apartment building — a screen door teetered off its hinges.

Bennie crossed the alley and vaulted a back stairwell, bumping walls. A tight fit: steep steps in a narrow corridor. Drops of blood led the way. He smashed through a doorway into the main foyer, expecting the worst. Instead, he heard distant footsteps above, slowing. He found more stairs and risked a peek. A bullet missed him by inches and caught the railing. Wood chips showered him and sent him reeling against the wall. His legs went wobbly, his temples pulsed.

Island flashes: Jap/knife/blood/eyes.

Everything spinning.

Three floors up, a woman shrieked.

Straight courage brought him out of it. Bennie spit sawdust and hoofed.

He spilled onto the top floor with shaky legs, panting. An open apartment, ten feet away. He followed his gun past a blood-marked door, inching his way inside. An upended lamp shed eerie light on strewn furnishings: a wooden rocker, capsized; spilled flowers; a coffee table on its side.

There, on the floor: blood trails led a path toward the back. Bennie started that way when an old biddy lunged at him with a cast-iron fryer, catching him good on his right shoulder.

"Away! Away, now!" she hissed, waving the pan, wild and ghostlike in a white nightgown, her hair done up in curlers.

Bennie badged her. "RPD, Lady! Police!"

"Get out of here," she scoffed. "Both of you!"

Bennie snatched the pan from her. "Shh," he said, holding a finger to his mouth. He pointed toward the back, inquisitive. She nodded, spooked. "Please, go out into the hallway," he whispered. Reluctant, she tiptoed off. Bennie started to chuck the pan into an armchair and thought better of it.

He moved down the cramped hallway. His .38 in one hand, the frying pan in the other. Streaks of moonlight hit the bathroom door, revealing blood smears. Bennie crept forward a few feet and chucked the pan inside.

KERRCHING!

A shot hit the pan. An echo rang out. Bennie slid into the room and drew a bead on a figure hiding behind a ragtag shower curtain.

"RPD," Bennie called out. "We got a bus coming, so make it easy on yourself. We can talk at the hospital."

Bennie heard strained breathing. He took a step and stopped. Blood, all over the floor. He almost slipped.

Then, this choked-up Southern drawl: "Bennie Sherwood, is that you?"

Bennie wrestled his instincts, fighting with it. Then he said it slow, as if he were afraid of the answer.

"Skipper?"

From behind the curtain, a coughing fit ensued. Bennie steadied himself with the wall. He shuffled to the tub and drew the curtain back. Shit: Skipper Holly, laid out in a blood bath.

"Jesus," winced Bennie. "Come on, let's get you downstairs."

Bennie moved to lift him, but Skipper held him off.

"Nah, just let me lay here a minute."

"Skipper, come on, there's still time." Bennie heard commotion out in the hallway. Make it the old lady, rattling off to Jack.

"I thought you was them, come to finish me off."

Bennie couldn't stand it any longer. "Damn it, we're getting you out of here, *now*."

Skipper retched blood and phlegm all over the tub. Bennie reeled back, wiser. Lift him or let him sit, it didn't matter. He was a goner.

Skipper pulled a pack of smokes from his shirt pocket. Pulled one out and lipped it. He reached into his jacket and found a matchbook. He struck one, lit the smoke, and inhaled deep. A calm came over him, like some immeasurable peace.

"I heard about your old man, Bennie. A real shame."

"Yeah. Yeah, it is."

Skipper gargled blood and coughed as if his soul were coming apart. Bennie caught blood on his face and flinched.

"My mother," Skipper forced out, "she lives over on Grace. Works days at Tredegar. I want you to go and see her for me, tell her I died good, ok? Tell her I died doing something good for the war."

"Sure thing," said Bennie, grimacing. The smell of Skipper's wound made him gag. It was a smell he knew all too well.

"Do it right. Make it stick, Bennie. Make it sing."

Bennie nodded, speechless. He had comforted no less than seven men in their final moments on Guadalcanal. Here he was again, brothered up with a dying man in shit circumstances.

Skipper put the pack of smokes and matchbook in Bennie's hand.

"Save those, Bennie," wheezed Skipper. "You might need 'em."

"I don't smoke."

Skipper laughed at that, and then he gave out all at once, trembling as the light went out in his eyes. His neck went limp. Bennie jerked forward and caught his head so it wouldn't bang the tub. He let it rest against his arms, and then he just sat there, holding him.

CHAPTER TWO

MID-DAY LIGHT filled the Annex squadroom. Tables and chairs angled toward a lectern. Behind it, the wall-width case board loomed large. It was sectioned three ways: ongoings, warrants, and wartime protocol. Above it hung framed photographs of every department man killed in the line of duty. They ran in sequence: first to last, left to right, two rows deep. Bennie found the old man frowning down on him from the last spot. His stern glare, preserved for all time: coal black hair, cut short; misshapen nose, forever swollen; diamond-hard eyes, probing for weakness. Bennie half-expected him to reach out from the frame and thrash him as he turned away.

The room hummed with pencil work. Six men sat at a table and filled out forms while a sergeant watchdogged. Bennie slow-walked around them and made for the coffee station. He lit up at the sight of homemade crullers, a regular gift from a few of the cops' wives. He wolfed one and poured himself a cup of joe.

He shot a look out an east facing window. Broad Street traffic was heavy. Troop trucks and street cars, mostly. A few taxis, some buses. People on the move donned coats and scarves. Winter temps were chilly.

Bennie topped off his cup and took the hall to 202, the detective's lair. Twelve desks fought for space in a cramped room. No windows, dim light. An ever-present mix of smoke and must in the air. In a word, dingy, save for the wall-to-wall pin-up girls that gave it pizzazz. Rita Hayworth, Betty Grable, Jane Russell, Ava Gardner.

Bennie took up at his desk and leafed through the carbons in his mail tray. One was a summary of the weekend's arrests. He sipped his coffee and whistled. Some real doozies, he thought.

— Three claims of rape were tied to one man, a GI on liberty from Camp Peary, now in the hands of the MPs.

— A dozen break-ins were reported citywide; early hunches pointed to a youth gang.

— Drunk-tank overload: over a hundred civilians and military riffraff were drying out in the jails.

— Whispers of *Klan* and *Nazi* activity were making the rounds; everyone was to keep their eyes and ears open.

— And a scuffle at the Jefferson Hotel uncovered several hundred counterfeit ration coupons; their owner was a noted bagman for Senator Byrd.

Nestled in with the carbons was a handbill. It advertised a bond drive at Tantilla Garden this Saturday night. The shindig was sponsored by King Tobacco — the newest player in the city's tobacco game. Bennie felt his nerves flutter: TG was cooze central. If he went, maybe he'd meet someone.

Bennie pushed the carbons aside and drank his coffee. He was stalling. Jack had demanded his report on Pearl's before roll call today and he hadn't written a single word. He'd thought only of Skipper for two days straight. How resigned he'd been in his final moments, how accepting of death. As if he welcomed it.

A couple of chatty afternoon bulls made the lair. They ignored Bennie and talked amongst themselves. Bennie got a look at the wall clock. It was 3:40PM. He had twenty minutes.

Bennie forced himself from his desk and hustled to the typewriter. He fed it a sheet of paper and got to work.

Pearl's was but two days old and yet it felt like ancient history. Bennie prodded his mind and found the beats, tracking the events from the alleyway to the old biddy's bathroom. He made a direct aside to Jack on their missed flashlight signal, tossing it off as bad communication. He noted Niles' kill shot, recommended a psych eval, and asked to be personally involved in anything related to Skipper's investigation. He read it through a few times under his breath, checking for spelling errors and narrative clarity. Satisfied, he pulled it from the typewriter and signed it.

A check on the wall clock — *shit.*

Bennie jerked from the chair and darted from the room.

The squadroom buzzed: the night shift, filing in. Yawns and chit-chat circled the room. Bennie cut through the crowd and beelined for the coffee pot. Glares came his way. Five months on the job and still the resentment was hot.

Floor smacks and foot drags drifted in from the hall. The room got quiet fast. The sounds grew louder and louder until, finally, Chief Reed stormed the threshold, balancing on his walking stick as he lumbered through the room. The Cane moved like an injured bull determined to live, his defect be damned. He banged his rod against the wall as he lurched forward.

"Quit standing around," he barked. "This ain't the Commonwealth Club. We've got work to do, so put your asses in seats, ladies, and get your eyes forward."

The room scrambled for chairs. Bennie chose to stand and leaned against a pillar. Jack slinked into the room and hugged an opposite wall. He and Bennie exchanged curt nods.

The Cane took up at the lectern. "By now, you've all heard about Pearl's, so I'll skip the summary and cover results. Detective Mills is in stable condition and the recovered goods represent at best one percent of what's available on the street."

The Cane let the words ring out.

"In other words, ladies, horseshit! We must do better. Our soldiers demand it, the people of this city demand it. We now know for certain that Pearl's operated a side menu of rationed goods, and we suspect that other dives around town have the same racket going. We'll start there. I want inquiries into diners, confectionaries, nightclubs. Go as plainclothesmen in teams of two. Blend in, soak up the atmosphere, glom what you can. Imbibe if you must to keep cover, but one drink only. I won't have any stumblebums on the job. Now that we've shut down one operation, business is sure to pick up at another. The time to strike is now! Jack has a list. See him for assignments so you don't double up. Any questions?"

A vice bull piped up. "We got a line on Pearl's owner?"

From the back of the room, Jack said, "We ran down the business license on file at city hall. The owner knew zilch about under-the-table perks. Said a cousin ran the place. He's MIA."

Shrugs around the room. The Cane took up again.

"Now, before we move on, I invite you to look around the room and notice the new mugs we have with us today. I've asked a few of our more dutiful auxillary officers to join the night squad until we get this mess under control. Introduce yourselves and make nice, they'll be with us for a while."

Bennie scanned the room. Sure enough, the six paperwork men sat amongst the regular night corps. None of the other officers said a word to any of them.

Most of the AOs who came to the department were too old to fight for Uncle Sam. The rest were an even mix of 4F rejects, schlubs, and men generally unfit for the RPD. Each one got a temporary badge and a limited range of assignment. They were forbidden to work alone and got little respect from bona fide cops.

"Now," said The Cane. "It has come to my attention that policemen-led convoys en route to Camp Lee have been stopping off at Miss Westerman's and Miss Potter's on their way through town. No doubt bribes have been involved. I'm here to tell you this will stop immediately! Cherry and Doris have no problems drubbing up business on their own, I'm certain they don't need our help. Is this understood?"

Hushed grunts swept the room.

"Gentlemen, we may be short on men, but I will not hesitate to quit the next man guilty of this horseshit. As you can see, in this very room, we've plenty of men ready to take your place. And you'd do well to stay out of the cathouses yourselves. We've got enough VD in this city already."

Feet shuffles and shifty bodies: Bennie figured at least half the room was infected.

"Last order of business from me," said The Cane, a

smile taking shape on his face, "is a promotion. Niles Hunter, please come forward."

Niles shuffled to the front. He looked rather sullen for someone about to be promoted. Taking a life will do that to you.

"By now," said The Cane, proudly, "you've all heard of Niles' courageous behavior at Pearl's. With our desks in such need of standup men, it's my great honor to elevate him to the role of Junior Detective. He'll join the Victory Squad, effective today."

Niles and The Cane shook hands as claps and applause made the room. Niles looked altogether uneasy and faked a smile.

The Cane tore out of the room, his rod and legs striking desks on the way out. Jack took up in front and surveyed the crowd. He was 5'10", trim. Young and healthy, with good hair. A Marine Corps recruiter's wet dream. He would have served, too, were it not for the draft deferment he'd elected on account of the department's manpower shortage. He would have made a hell of a drill sergeant, thought Bennie. Rigid demeanor, cold eyes, all the warmth of an icicle.

"Good afternoon," said Jack. "For the benefit of our temporary recruits, I'll review our recent caseload and address our priorities moving forward."

Jack drug the lectern to the side. Everyone got a good look at the ongoing section of the case board. "On the night of Wednesday, December 1, 1943," he said, "a delivery vehicle carrying approximately 500 pounds of sugar was hijacked as it traveled from Petersburg to Richmond. The way the driver told it, he came upon a stopped car with a raised front hood. Suspecting engine trouble, the driver offered assistance, but was instead held up by two men with 12-gauge pump shotguns. According to the driver, these men wore gas masks and demanded the truck's keys. Without resistance, the driver complied with the request and watched as the two men drove both the car and the truck away."

Jack shuffled over to the warrants section. A couple of bulls scribbled notes. One of them craned Bennie's way and shot him the bird.

"The driver," Jack said, pointing at Skipper's mug shot, "was this man, Skipper Holly." Skipper, a mug-shot regular, smirked for the camera.

"As most of you know," Jack continued, "Mr. Holly died as the result of a gunshot wound sustained during the raid on Pearl's. His presence there leads us to believe he was in on the truck hijack from the beginning. While we may never know what truly happened, one thing is decidedly clear. The market for these goods is hot and if we don't get a leg up on who's responsible, we may never get in front of it. I want you all to think hard about everyone you see. Where are they going? How are they getting there? Do they look as if they can afford the car they're driving, or the clothes they have on? We've been at this war awhile, gentlemen. People are tired of sacrifice, they're cutting corners. It's our job to stop them. Any questions?"

The room shrugged. Jack smacked the case board. The room jumped.

"This isn't a joke, gentlemen," he said. "I expect you to plug hard out there and put a stop to all this."

The room chorused in agreement. Jack tacked a list to the board.

"Here are the assignments the Chief told you about. Detectives will pair with aux — "

Groans swept the room en masse.

"Enough! These men are here to help us, so put a lid on it. Detectives will pair with auxillary officers and take on two locations a night. Reports on the previous night's scouting are due before the following day's roll call. Is this understood?"

Assertive yeses across the board. Jack scanned the room, hunting for dissent. He met Bennie's eyes and went somber.

"Also," Jack said, pointing at the framed photograph of Bennie's father, "we're still on the hunt for any information concerning the murder of police lieutenant Samuel Sherwood. If you need a refresher, the details surrounding his case are here on the board."

The men looked around: at the walls, at the floor, at each other. They shrugged their shoulders and bit their fingernails.

"Alright," said Jack. "Dismissed."

The room got to its feet fast and made for the assignment list. Men partnered up and left the room in twos. Bennie checked the list. He was on it alright, sans a partner.

He found Jack at his desk. His office was quasi-spartan. Two chairs slanted toward an oak desk, bare save for a pad, a pen, and a stack of summary sheets. The walls were free of decoration. No war bond posters, no VD warnings. Just a prim row of essential department reports tacked in place along a very straight line.

Jack looked up from the report he was reading and said, "What is it, Detective?"

Bennie said, "How's Mills?"

"Mills is fine."

"Good. That's good to hear."

"Anything else?" Impatient Jack.

"It's just…"

"What?"

"I'm on my own. Nobody to partner with tonight. What about Niles?"

"I've put Niles with an AO for this assignment. He demonstrated a good deal of courage at Pearl's. I need that sharpness out on the streets tonight."

"But if I hit a few of those joints solo, I'll stick out like a sore thumb."

Jack sighed. "Fair enough. Visit Mr. Holly's mother and see what you can learn about his life and his employment history. Start there, and see where it leads us."

Bennie was terrified, remembering his promise to Skipper. "No one's been to see her yet?"

"She knows of her son's passing, but not of the circumstances. Perhaps you could design a more… noble scenario."

"You'd be ok with that?"

"I'm ok with anything that gets us a lead. I'll expect word from you on the matter later today."

Bennie turned and made for the lair. Knots began to take shape in his stomach. Christ, he thought. What do I say to her?

As Bennie passed The Cane's office, the elder Reed's voice boomed into the hall.

"Bennie Sherwood, a word."

Bennie cut over to The Cane's office, thankful for the distraction. He stepped inside and looked around, marveling at the history. Cop clippings crowded the walls. Framed photographs of past police chiefs hung above them.

"Shut the door, son," said The Cane. "Let's jaw a bit."

Bennie eased the door closed and leaned against a file cabinet. "What can I do for you, Chief?"

"How are you faring after the other night?"

"Pearl's? Just needed some rest. Slept all of yesterday. I'm here, I'm ready."

The Cane took his time. "I was worried it might have been a little too... close to home."

Bennie felt his nerves quiver. It had been just over a year since he'd left the 'Canal. He could still smell the jungle, here and now, and feel its damp air on his skin. "I'm fine," lied Bennie. "It's in the past, over and done with."

"And what of the other men here? Have they warmed to you yet?"

"Not exactly."

The Cane scowled. "You can blame that on me. I jumped you to Detective in deference to your father. Didn't think they'd hang you out to dry over it."

"Maybe it's better I work alone. He always did."

"You're right about that," said The Cane. A knowing look passed between them. The old man had been a lone avenger, always off on some crusade. "In any case, if anyone gives you any shit, send them to me."

"Yes, sir."

The Cane's phone rang. He picked it up and barked a greeting. Laughs followed. "Hold on," he said, shouldering the receiver. "Be safe out there, son."

Bennie nodded and turned to leave. The sight of a familiar photograph stopped him: The Cane, the old man, and himself at 12, celebrating the downfall of a Church Hill whiskey still.

CHAPTER THREE

BENNIE STEPPED OUT of the Annex and saw them right off. Three newsboys, chumming down at the corner, fishing for police scoops. One of them honed in on Bennie and beelined his way.

"Say, pal, are you with the cops?" A kid, maybe 16 years old. He sported a crewcut, a bow tie, and an ear-to-ear grin.

Bennie just nodded. He was suit-and-tied, his badge out of sight. Department regs mandated plainclothes attire for all case men.

The kid feigned a bow and rattled off a rehearsed spiel. "Archie Smith, at your service. I'm an up-and-comer, as it were, making my way through the mean streets of Richmond by way of the newspaper business. I'd be grateful for any tips or leads that get the copy editor off my back and helps a few dollars change pockets, if you catch my drift. What do you say?"

Bennie let out a smile. The kid had charm. He thought back to those arrest carbons. That bit from the Jefferson was juicy and might get the kid some ink. But before he could say anything, Archie's eyes went wide. "Say, you're Bennie Sherwood!"

"And what if I am?"

"You're big news, is what. Say, you guys any closer to figuring out who clipped your old man?" Just like that, like it was no big deal.

Bennie scowled and started to walk away.

"Nobody clipped my father, you runt. He died in the line of duty, serving the people of this city. Now scram."

"Hey, look, I'm sorry," said Archie, on Bennie's heels like a stray dog. "It's just, he used to talk about you, you know?"

"Who?"

"Your old man. He used to talk about you all the time at the news briefings. Say, what was it like on Guadalcanal?"

Bennie's stomach knots twisted, his palms got clammy. "Hell, you outta know, it was all over the papers."

"You bring home a Jap sword?" This kid and his big eyes, all excited.

Bennie thought of his island keepsakes: acute memories of death and dysentery; a newfound respect for life and all living things; a distrust of any and everything *Jap*.

"No, kid. No Jap sword."

"Say, you want to get together on *that* story?" Archie talked lightning quick. "Tell me how it really was, I might even get it front page. Boy, the inside scoop! My boss'll have berserks! What do you say?"

"Yeah, kid, I don't know. Listen — "

"I'm telling you, your old man, he'd gush about you being this big war hero."

A knot in Bennie's stomach strangled itself. Bennie grabbed the kid by his collar and glared daggers into him.

"You quit my old man, you hear me?"

Archie swallowed hard and went cold. "Yeah, ok, sorry."

The kid hurried off. Bennie felt his pulse skyrocket. He got dizzy. There, by the curb, sat his unmarked Roadster, an all black job with thin white lines along the length of both sides. He lurched toward it and steadied himself against the door.

Deep breaths righted him. Inhale, exhale, repeat. Just like they taught him. He threw himself inside the car, fired it up, and pulled out onto Broad. He shot a quick look back over his shoulder, scouring for Jap ghosts.

Ms. Holly looked up at Bennie from the thinning couch on which she sat and surveyed him with tired, glassed-over eyes. She was older than Bennie remembered, an irrelevant detail that he dismissed, considering. She had the colorless look of someone who'd not eaten in several days and, despite her meager frame, appeared altogether immovable from the couch. She brushed frayed, unkempt strands of hair from her face and said, "Yes, I do remember you. Baseball, I believe it was."

"Yes, m'am, before the war."

"*That's* right. He did talk about you from time to time. Bennie this, Bennie that. And then you went to war, is that right?"

"Yes, m'am. With the Marines."

"And here you are, all in one piece. Poor Skipper. He so badly wanted to go."

Bennie hadn't seen the autopsy report yet. "If you don't mind me asking, Ms. Holly, why couldn't Skipper serve?"

"Perforated ear drum. You want some coffee?"

"Yes, m'am, that'd be just fine."

She rose from the couch slowly, like an animal come to

stand after a long rest, and hobbled to the kitchen. Alone now, Bennie was too nervous to sit, so he stood and took in the room. As living rooms went, it was worse for wear. Clothing was scattered over the couch and chairs. Liquor empties littered the floor and an ashtray overflowed with butts on a side table.

Bennie found signs of life on a front window sill. Photographs of Skipper, all in a row: Skipper at 10, devouring cotton candy by the seaside; Skipper at 18, receiving his high school diploma; Skipper, more recent, a resigned look on his face, standing beside snazzy wheels. A Chevy convertible. '38, maybe.

Ms. Holly returned with the coffee. "I've just a little sugar left, but you're welcome to it."

"No, thank you," said Bennie, reaching for his cup. Nerves almost sent it toppling over. He downed it in three gulps. The heat gave him a rush and he said it fast. "Ms. Holly, I've come to tell you how Skipper was killed."

She paused mid-sip. "Oh?"

"Yes," said Bennie, slowing himself down. "On New Year's Eve, Skipper was dining at Pearl's, a local diner, when two men held the place up. They demanded the owner empty his register, but the owner refused, so the stick-up men threatened to harm the patrons until he complied. Two witnesses have confirmed that Skipper tried to intervene on the owner's behalf and was killed in the process."

Ms. Holly set her coffee down and reclined into the couch. Tears welled in her eyes. After a time, she said, "Why wasn't this told to me when they came to tell me he was dead?"

Bennie cleared his throat. "The location of the shooting is part of a larger investigation being carried out by the department. For security reasons, we have to keep that information private." Bennie felt as if bullshit were oozing from his ears.

"Well, what about the two men? What's going to happen to them?" She was getting angrier by the minute.

"They were killed resisting arrest, Ms. Holly."

"Well, then, I want to see their bodies, I want to see their faces. I want to see who did this to him!"

Bennie wasn't sure how much longer he could keep this up. "Ms. Holly, that's not a good idea. And anyway, I don't believe it's allowed. Only kin's allowed at the morgue. You're welcome to see Skipper, if you'd like."

The words rolled off his tongue before he could stop them. Ms. Holly recoiled in horror and sobbed. Bennie felt like a heel. He wanted to crawl back to Guadalcanal and bury himself in the sand.

When she could cry no more, Ms. Holly wiped her eyes with a handkerchief and sat up. She took a drink of coffee and reached for her purse. She pulled out a pack of River City Sovereigns, a homespun brand of King Tobacco cigarettes, and lipped one.

"Would you like one, Detective?"

"No, m'am. Thanks all the same."

She lit the cigarette and took a long pull. Calm found her and steadied her breath. She was thousand-yard-stare lost. Bennie knew the look well. He forced life into his legs and moved to leave when she spoke.

"Skipper didn't start smoking until after he was working for King. They gave him a pack with his pay and he often shared them with me."

"King *who*, Ms. Holly?"

"Why, Mr. *Jedidiah* King. You know who he is, don't you?"

27

Bennie knew *of* him. Man about town, head honcho of King Tobacco, a high society type. Squadroom rebop had him pegged as a strange cat who frequented Jackson Ward jazz clubs in his off hours.

"Yes, m'am, I'm aware of him."

"He might be the nicest man in this whole city. He took Skipper in for a job when no one else would. Treated him real nice, too."

A lead, thought Bennie. He pulled out his steno and started to take notes. "Ms. Holly, do you recall when Skipper went to work for Mr. King?"

"Oh, about a year after Pearl Harbor. When Uncle Sam wouldn't take him, he knocked around town, mad as hell. He didn't want to do anything but go to war. He'd get drunk, get himself into a scrape. Even got himself locked up a few times. I think it was during one of those spells in jail that a fella offered him a job working for Mr. King. After that, he didn't get into anymore trouble."

Bennie's heart sank as he jotted notes into his steno. He couldn't look her in the eyes.

"Ms. Holly, by any chance, do you recall this person's name? The one in jail that offered Skipper a job?"

"No. I never met anyone Skipper worked with, save for Mr. King." Suddenly, she grew alarmed. "Do you think he knows, Detective? About Skipper? Someone should tell him."

"I'll see to it personally." Enough, thought Bennie. "Ms. Holly, I'm so sorry about Skipper," he said, coming to his feet. "If there's anything the department can do for you, please let me know."

She beamed at him. "You look like him, you know?"

Bennie just stood there, too frozen to move.

"He was a good boy, wasn't he?"

"Yes, m'am, he was."

She sank into the couch and beamed at him a little longer before her eyes drifted off and away.

CHAPTER FOUR

BENNIE STEERED HIS unmarked eastbound and took Broad Street slow. A check on the gas gauge: running high. He had time to take it easy.

His chat with Ms. Holly had him feeling sad and nostalgic. He downed the volume on the two-way and let his mind drift *back*.

Spring, 1941. Bennie is 17 and attends high school. He lives with his father in the Church Hill district of Richmond. His mother is MIA, going on five years.

The old man is both caring and cantankerous. He is *the* most notorious detective on the RPD, known for his brash attitude and his penchant for fist work. He and Bennie share a love of baseball and bond over their abandonment.

Bennie is a so-so student and an excellent second baseman. Among his classmates is Jack Reed, son of another well known policeman, Lt. Stolmy Reed, aka The Cane. While Bennie ropes moonshots for the varsity baseball team, Jack toys with his Bunsen burner at the local science fair.

The talk of war makes Bennie uneasy. He cuts class, skeptical of his future. He finds solace playing scratch baseball on sandlots throughout the city. He meets Skipper Holly, a crackerjack shortstop. Together, they ace double plays and sip moonshine between innings.

Bennie's father threatens him with jail time if he doesn't return to school. A class assembly on his first day back redirects him. A Marine Corps recruiter talks war and service. Bennie gets this *idea*: if we don't help win the war, there won't *be* any baseball.

Bennie's decision to enlist levels the old man. Their last moments together are wrought with tears and silence.

Boot camp follows: six weeks of hell on Parris Island. Then, to New River, NC, and the First Marine Division. Bennie is made a mortar man and assigned to the 1st Battalion, 5th Marine Regiment, Delta Company. AKA the D-1-5.

The D-1-5 sails from Norfolk, VA, in May, 1942, en route to Wellington and Fiji. Bennie is restless and frightened. He's unnerved by the names of islands he can hardly pronounce, much less spell.

August, 7, 1942: Bennie's in the first wave to hit Red Beach on Guadalcanal. He endures three months of mosquitoes, torrential rain, and mass humidity. He drops 15 pounds. He develops a third eye in the jungle and trades his mortar for knives. He makes a friend of terror and hunts Japs in the night.

Wounds and malaria take their toll. Bennie is shipped to San Diego Naval Hospital in late November, 1942. His head hurts and he panics on a dime. He's unsure about his contribution to the war. He's a proud Marine but his bloodlust unsettles him. He begins to fear returning home. What will he do? Who will he be?

July, 1943. Eight months of recovery find Bennie's body on the mend and his mind on the fritz. He can move, run, and fight, but his thoughts are dark. His nightmares are worse.

On the eve of his medical discharge, Bennie receives a telegram from The Cane. The old man is dead, killed in the line of duty.

Bennie jettisons home. He finds the police department stretched thin. He's livid: inept detectives are bumbling his father's investigation.

He demands access to the case files. The Cane makes him a deal: work for me and you can lead the investigation yourself. Bennie is jumped to Detective Sergeant on account of his war service and his many years of exposure to police work. He's assigned to the Victory Squad, but ignores his assignments and devotes himself to the old man's case.

Five months pass. Lt. Samuel Sherwood's murder case goes nowhere while the local ration rackets pick up steam. The Cane threatens Bennie with dismissal: work cases you can *solve* or hit the road. Bennie puts renewed focus into the job. He finds that police work steadies his mind and calms his nerves. His clearance rate improves. His attention to the old man's case wanes.

The shift in priorities leaves Bennie in conflict. He mourns his father but enjoys his work. He longs for his Marine brethren but relishes his life as a civilian. He's prone to panic and overloaded with feelings of guilt and rage.

Tremors ran through Bennie's hands. He felt his body shake and jerked the car into an adjoining lane. Horns and screams came his way.

He curbed his wheels and caught his breath. That trip down memory lane had him on overdrive.

Lying to Ms. Holly rankled him, too. He sought to admonish his guilt with work. That promise to her: follow up with Mr. King. Make it happen *now.*

Bennie took to the sidewalk in search of a call box. He saw one two streets up and upped his pace. Along the way, he passed a few newsboys hawking the bulldog edition. It looked chock full of war news and Pearl's speculation. Bennie regretted his behavior toward that kid reporter. He should have been nicer.

He came to the call box and dialed the Annex direct: 3-8381. A dispatcher routed him to the records room. Bennie tapped the box, hopeful. *Ring, ring, ring, ring, ring...*

"Hello?" A deep, scratchy voice, care of Everett Brown, RPD records clerk. Cranky and pushing 60, Everett was an RPD lifer. Story was, he'd caught a bullet in the aughts and retired from field work, but had always harbored an itch for detective work.

"This is Detective Sherwood, Everett."

"Yeah, so?" Typical Everett: unimpressed.

"Jedidiah King," said Bennie. "What do we have?"

"What do you want with him?"

Bennie detected an air of excitement in Everett's voice. "I'm doing follow up on Pearl's. His name came up."

Everett whistled. "I'm not sure you'll find anything. He's pretty clean. Bond drives, charities. Top notch tobacco, too."

"Well, whatever it is, I'd still like to dig into it. How about carbons on my desk within the hour?"

"Yeah, sure."

"Say, is Jack around?"

"No, why?"

"He asked me to report in on my afternoon."

"He ran down to Camp Lee, something about a new lead in the sugar hijack. Made a big deal about it, too. Corralled the squadroom and told everyone."

All systems go, thought Bennie. With the bulk of men casing hash joints tonight, Jack had to put in extra legwork. "I'll leave him a note when I stop in. An hour for those carbons, ok?"

"Sure thing."

Bennie hung up fast. He had an hour to kill. He weighed his options. He could run by the house, grab a drink —

A siren whirred alive and cut off his thoughts. Instincts sent him to the ground, panicked. He looked up, expecting the worst, but the sky was clear. No Jap planes. He looked in all directions to be sure. Nope, nothing.

The alarm stung the air. Bennie placed the pitch: a blackout siren. Lights extinguished all around him. Fines were the pits. He felt a headache coming on and started to sweat.

People scurried in all directions, puzzled and amused. The idea of an enemy airstrike at this point was far-fetched. Some Red Cross gals sidestepped him in a hurry. They laughed and shot him curious looks.

Bennie stood up and fumbled through his memory. His crib notes on air raid protocol came into focus. Everyone had twenty minutes to get somewhere and stay put.

The first blast quit. A chorus of relief took its place. Bennie cut through the crowd and kept looking up.

He came to his wheels and threw himself inside. His heart beat machine-gun fast and his hands throbbed. He jerked his unmarked from the curb and sped off.

He turned left off Broad and zig-zagged streets. He

found a quiet alleyway and parked. Peace and quiet, for the moment. Then, the next siren spun on. The noise made him twitch. He forced himself to relax with deep breaths and neck rolls.

A light sound caught his attention. Someone, far off. *No, wait,* he thought, *here in the car.* He upped the volume on the two-way and heard, "All available units, please report in." The sweet, warm voice calmed him. Volunteer war wives ran the Annex radios at night.

She repeated the message a few times. Bennie felt stiff and afraid. He thought of hesitation and cowardice in the jungle.

He grabbed the receiver and said, "HQ, this is four zero seven, reporting in."

"Roger that, four zero seven. Where are you located at present?"

Bennie shot a look around the alleyway. He lied and said, "Lombardy at Broad, heading east."

"Roger that, four zero seven, you're not too far, and I can't get anyone else. We've had repeated calls from a Jackson Ward hotel. They started calling a few minutes ago and say they won't let up until we send someone."

Gut flutters unnerved him. The Ward was oft ignored at night. Non-stop calls could mean something serious. "Roger that, HQ. Anything else?"

"Let me see... We've had multiple reports of someone impersonating a neighborhood warden in Oregon Hill. Two men fought and broke windows at a diner on 3rd. And..." She broke off and giggled. "A very drunk man in Confederate garb refuses to leave the Capitol steps. He claims to possess the reincarnated soul of Robert E. Lee."

Kid stuff, thought Bennie. Unfit for a Marine. "Roger that, HQ. Which hotel in the Ward?"

"The Apollo. You'll take it?"

"I'll take it."

"Roger that, four zero seven. 514 North Second Street. I'll mark it here on the log. You're to see the bellhop."

Bennie evened his nerves and took his time reaching Two Street. The Deuce, they called it. The heartbeat of Jackson Ward. A crowded mix of business and pleasure. Along a three block stretch from Broad to Leigh, almost every square foot belonged to a shop, hotel, or club.

Bennie parked his sled a block away and took to the Apollo on foot. The trek juiced him and gave him time to shore up his nerves. Music spilled from apartment windows on either side of him. Jazz to his left, blues to his right. Late night jam sessions that were just getting started.

The Apollo Hotel was a two-story social club in the middle of the 500 block with old bricks and peeling paint. A mob had assembled outside. Bennie slowed his approach and counted three dozen men and women in congregation. The group went radio silent when they saw Bennie. Voodoo eyes came his way en masse. Bennie pulled out his badge and held it up for everyone to see.

"I'm Detective Sherwood with the police," he called out. "Could someone direct me to the bellhop?"

No response. Bennie scanned the group one by one. He met stone-cold eyes on every face.

Raised voices came from inside the hotel. Bennie dodged the crowd and darted inside. He found two Negroes in the lobby. A seasoned man with a bow-tie and a young woman in a maid's uniform. Just beyond them, dining tables and chairs faced a small stage. Bennie turned out his badge again and said, "I'm looking for the bellhop."

"That'd be me," said the man.

"You called in a complaint?"

The man pointed at the stairwell. In an unsteady voice, he said, "Room 211."

The voice put Bennie on edge. He eased onto the well-worn stairs and padded the steps. Faint memories of Pearl's spooked him. In the far distance, he heard the third blackout siren come to life.

The stairwell spilled into a long hallway. There were five rooms on either side. Bennie tiptoed into the hall and saw big drops of blood on the floor. He pulled his gun. His body started to tingle.

The door across from Bennie opened. He whipped his gun in that direction. A little girl in a rose colored smock popped her head out. Big, chestnut eyes, full of fear. She saw the gun, screamed, and slammed the door shut.

Bennie felt his legs lock up. His breathing ramped up. He looked left, then right. *Shit.* All alone in the jungle, again.

The man called to Bennie from the stairwell. "She ain't gonna hurt you," he said. "We just can't get her out of that room."

The man's voice unfroze him. Bennie took a few steps toward 211, skirting blood. The door to the room was just cracked. Bennie two-handed his .38 and elbowed the door all the way open. He looked inside and felt his knees buckle.

Two slain bodies lay atop the bed, both of them naked. A white man, a Negro woman. Bennie edged closer to them. Signs of struggle marred both bodies: bruises/ fingernail scratches/torn hair.

The dead man's neck looked all wrong. The dead woman's eyes looked at Bennie. A river of blood seeped from her back, down the bed sheet and onto the floor. Bennie saw flashes of the old man's morgue pics: stab wounds, all across his back. A jungle memory surfaced: his unit's first staff sergeant, cut up like pieces of meat in a butcher shop.

Bennie went cyclone dizzy. He lost his balance and spun backwards. He hit a wall and saw a window. He threw it open, stuck his head out, and vomited.

The third blackout siren sounded its final burst. A chorus of *Amen!* came from the street out front. All around Bennie, lights began to switch on.

His dizziness faded and he heard this *sound*. Down the block, that jazz session kicked up the volume and really started to cook.

Chapter Five

THE SQUADROOM WAS packed wall to wall, every desk accounted for: vice, robbery, homicide, traffic, and Victory. Juvie, too. Even the paint shop men showed up. Wartime news announcements came over the radio thrice daily. On-duty cops not on patrol or call-outs were expected to attend. The Cane enforced a strict behavior policy: inattention earned you a stretch of parking meter detail and three laps around the Capitol.

The radio sputtered noise and hum until The Cane smacked it with his rod. Now, big band crescendos and snare hits blared from the speakers. The broadcaster spoke slowly and with purpose: "On this day, news from Berlin..."

War sounds flooded the transmission. The rat-tat-tat of gunfire gave Bennie tingles bone marrow deep. He heard gasps from the back of the room. One of the secretaries had a brother fighting in Europe. She went sheet-white and wrapped her arms around herself.

The announcement continued: "...RAF Lancasters have trounced Berlin with more than 1,000 long tons of bombs, the Sixth Army has advanced into New Guinea, and Marines have expanded their hold on Cape Gloucester..."

Bennie tensed at the thought of his fellow boots in battle. That was *his* group on the Cape. A world of wrong hit him, and he wished he was with them.

The transmission wrapped up. In summary: the war was far from over. Radio ads stole the spotlight. Dean Martin told them to save their cooking fats. Bennie thought of his own kitchen and felt bad. He never ate at home; he wasn't doing his part.

"Right," boomed the Cane. "Now, listen up. It's been an ugly night around here, and today won't be much better. We've got a terrible mess on our hands and the press is hounding us for information. I'll make an official statement shortly, but I want it known: *no one* is to say *shit* about the Apollo to anyone without my say so. Is that understood?"

Feisty *Yessirs* made the rounds.

"Good. Jack, Bennie, you two with me. Downstairs. Everyone else, you know what to do."

Bennie lumbered to his feet. His legs felt wooden. He'd not slept much during the night. Ghoulish stab imagery had kept him awake. Cue the slideshow — the old man's morgue pics and the Negro woman's back wounds. He shook blood into his legs and found his stride. He followed Jack and The Cane into the hall.

Bennie said, "You think he's ready to spill?"

The Cane said, "He damn well better be, or he'll find my stick up his ass." Jack flinched at the idea.

They made the first floor and headed toward the rear of the building. Bennie got chills. He had never liked this part of the Annex, where muted lights kept the shadows close. He angled his eyes this way and that. *Hey there, Jap bogeyman. Come out, come out, wherever you are.*

Jack said, "I don't think we'll have any problems with Johnson. He spent the night in jail and I'm sure he doesn't want to return."

"What'd you charge him with?" asked Bennie.

"Renting rooms."

They came to the interrogation hall where a uniformed officer watchdogged a trio of 6 by 8s. Large panes of glass provided one-way views into each one. Three furnishings a piece, a desk and two chairs. Only A1 boasted occupancy — the Apollo's bellhop, snoozing in a chair. The uniform braced himself as the Cane approached.

"He make any requests?" barked The Cane.

"No, sir."

"To relieve himself, or be fed?"

"No, sir."

"He make any untoward comments about the department or the military?"

"No, sir."

The Cane turned toward Jack. "You want to take him?"

Jack stewed on the question. Bennie clocked a tension in his face before he turned to Bennie and said, "See what he knows. You were first on the scene, you may know best if he starts to dissemble the truth."

Bennie's gut shivered. Many a time he watched the old man bounce between these three rooms like a natural, working his fists on those who deserved it and his charm on those who didn't. Bennie wondered if he had the same instincts.

The Cane broke the silence. "Is that going to be a problem?"

Bennie said, "No," and yanked the bellhop's file from

Jack's hand. He gave the report a glance and entered A1 with force, slamming the door shut behind him. The bellhop jerked to life, as if he had been slapped awake.

Bennie circled the room as he talked. "Mr. Johnson, my name is Detective Sherwood. We met last night. Do you remember me?"

Mr. Johnson let out a canyon-sized yawn and blinked his eyes open. He looked up at Bennie and placed him from memory.

"Yeah."

Bennie studied his file. "Your full name is Cornell Roosevelt Johnson. You're 57 years old. You're packing beefs for B and E, robbery, and operating a shoe shine stand without a license."

"So?"

"Not exactly a model citizen, are you?"

Mr. Johnson pinned a strained look on Bennie. "And cops are?"

Bennie ignored the suggestion. "You're the bellhop at the Apollo Hotel, is that correct?"

"Bellhop, bartender, cook, on-call doc. Shit, I do it all, day and night."

"Are you a pimp, too, Mr. Johnson?"

"Hells no! All's the shit I hafta do, when you think I got time to run trim?"

"I think you've got time to run hot sheet rooms."

"Folks need a room, I rent 'em one. Why should it matter to me what they need 'em for?"

Bennie pulled a morgue photo from the file. It was of the man found in the hotel room — white/early 30s/curly hair/a scar down the right side of his face. So far, no ID.

"Did you rent a room to this man, Mr. Johnson?"

Mr. Johnson regarded Bennie as if he were an exotic

animal or plant. "You sure you work for *this* city's police department?"

"Certain of it. Why?"

"'Cause no policemen 'round here ever call me any kind of Mister before."

"Just answer the question. Did you rent a room to this man?"

"No. I never even seen him come in."

"Had you ever seen him before?"

"No."

Bennie eyed the report. "Why isn't Josephine Scott listed in your check-in ledger?"

"Who?"

"Josephine Scott, the woman we found in room 211. Why isn't her name in your book?"

"Because I didn't see her come in neither, that's why."

"And why'd you not see Miss Scott or the man she was found with enter the hotel, Mr. Johnson?"

"Because we was out back, putting out that fire."

Bennie was certain Mr. Johnson misspoke. He checked both sides of the report. "What fire? You didn't say anything about a fire last night."

"That's cause you were pulling two dead bodies out of my hotel and throwing me in jail."

"Where was this fire? And what time did it start?"

Mr. Johnson just looked at him.

"You want to spend another night in jail, Mr. Johnson?"

"Shit, you take me back to jail all you want. Couple of boys in there run a dice game, I won me five whole dollars."

Bennie felt a headache coming on and dismissed his patience. "Just answer the question!" he yelled. "What time did the fire start?"

Their ice-stare stretched a long beat. Finally, Mr. Johnson said, "I think it was just about eight o' clock last night, right before that first siren come on."

Bennie felt his skin tingle. The old man's voice filled his head — *There are no coincidences.* "You're sure about that time?"

"Only thing I'm sure 'bout are those two bodies in my hotel and being thrown in jail for no good reason."

Bennie pressed. "Are you *sure* about that time, Mr. Johnson?"

Mr. Johnson popped sweat. "I didn't kill those two people."

"That's not what I asked you."

Mr. Johnson took his time and said, "*Yes.* I know's it was about eight o' clock last night cause that's when me and Della eat dinner."

"Della works for you?"

"She does. For that I cut her a break on the rent, on account of she and her daughter live upstairs. Her man's overseas."

Bennie flashed on that moment — pointing his gun at that little girl.

"Go on."

"We's just finishing up when we see the smoke through the back window. We run out, and hell if my paper bin ain't on fire."

"Paper bin?"

"For the scrap drives. Newspapers, magazines, old books."

"How noble of you."

"Shit, it ain't me. Della make me do it. Hell, she got the whole neighborhood involved. Now we collect it all at church on Sundays."

"How'd you put the fire out?"

"Neighbor across the alley got a fish smoker. He keeps pails of water nearby, so me and Della run across and grab 'em."

Bennie's instincts criss-crossed — the killer knew about the blackout, the Apollo's thin staff, *and* the paper bin.

Mr. Johnson said, "So?"

"So what?"

"So is that enough? I gotta get back to the hotel, we gotta clean up those rooms. Poor Della's all by herself."

Bennie's mind popped with an idea. "Did you tell any of the cops about the fire last night?"

"I told you already, no. You's too busy hauling my ass to j —"

Bennie lit up out of the room.

"*Hey now*! You gonna let me out of here?"

Bennie darted from A1 and found the Cane outside the room.

"Where's Jack?"

"He's on his way to the Apollo now. That's good work, son. If there's anything left from that fire, he'll find it."

Bennie could hardly contain his excitement. "Chief, it's just gotta be connected. The blackout was orchestrated, this was all a setup."

"Son, you don't know the half of it."

"What?"

The Cane sighed. "Someone boosted a filling station during the dimout and made off with all of its damn gasoline."

CHAPTER SIX

BENNIE STOOD OUTSIDE the place and double-checked the details from his steno: Digby's Service Station, 3716 West Broad. Off Hamilton Street, out near Tantilla.

He stepped inside and found the place quiet. A small office looked out on three car bays. Business must be good — a car in each bay, the lot out front full of repair jobs.

Behind him, a strong female voice said, "Excuse me."

Bennie turned and put eyes on a beauty. Thick, auburn hair, tied up in a yellow bandana. Olive green eyes that would give any man pause. Oil smudges on her cheeks and nose. Ditto her chambray jumpsuit and leather gloves. She smelled like gasoline and made Bennie think of Rita Hayworth.

She said, "You're with the cops?"

Bennie found his voice. "Yes, I'm Detective Sherwood."

"Took you long enough."

"It's been a long night and we're short-handed. What can I tell you?" A yawn forced its way out of him.

"For starters, you can tell me who stole our gas." Feisty, quick. Bennie's nerves fluttered.

"Let's start with what you know, Ms...?"

She let it go unanswered for a few beats. "McKenna. Imogene McKenna."

"Is that your maiden name?" It just raced out of him.

She dead-panned him for a full beat. Then, she said, "We came in this morning and found every bit of it gone. Three barrels, our pump hoses, even a dolly we'd rigged up to move it all around. Only drops left are what we have outside."

The sound of glass breaking stole her attention. Inside the station office, an older man fell across his desk and cried.

"Excuse me," she said, jogging toward the office. Bennie watched her go. She was swift and agile, like a cat on the hunt.

One of the fingerprint men caught Bennie's gaze and shot him a knowing look. Bennie deflected it and put eyes on the room. The walls were filled with car diagrams and ration point breakdowns. Car bay 1 housed a steel colored Ford with front end dents. Bay 2 held a Plymouth with cracked windows. Bay 3 harbored a dark green Chevy convertible with its top down. Snazzy wheels, the best of the bunch. Bennie wrote down the plate numbers and details of each one.

"So, what do you think?" she said. She'd crept up on him unnoticed.

"About?"

She frowned. "You're not much of a detective, are you?"

The jibe needled him. He gestured toward the office. "Is that Mr. Digby?"

"Yes, but I'd prefer we not bother him with all this just now."

"Why not?"

She paused, forcing the words. "A telegram came this morning. His son's not coming home."

The muscles along Bennie's back tightened. How the old man must have dreaded the telegram boys.

"Say," she said, eyeing him askew. "Why aren't *you* in uniform?"

"Detectives wear plainclothes most days, m'am."

"That's not what I meant."

"I served with the Marines. Did time in the Pacific."

"Why aren't you with them now?"

He let it go unanswered for a few beats. He said, "Let's take a look at that jimmied door."

The back entrance to the car bay had been crowbarred open. Jagged splinters sprung from the jamb like some kind of booby trap. Wood shards dotted the ground and crackled under Bennie as he studied the doorway. Imogene stood just inside with her arms folded, watching him with a cautious eye.

"Does Mr. Digby have any enemies?" he asked her.

"Not that I know of."

"Any other break-ins since you've been here?"

"No."

"Anything else taken? Money? Tires?"

"We checked. No."

"How about ration points? You handle any of that?"

"No, I just work on the cars. You'll have to ask him about those."

Bennie craned his head for a better view of the office. Mr. Digby hung his head and wept. Bennie settled his gaze on Imogene.

"Where were you last night, Ms. McKenna?"

"Behind a wheel. I drive a taxi a few nights a week."

Bennie scribbled in his steno pad. "What company?"

"Confederate Cab."

"What time?"

Imogene got wide-eyed. "You don't think I had anything to do with this, do you?"

"Don't get hot, it's just procedure."

"Who says I'm getting hot? Mr. Digby and I wrapped at 5. I drove from 7 to 2."

"What about the other mechanics?"

"There are no other mechanics."

"So, you're the only…"

"*Yeah*, I'm the only one."

"I'm sorry, I didn't mean to — "

"Listen, you got any more questions for me, Mr. Detective? 'Cause I got a lot of work to do."

"No, thank you, that's all for — "

She walked off before he finished, dismissing him with a quick turn. Bennie watched her grab a wrench and go to work on the Ford. His eyes lingered on her svelte figure and the back of her neck.

"Detective?"

Bennie jumped. One of the lab men was standing right next to him. Sleep deprivation had him on edge.

Bennie stifled a yawn. "Yes?"

"We've gathered about two dozen latents, sir. Hopefully we'll get a few matches that lead us in the right direction."

Bennie gestured toward the office. "No way we'll get an elimination set off him today," he said. "Run what you find through our file cards and cross check against the ones we got from Pearl's. Maybe we'll find a match."

"Yes, sir."

"You guys can shove off. I'll see what I can get out of

him."

The lab man walked off. Bennie risked another peek at Imogene on his way to the office. He caught *her* stealing a look at *him*.

"Mr. Digby, I'm a police detective. I'm truly sorry for your loss, I am, but I need to ask you a few questions. I promise it won't take long."

Mr. Digby wiped away his sobs with a shammy cloth. He looked to be about sixty, a frail man with thinning hair. He sat on a busted-up sofa that doubled for a bed. Newspapers and a torn blanket were thrown over the back. A lumpy pillow lay off to the side. The room smelled of corn whiskey and body odor. Mr. Digby said, "Alright, go ahead."

"This your service station, Mr. Digby?"

"Yes."

"How long have you owned it?"

"Five, six years. I don't remember."

Bennie shot a look around the room. "Do you live here, Mr. Digby?"

"Yes."

"Where did you live before?"

"What? Uh, my home, but I need to stay here. For now."

"And why is that?"

"My... my roof leaks. Damn it, what does this have to with anything?"

Bennie jotted notes in his steno. "I take it, then, that you weren't here then when the break-in occurred."

"Yeah, that's... that's right. I wasn't here."

"Have you any idea what time the break-in did occur?"

Mr. Digby drew the cloth to his face and fought back a

sob. "I... I... I was at the Wigwam. I drank for a bit, and then came here. Must have been 2, 3 in the morning when I got back."

"And you didn't see the back door?"

"No! No, I use the front. I use the front door."

"Can anyone confirm your presence at the Wigwam?" Bennie scoffed at the idea of a follow-up. The Wigwam was a 7 mile hike up US 1.

"What?"

"Who were you with at the Wigwam?"

Mr. Digby barked at him. "Oh, I don't know, people, just regular people! Just like me."

"Can you think of anyone who'd want to hurt you, or bring harm to your business?"

Mr. Digby looked up at Bennie with angry, bloodshot eyes. "How... how can you ask me that, today, how could you? How could you say such a thing? We all have enemies, every one of us! Their names are Hitler and Mussolini and Tojo! And *they* killed my son. THEY KILLED HIM!"

"Mr. Digby, I'm — "

"Go, get out, GET OUT!" Mr. Digby grabbed some newspaper, balled it up, and threw it at Bennie in a fury. It sailed through the air with all the force of a feather as Mr. Digby burst into tears and tore the rest of the newspaper to shreds.

CHAPTER SEVEN

THEY WERE HUDDLED up in the Cane's office. Stuffy air made the room feel tight. Bennie shuffled in his seat and eyed them both. The elder Reed sat at his desk, chomping a cigar. Jack leaned against the wall with an eye out the window.

"You couldn't have known he was going to unload on you like that," he said. "Anyway, it's done. You got a few answers out of him, and now you have something to work with."

Bennie was still on edge. "You think he'll file a complaint?"

The Cane almost laughed. "He wouldn't dare."

"He may have been under emotional duress," added Jack, "but you were just doing your job. Plus, if he was as skittish as you say, I'll bet he's in on it."

"I second that idea," said The Cane. "You want it, son? Be good for you. A case all your own."

Bennie bit his lip for time. The thought of seeing *her* again jazzed him. "What about the Apollo?"

Jack said, "I'm taking the Apollo, with some assistance

from homicide."

"But I was first on the scene," said Bennie, indignant. "It's mine."

Jack and The Cane shot him awkward looks.

Bennie didn't get it. "What?"

The Cane said, "You're not ready for the Apollo, son."

"Why not?"

Jack said, "Two of the attending officers on the scene reported seeing you in an unsteady state after you'd discovered the bodies. And a Negro on site saw you vomit out of room 211's window. Maybe seeing those bodies… triggered something."

Sweat pooled on the back of Bennie's neck. He felt a tremor coming on. He slid his hands under his thighs to hide it.

"Anyone could have reacted like that! She was all cut up, his neck was broken. Hell, I can handle it!"

"Your behavior says otherwise, son," said The Cane. "You're not ready for this. Not yet."

Bennie sank into his chair. He felt as if he'd been found guilty of some grave crime.

The Cane wouldn't have it. "Don't get sour with me, son. Or yourself. Not now. This is ugly, ugly business. Maybe the worst we've ever seen. I need every one of my men in tip top shape, not feeling sorry for themselves! Hell, this is gasoline we're talking about. Now, in the middle of all this! I've had half a dozen calls from the OPA already, and that's just this morning. You can either get on board with this or I'll detach you from Victory and find something more suitable. Perhaps you'd like to slum it in traffic awhile, eh?"

Bennie righted himself and held his head up. "Fine. I'll work the gasoline, but I want to know — this morning, my questioning of the Apollo's bellhop gave us a lead. What do we know about that fire?"

"The fire may have given us our best lead," said Jack, gloating. "We found a used matchbook from Tantilla Garden among the ashes. And two eyewitnesses say they saw a well-dressed man enter the Apollo just before the blackout sirens took up."

"What're you thinking?" asked Bennie.

Jack grinned, loving it. "I think it tells us we're looking for a well-heeled big shot who slums in the Ward, kicks his heels at the Garden, and offed these two vics for kicks."

Bennie could hardly hold it in, *this feeling* he'd had all day long. "Jack, it's gotta be connected. Same MO, same locale — "

Jack shrugged, dismissive. "Bennie, your old man's death was a tragedy, but an isolated one. *This* — the Apollo, the gasoline, Pearl's — this represents something bigger, something orchestrated. Somebody with serious juice pulled all this off."

"And we're gonna get him," added The Cane, drawing on his cigar, a Cheshire grin slowly taking shape.

Bennie felt lost. Together, the two Reeds came off like mischievous boys just off some illicit adventure. "You've got a lead?"

"You've heard the name Jedidiah King, haven't you, son?"

The connection jolted Bennie. "Well, yeah. As a matter of fact —"

"Yes, yes, Everett told me. Study the man all you like, but you are *not* to approach him, do you understand?"

"But, sir, I told Ms. Holly — "

The Cane slapped his desk. "You are *not* to approach him! Is that understood?"

Bennie shifted in his chair. "Alright, ok, I'll stay away from him. But how — "

"We think King is behind a string of wartime offenses," said Jack. "We've been onto him since you were overseas but we've never had a lead that stuck. This might be it."

"He's high profile, Bennie," said The Cane. "We can't go after him with anything flimsy. It's gotta be a *unified* effort, understand?"

Unified hit him wrong, as if they were worried he might slight their agenda. He stewed on it for a moment, and then it hit him.

"You think he had something to do with my old man."

The Cane took on a grave tone. "You will *not*, I repeat, *not* go after King on your own. We're just now connecting the dots, we can't afford to be short-sighted."

"*Short sighted?* I worked the case for months, I covered everything, why didn't you — "

"Because we didn't have enough to go on," said Jack. "We still don't, but we're closer."

"Don't let it take over, son, we don't *know* anything. Not yet."

Bennie felt his insides go cold, felt his bones freeze up. He got that bombed out feeling, like he was pinned to the ground, waiting for the next attack. Only he was tied to a chair and his own unit had opened fire *on him.*

"Then, what do we know?" he barked. "Those two bodies at the Apollo, how do they tie in?"

Jack said, "We've got the dead man's morgue pic making the rounds. No bites yet, but we're hoping for an ID."

"What about the woman?"

"What about her?" snapped the Cane.

"Well, she was murdered, too."

The Cane snarled. "She's just another spade in the wrong place at the wrong time."

"Then what about the alarms? We all know they're a factor."

"The mayor's office is on it," said Jack, a forceful tone in his voice. "Orchestrating a blackout under false pretenses is grounds for treason. We expect severe penalties for those responsible and are to stay out of it."

Bennie was both miffed and impressed, still in awe of the contradiction that was Jack Reed. Jack had been the shy type in high school. All study, no girls. Now, he had *gusto*. A top cop in line for a captaincy, maybe more.

Bennie said, "Fine, I'll work Digby. But I want *in*, understand? If this goes the distance, I want to be a part of it."

"Then do your part and do it right, son," said the Cane. "If we all work together, we can bring this horseshit to an end."

Bennie greeted his desk with a kick and a smack. The other bulls in the room looked his way, annoyed. Bennie ignored them and sank into his chair, fuming.

A present on his desk frosted his attitude: those carbons on King he'd requested from Everett. Bennie pulled out his steno and made quick notes.

- Full name: Jedidiah King; MI unknown
- Sex: Male
- Race: White
- Age: approx. 48; 1895 listed as birth year; no month, no day.
- Height: 6'
- Weight: 160 lb.

- Build: Lean
- Eye Color: Blue
- Hair color: Light Brown
- Scars: None visible
- Traits: Haughty, reserved; generally puts on airs.
- Dress: Often suited; upscale casual.
- Marital status: Single
- Residences: a swanky pad in Windsor Farms, 3 acres +; also rumored to own a river house on the James.
- Immediate family relations: Unknown
- Business affiliations: Proprietor of King Tobacco; Commonwealth Club board member; chief trustee of the city boy's home
- Frequent haunts: Tantilla Garden, Tilly's, the Westwood Club, the Jefferson Hotel, and several Jackson Ward nightclubs, chiefly Slaughter's Hotel and the Hippodrome
- Notable Colleagues: Mayor Ambler; Governor Darden; Senator Byrd
- Police record: none

An addendum to King's background was scribbled on the back. It pointed out that King didn't operate his tobacco business alongside the big boys on the Row. He did buy his tobacco from them, direct, but his manufacturing setup was a few blocks away, in a warehouse off Franklin.

A hell of a man, thought Bennie. King had money *and* clout. He ran in powerful circles, but he'd be easy to tail. The man was a social butterfly.

Angles formed and stretched in Bennie's mind. King frequented both white *and* Negro nightclubs. Was the man for mixed-race fraternization? Did he dig on Negro culture, or did he troll the Ward for prey? Was he Klan?

Shit — was he *Nazi?*

Bennie's mind veered farther off course: *maybe* the truth lies with Josephine Scott. Bennie thumbed through his steno and found his Apollo notes. Her post-mortem details were meager: 5'10", late 20s, no fingerprint on file. Lab men were slow to provide Negro pics, so Bennie braved his memory for the rest: ash brown skin, raven black hair, an exotic face. Bennie wondered: did she only truck with white men? Bennie scribbled a new note: check Negro papers for her obit details.

His head hurt. He rubbed his temples, rolled his neck. His mind throbbed with a question, on and off like a neon sign: did King have something to do with the old man?

He had to find out. To hell with the Reeds. As long as he did his job, he could play his own angles from the shadows. Just like in the jungle.

He folded the King carbons into his steno and rose from his seat. On his way out, he made eyes with a new Rita Hayworth on the wall. He left the room, thinking Imogene McKenna looked better.

The squadroom was quiet. A few cops hobnobbed around the coffee station. Bennie caught whispers of their chatter as he crossed the room.

"How about that dimout?"

"I bet somebody took a bribe!"

"Some lowlife in civil defense is gonna get it!"

Bennie made the case board. A few restaurant reports had already come in. They were fastened together, dangling from a nail in the ongoing section. Bennie pulled it down and quick-thumbed it front to back. The threadbare findings were arranged in alphabetical order. Not much to tell, apparently.

Bennie thought back to his questioning of Hollis Digby earlier that day. The man said he'd been at the Wigwam last night until around 2 or 3 in the morning.

Bennie flipped to the front page of the reports and found the assignment roster. Two-man teams and their destinations ran the full page. Bennie finger-tracked it to the bottom.

Well, look at that.

Det. Niles Hunter and his AO stooge were assigned to the Wigwam last night.

Bennie *re*checked the filed reports. Nothing from the Wigwam.

Bennie glanced at a wall clock. It was 10PM. He yawned big. He had two hours left on his shift. He grabbed a phone and dialed First Station. Three rings got him a gruff voice.

"First Police Station, Brown."

Bennie pulled a face. Arthur Brown was bottom-rung RPD. He'd failed the police academy, but gotten in on the good word of his uncle Everett, he of the Annex records room. Officially, Arthur was a clerk, pushing papers for the station's desk sergeant. Off the record, he was Captain Rivers' resident goon. He was rude, unkempt, and Bennie didn't like him.

"Arthur, this is Sherwood, out of the Annex. I'm looking for Niles Hunter."

"I should care?"

"Cut the shit. Where is he?"

A weighted pause. "He's busy."

"For how long?"

"I should know? He and The Captain are in the middle

of something. Until when, I don't know."

Bennie played nice. "Can you get him a message for me?"

"I guess."

"Tell him I need info on his diner scout. ASAP."

"That all?"

"Yeah, *that's all.*"

Bennie hung up before Brown could say another word.

CHAPTER EIGHT

BENNIE STEPPED INTO Doyle's Grill, a hash joint a few blocks from the Annex, and found a thin crowd. The lunch rush had come and gone.

He walked the aisles, scanning tables. Familiar sounds buzzed around the room. War talk among the diners, the Andrews Sisters on the radio.

He found Niles in a corner booth, fumbling with his hands, lost in thought.

"Found you."

Niles looked up, startled. "Hey," he said, pulling his hands into his lap. "You got my note." Bennie couldn't be sure, but he thought Niles' hands looked bruised. He slid into the booth, relieved to be off his feet.

A waitress made the table. Bennie ordered a cheeseburger and coffee. She brought the coffee right away and left them alone.

Niles eyed him sideways. "If you're looking to congratulate me, can it. One more cop slaps me on the back, I'm gonna deck him."

Bennie laughed. "Fine. Have it your way. But me? I'm

gonna celebrate, just the same."

"And just what's got you buzzing?"

"I'm gonna have a bonafide partner, is what." Bennie tipped his coffee cup and smiled. He *was* jazzed. No more going it alone.

"Right. You and me, huh?"

"That's right. But not until next week, I hear. What's The Cane got you doing?"

Niles soured. "I'm helping Captain Rivers, out of First. Something he needs a… hand with."

Bennie was puzzled. "Well, hell, man. Don't get too excited. It's not like you just got bumped from a shit traffic detail to a beaucoup desk."

Niles feigned a smile. "It's not that."

A few beats passed. Bennie made a guess. "Pearl's."

Niles fought with it. "It was him or me, you know?"

"Right."

"Comes with the job. Somebody draws on you, you might have to put 'em down."

"Exactly."

Niles reached for his coffee and nearly spilled it. His hands shook. *There, yes — bruises on his knuckles.*

Their waitress brought Bennie's cheeseburger. His stomach growled at the sight of it. Medium-rare with ketchup. He thought of his brothers in the Pacific and felt guilty.

They sat for a time in silence. Bennie eating, Niles thinking. The weight of it — taking another man's life — hung over the table like a dark cloud. It stays with you, becomes a part of you. Like your hair color or the shape of your face. You're not the same man afterwards. Bennie certainly wasn't. And from where he was sitting, it didn't look like Niles was, either.

Niles broke the silence. "What is you wanted to know?"

"Two nights back, the night of the blackout. You worked the Wigwam, right?"

"Yeah, what of it?"

"Tell me what happened."

"Well, we cased the joint for a few hours. For the most part, folks used cash for their food and drinks. But then a few people put up *extra* cash, even a few coupons, just like we thought, as if they were gonna get something more for their money. But the owner wouldn't have it. He acted all high and mighty, going off about sacrifice and the war. *Big* dramatics. He even threw a few guys out over it. But it all rang fake. It was as if..." Niles trailed off.

"Yeah?"

"It was as if he knew we were there. Like he was putting on a show."

Bennie's mind clicked: someone tipped the restaurant owners to The Cane's investigation.

Niles got it, too. "You think we got a leak?"

"Yeah, I do."

Niles shook his head. "The Cane's gonna be *pissed*."

Bennie nodded. "Look, while you were there, I wonder if you noticed someone. An older man. Thin, maybe 60. Not too much hair, a long nose."

Niles searched his mind. "*Yeah*," he said, remembering. "I saw him. That one? He had a load on."

"He say anything memorable?"

"You know, there *was* something."

"What?"

"We were at the bar, me and the guy who went with me, trying to get a read on the joint, when I heard the bartender offer to drive your fellow home."

"That bad, huh?"

"And your guy, what's his name?"

"Digby. Hollis Digby."

"Digby said no way, I can't go home. So the bartender pressed and asked why. Digby said he wasn't safe at home. Said he was a target and that they'd get him at home."

Bennie thought back to yesterday. Digby said his roof leaked. And he'd clearly been sleeping in his office.

"You know," continued Niles, "I didn't think much of it last night, but it does ring strange, thinking about it now. At the time, I just figured the guy was spooked on the war."

The waitress returned and refilled their coffee. When she left, Bennie said, "He say anything more about it?"

"Nah. Right about then they closed up and we hit the road, same as everyone else."

"What time was that?"

"Eleven, eleven thirty."

Bennie pulled out his steno and checked his notes. Digby said he didn't return to the service station until between 2 and 3 in the morning.

Niles fidgeted with his hands under the table, nervous. "What's, uh, what's all this about? Did I screw up?"

"No. Actually, this helps, a lot. Digby runs a service station out near Tantilla. The night of the blackout? Someone lifted all his gasoline."

"Holy shit."

"I talked to him yesterday. He's hiding something."

"What?"

"I can't be sure, but I think he was in on it."

Niles whistled. Bennie nodded and sipped his coffee. After a beat, he said, "What happened to your hands?"

Niles looked surprised. "What?"

"Your hands, they look swollen. What happened?"

"Oh that? Just went hard in the ring today, is all. Sparring with a recruit this morning."

Bennie switched gears. "The feelings you have, about Pearl's. Some of 'em will pass, some of 'em won't. It's a part of you now, taking a life. Better get used to it."

Niles went pale. "That's some bedside manner you've got."

"Better to get out in front of it than let it sneak up behind you. Take it from someone who knows."

Niles brought his voice down to a whisper. "You think they gave me Victory because I shot that Negro?"

"Hell, no. Put that away. You *earned* Victory. Don't think like that, not for a second."

Niles' face was a puzzle. He was clearly a man in conflict. He slid from the booth. "Look, I gotta motor," he said, leaving a few dollars on the table. "Settle up for me?"

"Sure."

Niles stood and dug his hands into his pockets. He put on a smile and said, "I'll, uh, see you next week, yeah?"

Bennie tipped his coffee cup and nodded. Niles turned and left in a hurry. As if he couldn't wait to leave.

Bennie waited until he was gone. He left the booth and walked over to the serving counter. Through an open window, he could see into the kitchen where a cook was manning the grill. Sweaty, unshaven, on the move. He felt Bennie's eyes on him and looked up.

"Whaddyaneed?" he snapped.

Bennie raised his badge and said, "I need to use your phone."

The cook froze for a moment, as if he didn't understand. Then he jerked his head to the right and barked, "Up at the front."

Bennie found a phone at the server's table. He asked the

operator to patch him through to the Mosque. "Connect me to police training, please."

A few beats later, a droll voice said, "Police Academy."

"This is Sherwood, out of the Annex. Who's this?"

"Williams. I'm the watchman over here."

"I'm looking for anyone who's been around the gym this morning."

"I've been here since 7AM, what do you want to know?"

Bennie said the name slow. "Did Niles Hunter come in this morning? Most likely he would've sparred in the ring."

Williams made clicking noises with his mouth as he thought it through. "Hunter, Hunter... nah, don't think so. He does a bit of boxing for us, doesn't he?"

"Yeah."

"Nope, not today. I woulda seen him."

Bennie thanked Williams and hung up, miffed. So Niles *was* lying. What the hell did he have to hide?

Bennie started for the booth. He still had to pay and grab his coat. He passed the kitchen on the way and peeked inside. No cook, just fry smoke. Bad smells, too, something burning.

He ducked inside and found the grill unmanned. A mess of burgers and eggs were charred, black as night.

The manager burst into the room and looked around, aghast. "Holy Jesus, what gives? Where's Freddie?" He saw Bennie and flinched. "Who the hell are you?"

"I"m a cop. Where's the cook?"

"Hell, you're the one in here. Don't you know?"

A draft circled the room. Cold, frigid air. Bennie turned a corner and found a back door wide open.

He darted outside and spilled into an alleyway. A look in either direction yielded the same view: not a soul in sight.

The cook was *gone*.

Bennie hit 204 — the records room at the Annex — and found Everett Brown lounging in his desk chair, skimming the paper.

Bennie walked over to the desk and said, "I need to run a check, Everett. On the double."

Without looking up, Everett said, "I don't do *on the double*."

"Goddamnit, Everett, this is serious!"

Everett peeked from behind the paper. "If you want *on the double*, son, you'll have to do it yourself. If it's just a file card you want, the drawers are over there." Everett gestured to the other side of the room with a nod.

Bennie shot him a long glare before he crossed the room and stood before a row of file cabinets. He checked his steno to be sure. The cook's name was Freddie Graham. Bennie opened the drawer labeled F-G-H and began to leaf through the cards. He came to the Gs and skipped ahead.

— Gibson, Gosling, Gray, Grayson, Green —

No Graham.

Bennie slammed the drawer shut.

"Hey!" barked Everett. "Don't be taking your frustrations out in here. Get your ass over to the gym if you want to throw things around."

Bennie made for the door. "Fuck you."

Everett threw his paper down and stood up. "You can't talk to me like that! You entitled prick, if your father was here — "

Bennie kicked his desk. "But he's not! *I* am, and I'm getting nowhere with the likes of you, sitting here with your feet up. I'll talk to you different when you do some real police work."

Everett didn't like that. "You better cool it, son. Hotheads get nowhere in this racket, certainly not with me. Now just what the hell is stuck in your craw?"

"Two nights ago — the night of the blackout — The Cane had everyone running checkups on diners to see who was cashing in on the Pearl's mess. The reports from every single one came back *thin* — no leads. I think someone tipped off the black market to The Cane's investigation and *I've* got a name that might get us somewhere, but hell if he ain't a goddamn ghost."

Everett was intrigued. This was no run-of-the-mill file card check, this was real.

"You check open warrants?"

"Yeah, before I came in here. Nothing."

"Those file cards aren't the only way to track someone down. What's the name you're after?"

"Freddie Graham."

"What's he look like?"

"Black hair, little bigger than me. Rough features, I think. Only saw him for a minute."

"I'll see what I can find out."

"Aren't you gonna write any of that down?"

"I've got it, son, don't you worry."

Bennie was surprised. "Thanks."

Everett shot him a glare. "Something like this? I'm all for it, but have a cool head before you come in here again. I don't want to have to whip you."

Bennie started to laugh at the idea before he realized Everett was serious.

CHAPTER NINE

BENNIE FELT THE unforgiving floor underneath him as he woke.

Damnit, he thought. Not again.

He came onto his elbows and propped himself up, straining. His back felt like an old, creaky board, his neck like a tree trunk.

It happened all too often. He thrashed himself right out of bed while he slept. He looked over at his mattress. The sheets were bunched into a pile. His pillow was nowhere in sight. He got that uneasy feeling of relief at having the bed all to himself. No one to hurt in the night, no one to see him like this.

Yawns set him on course. He forced himself to stand, wincing, his body pulsing with shivers. He donned sweats and made for the kitchen.

He made coffee on the stove and stretched himself out. Two cups later, he was on to his morning routine: pushups, sit-ups, and squats, thirty counts each. He repeated the cycle four times, downed a plate of eggs, and poured himself another cup of coffee.

A short walk brought him to the dining room. It was drowning in paperwork from his caseload. Boxes on the floor, scribbled notes and newspaper clippings on the table. Along the easternmost wall, Bennie had crafted a makeshift timeline of relevant facts concerning the old man's murder. Field interviews, photographs, and canvassing reports were tacked into place over a five foot stretch. Bennie sipped coffee and reviewed it from the start.

January — June, 1943. While recovering in San Diego, Bennie receives several letters from his father. They're filled with talk of home front troubles and friction within the department. Bennie gets the feeling his father is lonely. It's there, but never explicitly said: *Son, please come home soon.*

July, 1943. Richmond is overrun with soldiers, prosties, and VD. In an effort to curb the illicit sex trade, police go all out on Wednesday, July 14, in a citywide crackdown. Houses of ill fame are shut down. Ladies of the night are rousted by the dozen. Most of the police force on duty that evening are involved.

That very same night, Lt. Samuel Sherwood, acting commander of Second Station, responds to a burglary call at Sears Roebuck. Hours later, an anonymous call directs police to a Jackson Ward alleyway where his deceased body is found. Cause of death: stab wounds to the back.

August, 1943. Bennie returns to Richmond, joins the police force, and is made lead on his father's case. His first order of business is a citywide dragnet. Bootleggers, numbers runners, and wife beaters are hauled in en masse — a carnival of men who'd run afoul of both the law and the old man's rigid ways. All of them have credible and verifiable alibis for that July night.

September — December, 1943. Bennie chases lead after

lead and gets nowhere. His Victory squad work takes precedent. The old man's death remains on the case board as an ongoing, but is all but pushed aside in favor of more pressing and immediate crime.

Bennie reached the end of his timeline and sank into a chair at the head of the table. He set his coffee cup down and reached for a folder, bracing himself. He fished out a few glossies and laid them on the table. Crime scene snaps from that July night. The old man, face down. Three side views and a bird's eye.

This — knifing someone — this was big and personal. This was not random. This was *war.* Bennie knew.

He heard the voice again and his head started to hurt.

You'll never catch whoever did it.

It's been too long.

You let it slip away.

It was the voice of Tokyo Rose, taunting him. Her broadcasts sought to spoil the morale of American troops.

Tears began to well in his eyes. Here he sat — a man of war who lived to tell the tale — while the old man rotted away in Hollywood Cemetery.

Bennie had thought many times about reenlisting. If he couldn't find the old man's killer, why stay? Better to go back and kill more Japs.

Why, indeed.

Bennie pushed tears from his eyes and yanked Dougie Swyers' official department photo off the wall. It was the one thing that kept him plugging away at the old man's case.

Swyers was a former policeman, dismissed in early '43 by the old man over indiscretions with underage girls. Afterwards, Swyers had managed to land a night security job at Sears Roebuck and was on duty the night the old man died. Bennie forced himself to study the man. Swyers vibed creep: bug-eyes, heavyset, no smile.

Bennie was certain: Swyers lured the old man to Sears Roebuck.

Either he did it or he was *in on it.*

Bennie had combed the city down to its cobblestones for Swyers. The man had vanished. But something needled Bennie, like a jungle instinct — Swyers was still here, somewhere.

Bennie stood and stretched himself out. He caught a glimpse of himself in a nearby mirror. He needed a good shave and a serious trim.

An idea *clicked.*

Bennie grabbed Dougie Swyers' glossy off the table and left the room, thinking of this old story his father used to tell.

Walter MacKaye held a barber's straight razor to Bennie's throat and said, "So. How many Japs you knock off?"

"Enough," said Bennie.

"That many, huh? You get to any of 'em up close?"

Bennie saw knife slashes on a Nip's face and said, "A few."

"Whooooee, boy," said Walter. "I surely can't imagine."

Walter lathered his neck and began to scrape. His thin gray-white hair capped a weathered face and ox-brawn. He still had that youthful zing in his eyes, even if he was pushing sixty.

"You're looking pretty good, Walter."

"For an old guy, you mean."

"What's your secret?"

"I like the women young and the whiskey straight."

Walter smiled as Bennie recalled his storied history with the RPD. He'd been quite the hellion in his 20s, racking up dozens of beefs for robbery and illegal trade. He made waves during Prohibition as *the* moonshine supplier for the East End. That is, until 1931, when two Treasury agents were gunned down during a raid on a still believed to be Walter's. No charges were ever filed, but Walter went into hiding, emerging some years later as a minor player in the city's thriving numbers racket. Popular opinion held that he engaged a high-ranking city official in a cover-up. These days, he was a gentle old dog, playing easy, offering up street tips in exchange for a lax attitude on his numbers setup.

"You see this scar?" Walter pulled back some of his thinning hair and exposed a cut along his skull. "Your father gave that to me." He smiled, as if thinking of a fond childhood memory.

"Oh yeah?" Bennie angled his head and pointed to his own facial scar. "He gave *that* to me."

Walter lit up. "What for?"

"For talking back."

Walter laughed. "Your father never came in for a cut or a shave, not once," he said, planing Bennie's jaw as if it were a delicate sculpture.

Bennie steeled himself and said, "He didn't trust you. He thought you should have taken the juice for those two Treasury agents."

Walter paused mid-scrape and digested the words. He held the blade tight against Bennie's skin. "That's some bold talk for someone with a razor at his neck."

"Come off it, Walter. You knew how he felt."

"And what about you?"

"I say let the past be the past."

"Said the man with a knife to his throat."

Bennie cracked a smile. "Cut me some slack. I'm just the new kid in town. I call it like I see it."

Walter gave the blade some extra weight. "I say the Marines took your manners and didn't give 'em back. You best learn to hold your tongue."

Bennie strained to speak. "Or what? You hurt me and the Cane'll shut you down before dawn. Now come off this shit, I've got questions."

Walter finished the shave and threw a hot rag at Bennie. "You can towel yourself off."

Bennie wiped himself down. Warming tingles took over his face as he eyed the room. The place hummed with activity and smelled of pomade. Five other customers got trims while Benny Goodman jazzed up the radio. *Walter, you did alright.* Ten barber chairs and a corner office. His numbers op ran out of the back room. The barbers doubled as runners on their off hours.

"Walter, who's moving rationed goods around town?"

Walter got smug. "Who isn't? Every dope in town has tried to hock their coupons or their book at one time or another."

"I'm talking weight. Who's got the pull to work something like Pearl's?"

"Hell, if I knew, don't you think I would've told you by now?"

"You've been asked?"

"Of course I've been asked. The Cane's in here most every week. Listen, it's like I tell him every time. I'm small time, that's it. No more liquor. If I know something, I'll dish. Ok?"

Bennie fished Skipper's mugshot from his steno and held it up. "Do you know this man?"

Walter leaned in. "No." Right off, no pause. Bennie took it for truth. He pulled Dougie Swyers' glossy from his pocket and showed it to Walter.

"How about this one?"

"Who's he?"

"Dougie Swyers, *ex*-RPD. Night watchman at Sears the night my father died."

Walter's brain churned memory. *Click, click, click,* until his eyes went bingo. "*Right.* Heavyset guy. I remember him. He liked his hair parted on the left."

"Know where he is?"

Walter got cross. "And why would I know a thing like that?"

"Because you deal with the scum of this city on a routine basis, and Swyers is most definitely that. I'm coming to you because it's the kind of thing you might come to find out, if you did a little asking."

Walter chilled. "Alright, fine, I'll ask around. Say, you're a big shot detective now, why don't you find him?"

"Because the Cane's on my ass to work a Victory job and I can't double time it." Bennie got up from the chair and checked himself in the mirror. *Nice work.*

"What do you know so far?" asked Walter.

"Swyers vacated his apartment two days after my father was killed. No one I talked to has seen or heard from him since."

"Sounds like a man he doesn't want to be found."

"And a man who doesn't want to be *found* — " said Bennie, letting it just hang there.

Walter flashed a knowing smile. "Is a man who just might have something to hide."

Chapter Ten

BENNIE STEPPED FROM his wheels and relished the air. The cold soothed his freshly-shaven face. All around him, the sun was setting. Wisps of orange streaked the gray sky, growing fainter by the minute. Darkness was closing in. Bennie felt a shiver run up his back and looked in all directions.

No bayonet charges.

No screams of *Banzai!*

Relieved, Bennie quickened his pace. Not that he was in any real hurry to make his destination. It looks like a dark castle, he thought, nearing the building.

The city jail lived under the shadows of the Marshall Street viaduct. It was an altogether dismal spot, blackened with soot, three stories high. Bennie had crossed its threshold countless times over the years and still, walking up the pedimented steps, he still got that eerie feeling of dread.

He shot a quick look upward before heading inside. The viaduct loomed overhead, ninety feet up, like something out of a science fiction story. A walkway to the sky. Bennie recalled one of the old man's oft repeated gripes. Folks could stroll across the viaduct and drop things into the jail yard for the inmates.

Bennie stepped inside and recoiled, aghast. The putrid smell of vomit polluted the hallway. Bennie covered his face and ducked into an office just off the main stretch.

He shut the door, relieved, and found the intake officer catching z's in his chair. Bennie pulled out his badge and rapped the desk with it. The officer came to in a snap.

"Yeah, whaddya need?"

"What happened out there?" asked Bennie, gesturing to the hallway.

"A bunch of army grunts got loaded last night off some high test rotgut. Cheap, back alley shit. They all got sick when we hauled 'em in."

Bennie winced at the thought of it and told the officer what he was after.

"Well, you can have a look all you want," he said, nodding toward a stack of boxes behind the desk. "It's all yours."

"What happened to the file cabinets?"

"Hauled off and scrapped for the war." The officer came to his feet, rubbing sleep from his eyes. "I'm gonna go see if I can find me some coffee. You want some?"

"Sure, thanks."

"Don't thank me yet. You haven't had the coffee here."

Bennie went behind the desk and dragged a chair over to the boxes. He pulled out his steno and thumbed through it. *There,* from his visit with Ms. Holly: Skipper went to work for Jedidiah King in December '42. That meant his jail time probably came *before.*

The intake officer returned with a few cups of coffee. "The boys in the kitchen say its alright. I say, drink at your own risk."

The officer took up at his desk and fingered through a newspaper. Bennie thanked him for the coffee and got to work.

The boxes were a mess. The files were in shit order. They zigzagged through time and were often incomplete and illegible. Bennie made a mental note: let The Cane know ASAP and get some competent people over here on the double.

Two hours passed. Bennie worked while the officer snoozed. Eight boxes netted three finds. He yawned, stretched, and wondered if they were enough. He took to his feet, studying them as he paced the room.

June, '42. Skipper does a weekend for brawling at a local dive and slugging a cop. He's separated from the other parties and bunks alone.

August, '42. Skipper does two nights for burglary. It's a trio this time, busted for boosting booze. His cohorts are J. Godfrey and E. Moore.

January, '43. Skipper does three nights for being drunk in public and resisting arrest. His bunkmates are S. Caldwell, J. Gentry, and N. Ray.

Bennie's mind trips an alarm. It's there — the second one, in August, '42. He heard Ms. Holly's words in his head: *"I think it was during one of those spells that a fella offered him a job working for Mr. King."*

It made sense. By January '43, Skipper's got a job. He can afford to get blotto and sleep it off in a cell. But go back six months, he's a wreck, bruising his way to a night in stir. *Stealing* booze, not buying it.

Bennie committed to memory the names of Skipper's fellow burglars from the August arrest: J. Godfrey and E. Moore. It's got to be one of them, he thought, that recruited Skipper for King's outfit.

Bennie gave the intake officer a light shake on the shoulder. Light sleeper. He came to on the quick.

"Yeah, what?"

"I need to keep these," Bennie said, holding up the three arrest records.

"Fine by me. You know, I'm just now realizing who you are."

"Yeah?"

"Your father was a fine man and a damn good cop. It's a shame, all that mess."

"Thank you, and yes it is."

"I been hearing your name all over this place this past week. You had something to do with that diner business, 'bout a week back?"

"Yeah, me and a few others."

"That's what they been saying around here, but I gotta say, it sure is funny. You ain't got a scratch on you."

Bennie didn't follow. "And why's that funny?"

The officer took on a puzzled look. "Well, I mean, those two that come in here that night, they were — "

"What two?"

"Those two shines. I was here when they brought 'em in."

"I still don't — "

"Well, they were all beat to hell, and I just figured you all got into it, is all. Didn't mean no offense."

Bennie squeezed the arrest reports hard, puncturing them with his fingers. He felt this sudden void all around him, as if everything he'd ever known just up and slipped away.

He looked at the intake officer and said, "Show me."

Negroes had the eastern wing of the jail all to themselves. A regular paradise, Bennie thought. The cold in this part of the building was sharper, the foul odors more profound. Natural light and comfort were all but naught.

The intake officer led Bennie alongside a row of overcrowded cells. Bennie clocked seven men and a bunk bed to each 12 x 12.

"This one," said the intake officer, stopping by a cell near the end. Bennie followed suit and eyed the room. Three men slept on the floor, all in a row, like sardines in a can. Another caught z's leaning against a wall. The eldest of the bunch just stood in the middle of it all, wrapped inside a blanket, murmuring a hymn.

The last two laid on the beds. Bennie recognized them right off and recalled their names from the Pearl's writeup. He pulled out his badge and rapped it on the bars.

"You two, on the beds. Jefferson and Maurice, right? My name's Sherwood, you might remember me from the other night. The officer here tells me you two are pretty banged up from all that, is that right?"

No answer.

"I just want to know what happened. Maybe I can help you. Did one of the officers rough you up?"

No answer.

"Look, I'm not with First Station. I know Captain Rivers' reputation, I'm not with him. I work the Victory Squad, I'm on my own. You can trust me."

No answer.

Bennie steeled himself and put on a hard face. "I can also make it harder for you in here. *More* unpleasant, if you care to imagine that."

No answer. The elder one's singing kicked up a notch.

Bennie caught this look from the intake officer: *don't say shit like that.*

Bennie was out of patience. "Suit yourself," he said, turning to leave. "I'll make sure the officers here know your na —"

The one on the bottom bunk — Maurice — swung his legs around slowly and began to stand, wincing. He was clearly in a lot of pain. Bennie watched as he used the bunk to steady himself and start toward Bennie with short, careful steps.

The elder one's voice rose even more. He began to pace and nod his head in rhythm with a chorus.

With much effort, Maurice walked all of six feet, stopping just short of the bars. Until then, his face had been clouded by the shadows of the cell, but now, standing in range of what little light there was, Bennie got a better look at him.

Bruises covered his temples and cheeks. One of his eyes was nearly swollen shut. The other was so void of feeling, that days later, Bennie would quiver at the thought of it.

"Maurice, who did this to you?"

Still, no answer. The elder one's song reached its peak. Inmates from a nearby cell shouted obscenities their way, calling for him to quit his howling.

Bennie felt himself grow hot. "Damnit, who did this to you?"

No answer.

"Goddamnit, *WHO?*"

Still, Maurice said nothing as he lifted his tattered rag of a shirt just high enough to reveal his stomach. There, about where a doctor might find his left kidney, was a blackened spot the size of a large fist.

A *single* spot, pounded again and again.

A target, singled out with precision, like what you might see from a boxer in the ring.

Bennie hit White's on Cary Street for grub. The spot had sentimental appeal. A Sunday matinee at the Byrd followed by dinner at White's had been a favorite father/son pastime.

His badge got him a primo counter seat and a beaucoup meal: steak, eggs, and coffee. He hit a pay phone while he waited for his food. Calls to Niles' home rang and rang. Nobody home. Bennie tried the HQ switchboard next.

"Detective Hunter is on duty with the First tonight," said the dispatcher. "Would you like me to patch you through?"

Bennie thought better of it and declined. Don't rush it, he thought. Think it through, take your time.

He found hot food waiting for him when he returned to his seat. He could have inhaled it right off, but he paused and took a moment of silence. For the old man. For the D-1-5.

He downed his steak, wolfed his eggs, and gulped his coffee. He welcomed a full stomach. The day had drained him something fierce.

He mulled on Niles. It made sense now. Two days back, at Doyle's, Niles was all shifty, hiding his hands. As if he were afraid someone might see them.

Something clicked.

Niles was working First tonight. First was Captain Rivers' territory. Rivers was big and mean and liked to throw his weight around. Literally. The Cane gave Rivers carte blanche over his jurisdiction, just so long as his tactics didn't earn the department any unwanted ink.

Bennie tried on a narrative. *Maybe* Rivers was working Niles. Niles had just secured a promotion, a step up. He had a wife and two kids to feed. *Maybe* it came at a price.

A yawn forced its way out of him and broke his train of thought. It was as if his brainwaves demanded something new, some distraction to counter the day's revelations.

Bennie glommed an abandoned newspaper off the counter and thumbed through it. Front page headlines were 100% war. Skip 'em, he thought, and maybe you'll sleep better tonight.

He flipped to the metro section and got a rush.

Halfway down the page was an ad for a bond drive at Tantilla Garden.

This Saturday night.

Right — there'd been a handbill in his mail tray earlier this week.

And — the shindig was sponsored by King Tobacco.

Bennie got the heebie-jeebies. *He* might be there.

Bennie pictured himself at the event. It looked *wrong*. On his own, he would stand out, like a boot caught in the crossfire with no cover.

But *with a date* —

A waitress at White's gave him the number. Said she used it often for servicemen. Bennie ran it by a Chesapeake & Potomac phone op and got the address. Maybe he'd catch her in between fares.

Confederate Cab operated out of an old garage near the State Penitentiary. It was an easy find. A big Confederate flag was painted on the outside of the building.

Bennie walked into the cramped office and found the dispatcher behind a cluttered desk, warming his hands with a cup of coffee. Friendly fella, ready to help. "Need a ride, mister?"

"I'm looking for one of your drivers," said Bennie. "Imogene McKenna?"

"She's on the road. Cha' need with her?"

"Just looking to get in touch."

The dispatcher flashed an *Ah-ha* smile. "You carrying a torch, pal?"

Bennie's look said *you got me.* "Any idea when she'll be back this way?"

The dispatcher got protective. "Who's asking?"

"I'm a detective, with the RPD," said Bennie, holding up his badge.

The dispatcher's eyes went wide. "This a police matter?"

"No," said Bennie, emphatically. "I just knew she drove here. Look, I can come back —"

"With her, there's no telling. Could be two hours from now, could be any second."

Bennie was intrigued. "She give you the runaround?"

"Nothing like that. Just goes off on her own every once in awhile."

"And you let it slide?"

"Don't really bother me none. She drives good, does right by her fares, and gets her wheels back every night. Who am I to complain?"

"I'd think it'd be bad for business."

"Well, there's enough of that going around that it don't matter much. I say let her do what she wants. Especially after what she's been through."

Bennie played along, like he knew. "Right."

"I mean, what're you gonna do? They don't give out medals for *that.*"

"They should."

"You're damn right they should! I mean, if any of that happened to one of my girls, I'd just be sick about it, you know?"

"Yeah."

"Or my wife, even. Just sick." The dispatcher drifted off, lost in a dark thought.

"Well, listen," said Bennie, "could I leave a note for her?"

"Sure, sure," said the dispatcher. "Like I said, though, I never know when to expect her."

Bennie pulled the bond drive ad from his pocket and scribbled a note along the margins. "Give this to her, will ya?"

CHAPTER ELEVEN

BENNIE STEPPED INTO Murphy's Hotel bar and grabbed a stool. The room oozed whiskey and smoke. Dim lighting gave the place mystique while laughs and revelry made the rounds. A poker game in one corner, politicos in the other. It was ten o'clock in the morning and the world was on fire.

A bartender walked over and set a napkin down in front of him.

"'Cha having?"

Bennie badged him and said, "Breakfast. With coffee."

The bartender about-faced and made for the kitchen. City bigwigs and top cops got food on the house.

Bennie slipped his coat off and hung it on the chair. He reached into his front breast pocket and pulled out the letter.

Careful now, don't tear it.

He held it gingerly in his hands, as if it were the last letter of its kind on earth, worth millions.

To him, it was.

He slipped it from the envelope and began to read,

savoring every word.

V-Mail
Melbourne, Australia
Nov 27, 1943
Bennie!

How's tricks, pal? Swell, I hope. It ain't the same without you, but you already know that. Word got around about your old man and we're sure sore about it. Whoever did it, we sure hope you run the guy down. The girls here sure miss you, especially that nurse. But you've got my word, none of us took up with her when you left, and that's straight up.

By the time you read this, we'll surely be off to ▮ ▮ ▮ ▮, but we're good and rested, so pray for whoever we meet because they're the ones that need it most. When its all over with, we're coming to see you, so get ready. Jimmy says you owe him two sawbucks and Charlie wants his pocket knife back.

You could wish us luck, but you know it won't do us any good. Don't worry about the D-1-5, you know we'll come through. Take care, pal, we'll write again soon. Good luck and God bless you and to hell with the Japs.
Bob

Bennie read it three times through, stifling tears.

The bartender returned with his breakfast. Bennie thanked him and dug in. Eggs, toast, and bacon, gone in a manner of minutes.

A radio clicked on. War news flooded the room. The announcer ran down the week's developments, noting exciting demonstrations of Allied air power. Bennie raised his coffee cup in celebration as the room whooped and hollered. The broadcast continued, talking up the inevitable invasion of Western Europe and the pervasive sense of doom spreading throughout Germany. More raised glasses, more whoops and hollers.

A sudden backslap surprised him. A look over his shoulder: Mayor Ambler, right there. Several of his constituents stood nearby.

Bennie extended his hand. "Sir, it's an honor."

Mayor Ambler gave him a vise-grip handshake. "The honor's all mine, son. All mine."

The Mayor turned to his cronies, showboating. "This here, *this* is the real deal, boys. A bonafide veteran of the war. Of *Guadalcanal*, mind you."

Ahs and *Attaboys* made the rounds. Bennie felt his breakfast rumble. He forced a thankful smile.

"Stolmy tells me you're doing just fine on the Victory desk, just fine." The Mayor shot him a knowing wink. *Make me look good, son.*

"Yes, sir, that's the truth. It's a real pleasure to be working for Chief Reed. We're cracking down hard on the black market, I can tell you that."

More *ahs* and *attaboys*. The attention gave Bennie a rush. He got this bold impulse. He smiled for the cronies and pulled the Mayor in for a whisper chat.

"Sir, what ever came of your investigation into the OCD party responsible for our recent blackout hubbub?"

The Mayor gave Bennie a quizzical look. He lowered his voice and said, "Son, surely you're mistaken. That's on Stolmy's plate, not mine."

Bennie checked the squadroom clock. He'd made it just in time. Two minutes until afternoon roll call.

He caught his breath and shot a look out of the room's south facing windows. Just across Broad sat City Hall, a massive, gothic building that looked as if doom itself had been weaved into its stonework. It reminded him of the castles and monasteries they featured in newsreels, the ones now in ruins all across Europe.

Just behind him, some rank and file cops made a stink about the hash joint snafu. Those threadbare reports had everyone crying foul. Bennie sipped some coffee and listened in on the chatter.

"It's gotta be someone in the mayor's office," said one cop. "They've got clout with city bigwigs. They could be running a scam through the kitchens, skimming off the take."

"I think it's the jigs," growled a second. "They're working their voodoo shit all over town and wasting our time."

"Maybe it was the dead guy from the Apollo," said a third. "Maybe that's why he got snuffed."

"Nah," said the second. "He got iced for dipping his wick in the mud."

"Nix that," said the first. "If it *was* that guy, it was over control. Some kind of power struggle."

"Well, at least we know who he is," said the third. "Maybe now we can get somewhere."

Bennie craned his head toward the case board. Sure enough, a fresh carbon was tacked to the ongoings section.

Just then, the Cane stormed into the room at a furious pace and made his way to the front.

"Listen up, ladies. We're all thinking it, so I'll just say it. *Somebody* blew our cover the other night." The Cane sharpened his eyes on the room. "Maybe it was one of you. Whoever it was," he said, lifting his cane in the air like a sword, "no manner of kickback is worth my wrath."

SMACK!

The rod came down hard on the lectern. The room flinched.

"Should any of you care to feed me the responsible party," he continued, "you'll find me in your debt."

An infectious discomfort took hold of the squadroom.

"But," said the Cane, "all is not lost." He tore the new carbon from the case board and waved it in the air.

"We have a lead, so listen up. The dead male found at the Apollo has been identified as one Jack Gentry, a lowlife about town who drank and did little else. A records check on Gentry turned up zilch, but we scored an ID off his morgue slab pic."

Bennie got the shivers. Someone yelled, "How?"

"We got word from the street that local barkeeps were hot to find this chump who ran out on his tabs. Said chump had a scar down the right side of his face, like so."

The Cane moved a finger down his right temple.

"It just so happens that Jack Gentry had such a scar." The Cane held up the photo for everyone to see.

Bennie felt his knees buckle. His mind flashed to that night, those bodies on the bed — Jack Gentry's neck, bent all wrong.

The Cane said, "A waitress from the English Tavern gave up his name. Said Gentry was a regular, when he could pay up. Said his last time in the place was two weeks back. He drank himself sick and stormed out before anyone could stop him."

Someone piped up. "What about his draft card? Did he fight?"

Jack said, "We checked with selective service. Gentry's name was nowhere to be found. It appears he skipped this whole mess altogether."

The room exchanged puzzled looks. Bennie felt miffed.

Who the hell was this guy?

The Cane said, "Either way, it's a lead on our Apollo killer. Ask around about the man with the scar who liked to drink. It might get us somewhere."

The room grunted.

The Cane slapped the lectern. "Everyone got it?"

A collective *Yessir* made the rounds.

"Very well," he said. "Dismissed."

The room came alive and funneled toward the staircase. Bennie turned and started for the lair when he heard his name.

"Bennie," said Jack. "A word."

He and Jack took up in a corner, out of earshot.

"That's quite a get," said Bennie, "that guy's name."

Jack shrugged it off. "We don't know enough yet to say what's what. Could be a dead end."

"Still —"

Jack cut him off. "Look, I'm sure you remember our debacle at Pearl's," he said. "Well, the old bird who lives in the apartment where your pal Holly died has a bone to pick with the department. I'd like you to pay her a visit."

"What does she want?"

"An apology, a new bathroom, and a new frying pan."

Bennie tried to hide his frustration. "Couldn't one of the other men handle it?"

"The rest of the department is chasing a dead end. Perhaps you'd like to join them?"

Pushy Jack: gruff voice, hard eyes. Bennie didn't feel like arguing.

"Sure, then. I'll go and see her."

"Good," said Jack, starting to walk away. "And tomorrow, I want a report. Where you are with Digby and what's next. Understand?"

Bennie nodded and watched him go, wondering just why he was in such a hurry.

Bennie highballed the stairs that led to the old bird's apartment. He wanted it over quick. See the old biddy, move on. His fingers grazed the shot-up bannister and loosed more splinters. Bennie was surprised: no repairs yet.

He made the top floor and stopped just short of her pad. More of the same: no new door, just a shoddy jamb and hinge job. He readied his badge and knocked. An eerie sight made him flinch. Flecks of Skipper's blood were still caked to the wood.

A fragile voice sounded from inside. "Yes?"

Bennie checked his notes for her name before he spoke. "Ms. McGraw, this is Detective Sherwood with the police department. Could I speak to you for a moment?" The memory of her wallop gave Bennie's shoulder phantom pains.

Through the door, she said, "I've nothing more to say. I made my complaint and I'll surely make another if you don't let me alone."

"Ms. McGraw, if you'd only hear me out, I'm here *because* of your complaint."

Silence stretched three long beats before the door cracked open. Ms. McGraw peered from behind it, underdressed and unsure. "Were you the one who came before?"

"Yes, m'am," said Bennie, raising his badge for her to see, "and I apologize for my rude behavior. We were a little too preoccupied for manners that night." Bennie pocketed his badge and flashed his best smile. "Now, about your bathroom —"

She jerked the door open and spoke above him. "You don't look familiar."

"Well, it was a bit wild that night," said Bennie, "with everything happening. I wouldn't expect you to remember me. And I do apologize if I was rude, m'am. I was just doing my job."

"What night?" she said, growing irate. "I remember good and well that it was during the day. I may be on in years, but I do remember that much."

Bennie went along with it. "Yes, m'am, of course. Now, if you'd only tell me — "

"Don't try and hush me, you insolent young man! And why aren't you in uniform? You look of age. Why aren't you fighting?"

Bennie blanched and stood tall. He said, "Again, I apologize, but I've only been here once before, m'am, the night the man died in your bathroom."

She studied Bennie, bemused. "Well, of course I remember *that*, but I don't remember *you*. I thought you were the other man."

Bennie perked up. "What other man?"

"The one who came a few days ago, to look through the apartment. He said he was assessing damages, but then I never head another word from him or the police, so I made that complaint."

Bennie felt his skin tingle. "This man, Ms. McGraw, was he a policeman?"

"That's what he said. You think I'm making it up," she said, starting to get hot.

"No, m'am, I don't. Ms. McGraw, could I come in for a moment?"

"I suppose," she said, gesturing for Bennie to enter. "But let me get a robe on." Bennie shut the door and stood just inside the living room as she hurried off.

He could hardly stand still. His mind raced with potential visitors/motive: a rogue cop, looking for loose ends? An opportunistic reporter with a fake badge, looking for some truth?

Bennie looked around the room to calm himself while he waited. The place looked better than it had that night. Homely, all put together. A portable radio sat on the coffee table amidst wartime gimcracks and loving photographs of a young boy. Unfinished knitting rested on the seat of her rocker. Maybe something for the Red Cross, he thought.

Bennie's heart sank as his eyes found a nearby wall. There, above the well-worn couch, hung the cloth banner of irreplaceable loss: a gold star ensconced in a thick blue border.

"I don't have a proper window," she said, "so I hang it on the wall."

Bennie turned and found her standing next to him. "I'm so sorry, Ms. McGraw."

"You and everyone else," she said, exhausted of the sentiment.

Bennie changed the mood quick. "This man who came to see you, he badged you?"

"He did," she said. "He looked around the place for a bit and poked around in the bathroom for a time. Then he left in a hurry. He was quite rude. And, like I said, when I didn't hear back from him, that's when I made the complaint."

"Could you describe him?"

She clenched her jaw, her memory straining, and gave Bennie a good look. "He wasn't as tall as you, nor as trim. He was in dire need of a shower and better manners."

"Do you remember his name?"

Ms. McGraw pulled a piece of paper off the coffee table. She raised cheaters to her eyes and read off a name. "Sergeant Swain, he said it was."

A bogus ID. There was no Swain on any desk in the department.

"When did he come around?" asked Bennie.

She searched her memory. "It was Tuesday, just three days ago. I know because I always listen to Bob Hope on Tuesdays and this man interrupted the program."

"Do you remember anything else about him?"

"I remember he looked dissatisfied. As if he were looking for something he didn't find."

Bennie's brain shot blanks. Looking for what? "Ms. McGraw, do you mind if I take a look around?"

"Be my guest. Want some coffee?"

"Yes, m'am, thank you."

Ms. McGraw shuffled to her kitchen as Bennie tracked the hallway. He could still see blood marks on the walls and floor. When he made the bathroom, he flinched at the crimson streaks peppering the tub. It had been days since Pearl's, why hadn't it been cleaned?

Bennie moved in a circle, looking all around. He crouched and craned his head for a good look under the tub. Scuff marks marred the floor, as if someone had moved it in a hurry. Otherwise, nothing but dust and grime. Bennie came to his feet and took stock of the room. Towels, soaps, hairnets. Nothing suspect.

"Find anything?" said Ms. McGraw.

Bennie turned to find her standing just inside the room, holding two cups of coffee. Bennie took one and said, "Ms. McGraw, did no one from the department come to clean up afterwards? Or offer to fix the door?"

She pinned him with a sheepish look. "Someone did come, yes, but I was too... upset to let anyone in. I took a stab at it myself, but, as you can see, I didn't get very far." She sipped her coffee and rested her gaze on the floor. "My son would have fixed the door right. He was good at things like that."

CHAPTER TWELVE

BENNIE STEPPED INSIDE the Mosque Theater at Main and Laurel Streets. The swanky concert hall pulled triple duty. Music shows, police academy training digs, and anti-aircraft operations for the Coast Artillery Corps. Bennie sidestepped top secret types and made for the police gym.

Grunts and shouts led the way. The room smelled of sweat and talc. A dozen men pounded heavy bags, skipped rope, and did push-ups. Gunshots echoed from the shooting range down the hall.

Niles sparred in the ring. His opponent was an AO named Lewis. Lewis worked in the paint shop and did time on a civil defense beat. Rumor had it he went overboard on even the slightest infraction.

Bennie grabbed a ringside seat and watched them finish a round. Niles: quick feet, quick hands. Lewis: a tank on legs. Their back and forth went both ways. Niles went hard up close, hammering Lewis' ribcage with jabs. Lewis countered with powerful hooks and crosses.

One of his crosses put Niles on uneasy legs. He lost

ground and swung wildly, punching air. Lewis saw his chance and closed in, a big finish in sight. He landed a massive right hook that laid Niles on his back, gasping for breath.

Lewis stood over him, gloating. "Told you to pace yourself, but you rushed it."

Niles came to his elbows and spit blood. He glared daggers at Lewis, who just smiled and walked to his corner.

Bennie grabbed a pail of water and stepped into the ring. "You need a trainer," he said to Niles.

Niles took the pail and soup-bowled it. Dribbles soaked his chest. "I'll be fine," he said, rubbing his temples. "Just need a little ice and some aspirin." Bennie helped him to his feet and handed him a towel. Niles dried off and leaned against the ropes. "You want the real show," he said, "come tomorrow night. We got a thing going with Ladder 10, a fundraiser."

Bennie thought of tomorrow and got tingles. Would she show?

"I'm busy."

Niles took another drink from the pail. "So what's up? You wanna' spar?"

Bennie played it cool. "I know you don't start Victory until next week, but I need you for a job. The Cane okayed it and it won't take long. Would've grabbed someone else, but everyone's out working an Apollo lead."

"What's the job?"

"A warrant grab. Some wife beater out in the East End."

"That's First territory. They might mind."

"They're working the Apollo lead, too. Like I said, everyone's occupied. Come on, clean up. The sooner we do this, the sooner we can sign off."

"Alright, just give me a few to change. Meet you out front."

Niles made for the lockers. Bennie left the gym with butterflies in his stomach, hoping his plan didn't backfire.

They parked on Franklin, facing west, with a view up 28th. The house was in the middle of the block, near the alley.

Bennie said, "I'll come in through the back, you hold the front. That way, if he tries to rabbit — "

"I'll grab him," said Niles.

They nodded and set off on separate paths. Bennie hopped a fence and crept his way across a few yards, being careful not to disturb anyone's Victory gardens. He moved slow. It was dark, chilly, and hard to see.

He came to the house. Made the back steps and knelt beside them, feeling his way along the ground. No, not that one, not that one — *there*. He loosed the brick from the walkway and pulled out the door key, just like the old man had showed him, so many years ago.

Bennie restored the brick and padded the steps. He leaned in close to the back door, listening for sounds inside.

All clear.

He let himself in, shut the door, and eased his way into a hallway. His hands were outstretched, feeling for the walls.

He found a light switch and flipped it. He was in the common room. Lots of chairs sat around a big table peppered with playing cards, cigarette butts, and empty glasses.

Bennie left the room and walked down the hall. He

came to the front window and peeked outside. There, crouching behind a car, was Niles, ready to pounce.

Bennie cracked the front door and whistled. The whole thing reminded him of a midnight jungle raid. Niles came sneaking to the door on quiet feet. Bennie held a finger to his mouth and ushered him inside.

They moved back through the hallway and stopped in the kitchen.

"Where is he?" asked Niles. Jacked, ready to go. Bennie checked the icebox. Jackpot: deli meat, some cheese.

"Bennie, what's going on? Where is this guy?"

Bennie rummaged through a few cabinets next. No bread, but a good find: a bottle of mash, half full.

Niles, all rage. "Bennie! Shit, man, what gives?"

Bennie put the bottle on the table and turned to Niles. "My old man brought me here for the first time right after my mom left. Said if anything ever happened to him, to come here, that I'd be safe, that the other cops would take care of me."

Niles softened. Confusion in his eyes.

"The RPD keeps this place for a variety of off-book shenanigans," continued Bennie. "As you can imagine, it's good for private time with girls on the side. There's a few bedrooms upstairs. Others use it to dry out after a bender. And there's a weekly poker game, too. Being going on since, hell, always."

Niles looked around like he was in a foreign country. "And just what the hell are we doing here?"

"I'm gonna pour us a couple of stiff drinks," said Bennie. "And then you're going to tell me why you wailed on those two Negroes we hauled out of Pearl's."

Niles froze, as if he were a thief found out. Slowly, he went limp, steadying himself against the counter.

Bennie handed him a glass of mash and said, "Spill."
Niles said, "You better hand me the bottle."

Niles Hunter was a devoted family man. Married his sweetheart Cheryl Lee right out of high school. Theirs was a joyous union, fun and passionate. So passionate that just ten months pass before Cheryl Lee pops out a pair of twin girls. A welcome surprise, but a surprise nonetheless. The girls are just about 3 now, born in '41.

Niles' color blindness kept him from the fight, but he made his contribution here at home, building munitions at Tredegar. It paid well, but the long hours were hard on his new family. He got little face time with his girls, as they were often asleep when he arrived home.

He grew restless and unsatisfied. He started heading out with the guys after their shifts, hitting nightclubs and drinking. On one occasion, they happened upon a back alley brawl. A couple of GIs, going at it over some girl. A crowd had formed and bets were placed. Niles and his pals walked away with some extra scratch. They figured it was just a one time thing, a lucky break.

One of Niles' daughters was not so lucky. She caught a cough that wouldn't let up. Not only were medicine and doctor's visits hard to come by, they added up. Suddenly, Niles' paycheck was hardly making ends meet.

An idea came to him. A bad one, he knew, but he was desperate. He'd dabbled with boxing in high school and did alright. "It didn't disagree with me," he said. "I knew that much."

Meanwhile, the back alley brawls had become a regular thing, a way for guys to blow off some steam. One night, Niles went on his own, picked a guy out of the crowd, and decked him. "That way, I was justified. I had a score to settle. Or rather, the other guy had a score to settle with me." He was so confident he could win, he put money on himself.

His instincts were right. His bet paid 6 to 1. He walked out with double his paycheck. In cash.

"So you went back."

"Well, sure. But not right away."

Niles didn't want to make a habit out of bad behavior. Plus, his bruises scared Cheryl Lee and the girls. "I made something up, told them it was from Tredegar." He went back every couple of weeks, just to make some extra bread.

"What'd you do with all the cash?"

"Most of it I stashed in the garage. What I did bring home, I wrote off as bonus pay."

The Hunters were doing alright. Their daughter got better, the extra bills went away. Things evened out.

"So, you quit the fights, yeah?"

"Yeah. Pretty much. And then, one night…"

Niles' fight status had become legend around his Tredegar cohorts. They couldn't believe he just up and quit. "So, we're all out one night, and the guys are just egging me on, you know? So, we go, and I cave. What the hell, right?"

Niles took a long pull from the bottle. He wiped his mouth on his sleeve. "I wind up against some Marine. 6'2", big. Hell, I would have done better against a brick wall." Bennie stifled a proud grin as Niles told him how he'd lost, badly. And not just the fight, but a sizable portion of his self-respect, as well.

"It was bad. Real bad."

"But you went back."

"I had to."

Niles came from a long line of proud men, known for carrying their own. Standing tall on their own two feet. "I just couldn't go out like that."

He went back and lost. And then he lost again and again. He continued to lose until he'd drained his garage stash and then some.

"Jesus. And then what?"

"That's where it gets... a little strange."

Niles hit rock bottom in late '42. Right about the time Bennie was fighting off nightmares in San Diego. "I owed almost a grand to the guys running the fights. It was serious. I'd tried to get overtime work and couldn't. Too many people working, everyone getting paid. So I went to make a deal, with what I didn't know, when they direct me to someone new. A man I had seen around, checking in on everything, watching over the fights, like maybe he had a stake in 'em."

"And?"

"It was Captain Rivers."

"The Captain Rivers? Out of First?"

"That's the one. He says to me, 'I'll cover your debt if you come and work for the RPD'. I'm thinking, it's steady pay with a pension. I'm in. Only there's a catch. I would have to... assist investigations. When called upon."

The revelation of it hung between them like a bad smell. It was a smart play for Rivers, thought Bennie, letting someone else do the dirty work.

"So you've been doing this, what? A year?"

"Yeah, but the two Negroes, after Pearl's? That was it. I told Rivers afterword. 'My debt's paid.' No more, or he'd be on the receiving end."

"How'd he take it?"

"I didn't stick around to hear his answer."

"You and Rivers leave Pearl's with the two Negroes. What happens?"

Niles sighed. "We took those two to the auto shop. Rivers thought they knew something about that shipment, about something missing. I went at 'em for a time, but got nowhere, and then I just quit 'em. They didn't know anything."

"Anyone else there?"

"Just this guy Brown."

"Arthur Brown?"

"Yeah."

Bennie just shook his head.

"Now, Bennie, before we go on, there's something I want you to know."

"What?"

"I didn't enjoy it, you understand? I just… it was a lot of dough, and I didn't want the girls to know."

Bennie nodded. "What do they think of you being a cop?"

"Cheryl Lee don't like it much, but the hours are better. I see 'em more. It's alright. And now, moving to Victory — it's a good thing."

"Does The Cane know about your — ?"

"I don't know. Probably. There ain't much he don't know."

Bennie reached for the bottle and took a pull.

"It's my turn now."

The two of them gnashed salami as Bennie ran it down — Ms. McGraw's complaint, her apartment, her imposter cop.

Niles took a swig and thought it over. "So, the old bird said the man who showed up left disappointed, right? As if he couldn't find what he was looking for."

"Right."

"*Maybe* your pal Holly had something on him, something valuable."

Bennie followed Niles' line of thought. It was genius.

"The morgue."

"Yeah," said Niles. "And if we're lucky, they won't have torched his clothes yet."

Chapter Thirteen

NO SUCH LUCK, thought Bennie, as he stared into the fire of the incinerator. He was at the city morgue, in the basement of MCV hospital. He watched the fire blaze sun hot, feeding itself off an endless burn. Inside, Skipper's clothes had all but turned to ash.

"Put 'em in there just yesterday. Wish I'd a known."

The morgue attendant was rail thin and spoke with a slow drawl. His name badge read Sampson.

Bennie said, "How about recent IDs? You got a list hanging around?"

Sampson nodded and handed Bennie a clipboard with daily logs that ran a week back. Bennie fingered through them. *There*, three days ago: on Tuesday, 1/4/44, at 12:10pm, Ms. Luann Holly positively identified the body of Stephen Holly, her natural born son. Bennie got tingles: the box indicating that Skipper's belongings had been released to his next of kin was *un*checked.

Bennie said, "Personal effects found on a body. They're down here with you, right?"

"Yeah, but —"

Bennie held up the clipboard and pointed at Skipper's name. "This one."

The attendant squinted at the log. "Okay, just fill out a request. You'll have 'em tomorrow."

"No. I need 'em *now*."

"Look, they're already stashed away, and I'm off soon, so — "

Bennie shot him an ice stare.

Sampson huffed and copped attitude. He snatched the clipboard and zipped from the room.

Bennie stepped into the hall to wait. His stomach turned: the whole place smelled of formaldehyde. He found a seat in a folding chair opposite Sampson's desk.

Minutes ticked away. Bennie searched the room for something to occupy his mind. A war poster urged him to buy more bonds at payday. He scoffed at it, knowing full well he'd do just that.

Sampson returned, flustered. "Here," he said, holding up an evidence bag.

Bennie took it and emptied the contents onto the desk. A ration book spilled out, along with two dozen expired points, a numbers slip, and a napkin scribbled with Pearl's address.

"His mother didn't want any of this?"

"No, she was too distraught. She just saw the body and left."

Poor Ms. Holly. Bennie made a mental note: send flowers ASAP. He was disappointed. The items had little to no value. Numbers slips were only good day of. The expired points were worthless, ditto the napkin. Only the ration book had value. A sure hand could forge it and sell it on the black market.

Bennie said, "Burn it. All of it."

"You got it, right away." Sampson: suddenly eager to please. He returned the items to the bag quick.

Bennie made for the stairs, feeling hopeless. As he walked away, he wondered: who came down here to ID the old man?

Bennie sped onto Broad, nearly colliding with a bus. Home was but a short trip east, so he cooled his nerves and slowed. It was cold outside, getting dark. Evening had set, save for a few wisps of daylight fading into the horizon behind him.

He was just outside Church Hill when a jungle instinct needled him. He threw a look back and took inventory. A couple of taxis, an Army convoy, that bus. Nestled around them were a few prewar rides. Fords and Chevys, mostly.

Bennie hit the gas and threw a hard right at 23rd Street. Heading south now, toward the river.

A look back —

Bingo. One of the Chevys followed suit, a convertible with its top up. It was too dark to make out its true color.

Bennie kept a steady pace. He didn't want to spook it, not yet. He hit Main Street and bore right, westbound.

Another look back —

Bingo.

The Chevy did the same.

So, Bennie thought, I'm being tailed. The question was, who? Lose it first, then think.

Bennie tight-gripped the steering wheel and gassed it. Not too fast, he thought. Don't draw any unwanted attention.

An intersection loomed ahead. Bennie stole another look back: the Chevy, on him tight, gaining ground.

Bennie: eyes front, deep breath. He gunned it through a

red light, igniting a chorus of horns. A crossing bus just missed him, a mere yard from collision. A jaywalker escaped his path and sent a blue streak his way.

Bennie took the next two blocks easy. He risked another look back: that Chevy, still on him.

Up ahead, 14th Street. Bennie doglegged left and started across the Manchester bridge. A good sign: southbound traffic was light. Bennie zipped from lane to lane, threading a mix of cars and buses.

Bennie was heading south now, on Hull. Another look back — the Chevy was caught up in some gridlock, maybe eight car lengths back.

Bennie jerked his wheels right, then left, then right again. Old memories guided him to a dead end street between some warehouses. Bennie stopped near a field of overgrown weeds. Spooky place. Once, this had been the Manchester sandlot, a breeding ground for talent and wisecracks. Now, it was just a desolate patch of dirt filled with overgrown weeds.

Bennie found a spot in the shadows and killed the engine. From here, he had a clear line of sight on approaching cars. He sank into his seat and peered out the window. Nothing to do but wait.

Stalled time got him thinking. The tail car was RPD, all the way. The follow technique was textbook stuff, straight out of the academy. Bennie knew the signs well enough, having ridden shotgun alongside the old man enough times. Two hunches felt right: either The Cane didn't trust him to stay off King, or Ms. McGraw's cop imposter was onto him.

Lights up ahead. The Chevy was coasting the streets like a shark. It paused at the intersection, considering the dead end, and drove off.

Bennie breathed a sigh of relief. Give it twenty minutes, he thought. A big yawn took hold. Bennie closed his eyes and thought of days long gone: palling around with Skipper, cutting class, and finding glory in a well-turned double play.

CHAPTER FOURTEEN

RAPS ON THE driver's side window woke him. Bennie sat up and worked his neck. Bright sunshine held his eyelids at half-mast. He shook his head into focus and rolled down the window.

An older beat cop stood just outside. "Say, pal, you can't sleep here. You're gonna have to —" The cop paused, his head leaning in. "Say, aren't you Sam Sherwood's kid?"

"That's me," said Bennie, blinking his eyes open.

"Well, heck, I didn't know." The cop sized up Bennie's unmarked. "These department wheels?"

Bennie: foggy, slow with questions. "Yeah, that they are."

The cop lit up and whistled. "You on a stakeout?"

Bennie's very reason for being in the car, at this time, in this place, came back to him. "Not exactly."

"Ah, I see. Tied one on last night, eh?"

Bennie was thankful for the misunderstanding. The tail car had him spooked on other cops. "That'd be it."

The cop beamed in approval, recalling a memorable

bender. "Well, I know what that's like. Done that a time or two myself. Say, you can rest here as long as you want, no worry t'all."

"I appreciate that, Officer —?"

"Mitchell's the name. Cyrus Mitchell. I didn't know your father too well, being on this side of the river, but we crossed paths a time or two. Good man, your father."

"I appreciate that, Cyrus, and I'd be grateful if we could keep this between us. Victory Squad's got some high profile stuff cooking. Word gets out I'm a drunk, well — it might sour things."

"Oh, you needn't worry about me," said Cyrus, flashing a wink. "Hell, I ain't got anyone to talk to nohow. With all the AOs we got on now, there ain't nothing for me to do except walk this beat. Say, you boys need any help over there at HQ? I'm good on my feet and quick with a .38."

"I'll ask around," said Bennie, firing up the car.

"Boy, I'd sure appreciate that. I ain't got long left on this job, and I sure don't want to spend it out here in no man's land. Say, you ever get the guy that got your old man?"

"Not yet, Cyrus. Not yet."

"Well, keep at it, young man, and watch that drink, you hear? It's the devil."

Bennie snaked through Church Hill with a look in all directions. That Chevy was nowhere. He drove past his home on 28th Street and parked his wheels on Marshall. Two blocks down, facing east. An easy getaway route, if the need arose.

Bennie made his front door and found it unlocked. Probably just left in a hurry, he thought. He stepped inside, shut the door, and said, "Shit."

Someone had tossed the place.

Bennie ran through the downstairs. So many broken dishes littered the kitchen floor, he almost slipped. His casework was scattered all over the dining room; it would take days to reorganize it. Sofa stuffing caked the living room, like a fresh snowfall. Damn it, thought Bennie. Someone knifed the damn thing to shreds.

A run upstairs yielded more of the same. His bedroom was chaos: a pile of clothes on the floor, his mattress overturned. A walk down the hall was tricky: lumps of towels and shattered frames blocked his way. He came to his father's bedroom and stopped.

Nothing looked out of place. The whole room embodied stillness, as if it were a living photograph, a moment you could step into and feel but never change.

Bennie made his way back downstairs and into the kitchen. He found an unbroken cup and filled it with water. A long drink cooled him off. He took a seat at the table and let it all wash over him.

He felt it in his gut.

The sofa, knifed to shreds – it was the same MO.

His father's killer/the Apollo killer had been *here*, in the house.

Looking for something.

A tornado of emotion hit him — fear/worry/anger. He felt a dizzy spell coming on. He straightened his back, loosened his muscles. Inhale, exhale, repeat. Just like they'd taught him.

A clarity took hold.

The question now is not *who* —

The question is what?

What did he have that someone would toss his pad for?

Bennie jumped up and made for a hall closet. He pulled

a box from the top shelf and opened it. The old man's police commendations — untouched.

Back upstairs, to his own room. Over to the dresser, quick. He pulled a box from the bottom drawer and opened it. His war mementos — untouched.

The sight of them made Bennie quiver. His Japanese phrasebook, the stub knife he'd kept in his boot, a necklace of gold teeth cut from a dead Nip's mouth. He shut the box in a hurry, afraid of the items inside, and returned it to the drawer.

Standing there, in his room, Bennie suddenly felt as if he were caught in a clearing. Out in the open, all alone. Jap snipers circled him, only he couldn't see them, and they didn't shoot. They were just there, taunting him with their presence.

He sank onto his mattress, spent. He felt the shakes coming on.

Goddamnit — just fucking shoot me already.

He punched the mattress in frustration. It felt good. He turned, knelt on top of it, and hammered it with his fists, one after the other, screaming at the top of his lungs, so loud they could hear him all the way back on Guadalcanal.

Bennie stood in the middle of his room now, stark naked, and wondered what he should wear. Rest and a hot shower had calmed his rage. Now, it was time to get ready. The Tantilla shindig was tonight. He fumbled his way through the pile of clothes on the floor and fished out a collared shirt, a pair of slacks, and a blazer. He laid them on the dresser and pulled out clean drawers and some fresh socks. It still got to him sometimes, the clean clothes. Five months home and he still wasn't used to having them around.

He made his way down the hall, half-dressed. He stepped into the old man's bathroom and opened the sink cabinet. Bingo: a bottle of Old Spice, right there. Bennie took a whiff — it was still good. He massaged a few drops into his neck and felt the cool sting of relief. Something to the right caught his eye and he froze.

Holy shit, there's someone in the shower —

Wait, no.

It's just a shirt, hung up to dry.

Bennie's memory tripped six days back. He washed his bloody shirt from Pearl's in the sink and hung it to dry in the old man's shower.

Hanging next to it were the pants he had on that night.

Nerves sent a ripple up Bennie's spine as he replayed those last moments with Skipper. Just before he died, handing Bennie that pack of smokes.

Bennie grabbed the pants and rummaged through the pockets. The cigarettes were still there.

Well, look at that — they're River City Sovereigns.

Bennie took the pack, knelt down, and spilled the contents onto the floor: three cigarettes, some loose leaf crumbs, a cheap parchment liner, and a matchbook. Nothing of obvious value. No money, no ration points.

Bennie unrolled each cigarette and inspected its wrapping, front to back. No inscriptions, no scribbles. Ditto for the liner. The matchbook was from the Westwood Supper Club. Bennie flipped it open —

Holy Shit.

Scribbled on the inside flap was an inscription: JH M10 10P.

Chapter Fifteen

BENNIE STEPPED INTO the ballroom at Tantilla Garden and marveled at the scene. Johnny Pepper & The Salt Shakers, the house band, swung the room with *In The Mood.* Couples jitterbugged wall to wall and shook the maple dance floor with their moves. The room smelled of liquor and sweat and pulsed with heat. Blackout curtains covered the windows and oven-cooked the room. Two bartenders grabbed dangling chains and pulled the rollaway ceiling just open, ignoring the wartime edict. Cool air sent the room into a collective *Ahhh!* Hostesses weaved through the crowd with cups of ice and juice, mixing cocktails on the fly with brown bagged bottles. Frisky hands copped feels and tickles as the room spun with cheers and laughter.

Johnny worked the crowd as if he were a snake charmer, teasing them with a new tune. A few of the dancers near the stage worked themselves into a simmering frenzy. Snare hits and horn blares crescendoed and ignited a new dance. Bennie caught a contact high off the energy and let it ride. Action on the Canal had nothing on the Garden.

A voice purred into his ear. "Looking for a date, soldier?"

Bennie turned and found Imogene standing next to him. His heart skipped a beat at the sight of her. This was no grease monkey. Standing before him now was a War Belle Supreme, done up nice in nylons and a high-cut emerald dress. Loose-fitting rayon that really got Bennie's motor running. She had a playful look in her eyes and a Victory brooch made of sterling silver and faux pearl pinned to one of her lapels. Her quarter-inch heels click-clacked as she mimicked the crowd.

Bennie said, "Looks like I've got one now."

Her eyes darted around the room for a moment, as if she were looking for someone else. "Don't be so sure of yourself. This room's crawling with eligible men."

"So what are you talking to me for?"

"I want to see if you can dance."

"Just show me where to put my feet."

Imogene grabbed his hand and pulled him into the crowd. They started moving, all nerves and awkward steps. Before long, they found a groove and did the Lindy Hop and the East Coast Swing. They bopped and swayed in tandem with the room. They bumped into other couples and giggled. They bumped into each other and shared a nervous smile.

The Salt Shakers eased into a ballad. Couples all around them pretzeled up and got close. Bennie moved in, feeling bold, but her look held him off.

"Let's get some air," she said.

Frosty air welcomed them to the balcony. Imogene wrapped a sweater around herself and leaned against the railing. Bennie crossed his arms and kept quiet. He was too spooked to talk, afraid he'd blurt out the wrong thing. He kept hearing the cab dispatcher's words in his mind — *'They don't give out medals for what she's been through.'* Muffled sounds stole his attention. He looked over and saw a couple locking lips in the corner.

"Don't get any ideas, Mr. Detective," said Imogene, a sly smile on her lips. "That's *not* on the menu. And anyways, I haven't got all night. I had to switch shifts just to make this little rendezvous."

"So why'd you come, then?"

"I like this place, I like to dance, and I needed a night out. But these are my last good nylons. Tear them and you'll have one less eye to see with."

Bennie put his hands up. "You've made your point. Hands off."

"Good. Now, why'd you ask me out?"

"Isn't it obvious? I wanted to see you again."

"You could have just come to the garage."

"Not like that. Like this," he said, gesturing inside.

"Do you bring a lot of girls here?"

"No."

She pinned him with a suspicious look. "Don't kid me."

"No fooling, honest. Say, what about you? How do I know you're not here with a different guy every night?"

"You don't," she said, teasing him with a wink.

Police sirens sounded in the distance. Bennie turned toward them on instinct, concerned.

Imogene clocked his look. "Do you like being a cop?"

Bennie met her eyes. "Yeah, I do."

"You could be anything right now. There's so much work. Why do that?"

"It runs in the family and it's what I know. What about

you? You like working on cars?"

A grave look took hold of her face then, as if the saddest thought in the world just popped into her head.

"I'm sorry," said Bennie. "We can talk about something else."

"No, it's — " She fumbled with it, forcing a smile. "I love cars."

Raucous cheers came from inside. A GI skipped onto the balcony and said, "Hey, get in here! Some guy's sharing all his booze with everyone! Come on!"

The GI darted back inside. The couple in the corner broke free and followed suit. Bennie shot Imogene an eager look.

"You wanna?"

She smiled, grabbed his hand, and led him inside.

A mob had formed in a corner of the ballroom. They couldn't make him out, but a man in the center held court something fierce, as if he were the eye of a storm. The lot cheered as he passed out drink after drink.

Bennie and Imogene fell into the group, caught up in a riptide of moving bodies. The closer they got to the center, the more Bennie became sure of it. A woman just ahead of them called the man by name and confirmed it.

It was him, alright.

Jedidiah King held out glasses of booze for Bennie and Imogene and said, "Here, please, drink with us!" Bennie got a good look at him up close. On in years, but still youthful. Movie star handsome with a wolf's eyes and a politician's smile. Dapper threads: silk bow tie, three piece pinstripe, cordovan shoes.

"What are we celebrating?" asked Bennie, taking both glasses.

"Why, life, my good friend! I'd say that's cause enough, wouldn't you?"

"We couldn't agree more," said Bennie, handing one to Imogene, who took hers with reservation.

"To life, your health, and our nation's inevitable victory!" said Jedidiah, as the trio clinked their glasses together. The two men drank. Imogene just watched, her face growing with tension.

Jedidiah lowered his glass and peered at Bennie quizzically. "You look familiar. Tell me, have we met before?"

"I don't think so," said Bennie, tensing up. He spoke deliberately: "Name's Sherwood. I'm with the cops."

Jedidiah lit up. "Ah, yes, I remember now. Samuel Sherwood's esteemed son. It's Bennie, right?"

Bennie nodded, the hairs on the back of his neck rising.

"Delighted," said Jedidiah, extending his hand. "Jedidiah King, at your service."

Bennie forced himself to shake his hand. Locked eyes, firm grips.

"You must feel quite lucky," Jedidiah continued, "to have made it home in one piece."

Imogene broke her silence. "I'm afraid you must excuse me," she said, handing her drink to Bennie and hurrying off.

"Was it something I said?" mused Jedidiah.

Bennie lost sight of her, puzzled. Give her a moment, he thought, and seize the opportunity. He turned back.

"Since I've been home, Mr. King, I've heard a lot about you."

"All good things, I hope."

"Word is, you're a powerful man with powerful friends."

Jedidiah smiled. "Come now, Detective. Surely the talk

around the department is more robust than *that*. Yes, the war's been kind to my tobacco interests and success has earned me considerable influence. Which I use, I might add, to host events such as this and contribute to the overthrow of international tyranny."

"I'm sure Uncle Sam appreciates your support, Mr. King," said Bennie, "but I'm not sure he needs everyone quite so liquored up." A fight broke out near the stage. A GI and a Marine, trading jabs. *Oorah.*

"Ah, but that's just it, Detective," said Jedidiah, flashing a salesman's wink and lowering his voice. "The more they drink, the more bonds they buy!"

Two men called to Jedidiah from across the room. City councilmen, blotto on free hooch. Jedidiah waved to them, raising his glass.

Bennie steeled himself. Plant a seed, he thought. "You know, Mr. King, it's funny, meeting like this. I just ran into an old pal who said he's been working for you. Skipper Holly?"

King held his smile in check, as if he were posing for a photograph. Bennie caught the slightest of flicker in his eyes. "I'm sorry, Detective, but I'm afraid I don't know the name. You see, I've so many people in my employ, I've yet to meet them all!" King laughed to himself, amused by the idea. Quickly, he added, "I must attend to my guests, Detective, but, please, before I go, I wonder if you might sate my curiosity."

Bennie's body went rigid. "About?"

"The investigation into your father's death. How's it coming?"

Jungle rage bubbled up. Bennie held it off. "It's ongoing, Mr. King. As I'm sure you know, we've a mess of crime on our hands at the moment."

"That I do. Look, please call me Jedidiah, and accept the deepest of my condolences for your father. He was a fine man and an exemplary policeman. Our city is worse for wear without him."

"You knew my father?"

"Only as a fellow professional caught in the web of public life. I'd often see him at the boy's home functions I sponsor. A few pleasantries here and there, nothing more."

Bennie softened at the thought of the old man's hobby: recruiting sandlot players from the orphanage. "I appreciate your concern," he said, the words escaping him.

"I pray you find closure, Detective," said Jedidiah, betraying a hint of sadness. "It's not easy to come by these days."

A shout from across the room stole their attention. "Jedidiah, you old coot!" Mayor Ambler wobbled toward them, a Victory Girl under each arm.

Jedidiah sighed, downed his drink, and handed his empty glass to Bennie. "Please excuse me, Detective. I do hope you enjoy the rest of your evening."

Jedidiah turned and welcomed the Mayor with open arms, shooing off the Victory Girls. The two men embraced and howled with laughter, as if remembering some long ago mischief.

Bennie wandered the room, lost, his stomach twisting into knots. She wasn't on the balcony or the dance floor. He felt like a jilted teenager, stood up on prom night. Then, out of the corner of his eye, he caught a flash of emerald green near the stairs.

Bennie darted that way and cut through the crowd. He came to the stairs and took them two at a time. He spilled onto the sidewalk and saw her several yards off, charging across Broad. He tore after her, catching up as she made her wheels. He was out of breath: all this rash momentum catching up with him.

"Hey," he said, "what gives?"

She threw herself into her taxi. "I've gotta get to work. I've got to go, I'm sorry." Broken speech, slurs. Tears running down her face.

"Listen, whatever it is, I'm sorry. Did I say something?"

She caught her breath and composed herself. She looked up at Bennie and said, "No, it's not you. I just shouldn't have come, I'm sorry."

Bennie tried on some charm and smiled. "Look, we'll go somewhere else next time, somewhere quiet. Yeah?"

She took her time forming the words, fighting with it. "I'm sorry, no, I've… I've got to go."

The taxi ignited and sped off.

Bennie just stood there, in the middle of the street, and watched her go.

SUSFU

January 21, 1944 — February 17, 1944

CHAPTER SIXTEEN

SOFT, EARLY LIGHT snuck its way into the car. Bennie checked his watch — it was just after 6AM. He noted the time in his assignment ledger and threw a look at Digby's service station. He'd parked on Broad, facing east, just a short distance from Tantilla. From his point of view, he had a clear line of sight on both the garage and its front office. Nothing happening: no lights, no movement. He noted as much yet again — the state of affairs unchanged for three days straight — and tossed the ledger aside.

Bennie yawned and stretched. All night stakeouts reminded him of the jungle: fits of sleep, paranoia, sore muscles. A stench hit him hard: stale coffee and *his* BO. He rolled down a window, tossed the joe, and savored fresh, cold air, until an Army convoy whizzed by and doused him with exhaust. Bennie fanned away the fumes with an old newspaper. An eye on the street stoked a ghost memory: standing in the middle of Broad, two weeks back, watching *her* drive away.

Bennie threw another look at the service station — still nothing. He scanned his perimeter as he had the jungle, holding his gaze in all directions just long enough to register change. Nothing new, but still, he was suspicious.

Since he'd been tailed and found his home tossed, Bennie had taken to driving strange routes through town, never the same one twice. He drove circles through Barton Heights just to get here. He wound through Oregon Hill on his way to the Annex. And once, at night, he even cruised Jackson Ward, edging toward the Apollo, replaying that night. He'd yet to see that Chevy again.

A soft rap on the passenger side window made Bennie jump. He looked over and saw Niles, sporting a smile and carrying breakfast.

"Yikes," he said, sliding into the car. "Should have brought you a bar of soap."

"Stay awhile, it'll grow on you."

"That's what I'm afraid of."

Niles handed Bennie a fresh cup of coffee and a cruller. Bennie took a sip and a bite and nodded thanks.

"Don't thank me yet," said Niles, dropping a mess of paperwork in Bennie's lap.

"I should start calling you my secretary instead of my partner."

"Do that and you'll find yourself facing down one of these," said Niles, holding up a fist.

"Then I'll say no more," said Bennie, a smile escaping him. They sipped coffee and ate their crullers as Niles perused the most recent blotter.

"Anything good?" asked Bennie.

Niles smiled. "Yeah, looks like a couple of doozies," he said, skimming the sheet. "They pulled in some joker from Camp Lee who did a number on the town. Get this: the guy was a closet flasher."

Bennie nearly spit up his coffee. "How'd they nab him?"

Niles deadpanned him. "He shook his shit at the Miller & Rhoads' tea room."

Bennie howled.

"Sounds like those old biddies wouldn't stand for it," said Niles. They handbagged him into a corner and, uh, belittled his girth. Says here he sobbed all the way to the MPs."

They laughed as if it were the world's best joke.

"What else?" asked Bennie.

Niles flipped the sheet over. "Looks like some CI tipped Jack to a ration coupon job. He and a few of the boys laid in wait over at the War Price and Rationing board. Caught the perps by surprise."

"Good for him," said Bennie, peeved. Jack always got top notch collars.

A taxicab drove by. Bennie perked up and tracked it. *Not* a Confederate cab. His buzz deflated. He was desperate to find Imogene and ask her about those cryptic parting words, but she'd gone AWOL, ditching shifts at both Confederate and the garage.

"Couple of Negro boys are going up for jewelry theft," said Niles, still reading, "and there's enough syphilis in town to wipe out all of Japan. The Cane says if you're even suspected of stepping into a cathouse, you'll be docked a day's pay."

"Shit."

"You said it."

An extended beat. Suspicions percolated.

"You?" asked Bennie.

"Shit no," said Niles. "You've seen my two rug rats. That's enough to put any man off the snatch. You?"

Bennie shook his head, cold to the idea. Truth was, Imogene was the only woman who excited him.

Movement at the gas station stole their attention. Hollis Digby stumbled from one of his garage bay doors, swaying toward a rusted pick-up. He had the look of a man possessed, overrun by something crazed and unholy. His face was unshaven, his hair tangled like a nest of snakes.

"Bingo," said Niles. "You want to pick him up?"

"Let's see where this goes first."

They watched as Digby tried to fire up one of his pickups to no avail.

"Maybe it's out of gas?" snickered Niles. Bennie couldn't help but laugh.

Digby stumbled from the pickup, slamming the door. He lurched a few feet, reached into the bed, and pulled out a metal rod of some kind.

Then, with all the strength he could muster, he beat the truck with it. He wailed on it again and again, the violent crash of metal on metal ricocheting through the air.

Spent, Digby threw the rod to the ground. For a time, he appeared confused, looking about the cars outside the garage with great curiosity. As if he'd never seen them before.

And then, without warning, he undid his pants and began to urinate all over the lot, cars and all.

"Holy mother," said Niles, "he's off his rocker!"

"Come on," said Bennie, "I've seen enough. Let's get him inside."

They darted across Broad and made the lot, holding their badges high.

Bennie said, "Mr. Digby, we're police officers. How about we take this inside and jaw a bit."

Digby pulled his pants up — out of nothing but habit, Bennie figured — and eyed them with mistrust. "The fuck you want with me?" he said. "I ain't going nowhere. I gotta stay put, you hear me? Gotta be here for when my boy gets home." He teetered a bit then, rocking back and forth on his legs, like a weak tree in a strong wind.

Bennie and Niles shared a look. He really *has* lost it.

"We're not trying to take you away from here, Mr. Digby," said Niles, in a voice a father might use to calm his children. "We just want to take this inside. That's all."

Digby grabbed the copper rod from the ground and held it like a sword. "You two fuckers are gonna leave! *Now.* This is my property and you're not welcome here. Cops, you say? You're the ones that stole my gas and ran me out of business!"

Digby swung the pipe at them wildly. Bennie and Niles jerked and ducked to avoid it.

Out on Broad, cars slowed to check the scene. *Honey - look!* Bennie waved them off and signaled to Niles. Quick nods had them inching toward Digby.

The old man let out a war cry as Bennie moved in and absorbed a blow, wrenching himself around both Digby and the pipe. Niles wrestled it from Digby's hands as Bennie tackled the old man to the ground.

The cold concrete stung *hard.* Bennie yelped while Digby cried out. "You goddamn cops, you did this, you took everything, *everything!"*

Digby looked up from his spot on the couch, spent. "The hell do you want with me? Haven't you done enough?"

Bennie stood over him, catching his breath. It had taken them ten minutes to get Digby into the building. And then another five to get him here, into his office.

"I say again, the *hell* do you want with me?"

Digby had the look of a wolf now, a razor-sharp clarity in his eyes. Bennie felt for the man. He'd remembered that his son was dead.

"That business out there," said Bennie. "About cops stealing your gas. You meant that?"

"And what if I did?"

"We might could help each other, you tell us what you meant."

"And just how the hell could you help me? You heard what I said. Fucking cops."

Bennie pulled up a chair and took up across from Digby. Niles rifled through the papers scattered about his desk.

"The case on your break-in is still open," said Bennie. "If I show that your business suffered as a result of the crime, you could be looking at city money. There's funding for cases like this, I know it. Walk us through your predicament here," he said, looking about the room," and I'll see to it you're taken care of."

Digby let the idea of it sink in for a few beats. Satisfied that Bennie was on the level, he straightened his back and started right up.

"When my boy went overseas, I got restless, thinking about him. And I couldn't sleep. So I'd go out, get a drink, find some company. Anything just to be around people. And one night, I found me a card game. Won a few hands, felt pretty good. Went back a few times, did alright, so I kept it up. It kept my mind off my boy, you understand?"

Bennie nodded, thinking of his own father. How hard it must have been.

"Well, you know how these things go," Digby continued. "My luck ran out and I wound up in the hole, owing money to a couple of real shits. Two guys that said they were cops. They had badges, sure, but hell, if *they're* cops? Ain't nobody getting justice."

On a hunch, Niles described Captain Rivers and Arthur Brown for Digby.

"Yeah, that's them, as sure as all hell."

Niles shook his head and said, "What happened next?"

"They said, 'Whaddya got?' And I said I ain't got nothing but this place and it's for my boy. They'd have to kill me before I let it go. But then they figured they could just take the gas. They'd make a killing, what with the way things are now. Said that'd make it even."

"They staged the break in?" asked Bennie

"Yeah. Told me just to go off that night, so as not to be around. Said they'd make it look right, make it so I wasn't a suspect.'"

Bennie thought of the Apollo and the surprise blackout. "Did they say anything else about that night?"

"Just that no one would notice what they were up to. That, they were sure of."

Bennie and Niles shared a tense look. Rivers and Brown *knew* about the blackout.

Bennie stood up and forced himself to walk. He needed to move, for fear of implosion. He glanced at the car bays and remembered seeing *her* for the first time. He couldn't help himself.

"When I was here last, Mr. Digby, there was a mechanic here. A Ms. McKenna. Does she still work for you?"

"No, I sent her off. Didn't want her mixed up in all this."

Only one car remained in its bay, the Plymouth. "What about the other two cars you had here? There's only one now."

Digby looked confused. "What? Oh, those. They were just in for repairs. She finished them before she left."

"Do you know how I might get a hold of her, Mr. Digby? There could be something she knows that could help us."

Digby motioned to an address book on his desk. "Look in there, you'll find her address."

Bennie had to stop himself from racing for it himself. Niles flipped through it and found her details.

"Got it," said Niles, jotting it down in his steno.

"Are you going to be alright here, Mr. Digby?"

Digby took his time answering. "I... I don't know. It's not easy being alone, not after all this."

Bennie remembered a man, eager to help. "I think I know someone who can help you," he said. "Officer Hunter's going to stay with you awhile. We'll work something out for you."

Niles gave Bennie an *I am?* look. Bennie motioned for them to meet outside. "I meant what I said about the money, Mr. Digby. I won't let you down."

Digby gave Bennie a weary look as he reclined into the couch.

Bennie and Niles made their way outside and greeted the sunshine.

"The heck am I gonna do here?" said Niles, clearly annoyed. "We need to take this in. If Rivers and Brown knew about the blackout — holy shit."

"I know, but we need to *wait.* We've got to have more to go on. If we take this to The Cane now, Rivers will deny it, he'll work out a cover up. We can't risk it."

Niles sighed. A reluctant agreement. "Alright, fine, but we're gonna need some luck in all this and *fast.*"

Bennie nodded, scribbled into his steno, and ripped out the page. "Ring Third and ask for Cyrus Mitchell," he said, handing it to Niles. "Tell him Bennie Sherwood needs his help. He doesn't have to play nursemaid, just keep Digby company. Who knows, maybe they'll get on."

"And me?"

Bennie pulled five sawbucks from his wallet and handed them to Niles. "Use this and get him some chow. Things that might last a few days. No liquor, though."

"Alright. One of us has gotta check in, though. What'll I tell Jack?"

"Tell him we're close, but need more time. Two days at least. That should keep him off our backs."

"Got it. What are you gonna do?"

"I'm gonna see what Ms. McKenna knows about all this."

"Oh, I see," said Niles, tearing her info out of his steno and handing it to Bennie. "You play lover boy while I babysit."

"Look, she might know something."

"Just *get*, for crying out loud."

"Lay low, wait for my call. I won't be long."

Niles gave him a *Yeah right* look and made the jack-off sign.

Bennie turned and made for his wheels, resisting the urge to break into a run.

CHAPTER SEVENTEEN

THE ADDRESS WAS North Highland Park, a Queen Anne off Pensacola. Bennie parked a block away and checked out the pad, stalling. He told himself it was for caution, but he knew it was all nerves.

He bundled up and trekked to the front steps. Frigid air taxed him the whole way. He took a deep breath and rapped on the door.

A man answered. Older, with a face like a bulldog and a snarl to match. "Yes?"

"Is Imogene here?"

The bulldog got brash. "Who's asking?"

Bennie badged him and said, "I'm a police detective, sir. I need to speak with her about her former employer, Hollis Digby."

The bulldog's eyebrows raised at *former*. And then she was right there, in the doorway.

"What's happened? Is he alright?" True concern in her voice.

The sight of her sent a tremor through Bennie. The sweater and slacks she had on made her casual and regal all at once, like a Hollywood starlet on her day off.

"Former?" snapped the bulldog. "What's this all about?"

Bennie looked at her and said, "He's unsteady, but he's alright."

Relieved, she said, "Come inside. We'll talk in the parlor."

The McKenna home was a decorated affair. Pictures, portraits, and framed needlework hung on every wall. Bennie followed Imogene and her father into a well manicured parlor and was shown an armchair.

"Papa, the detective and I are just going to talk about Mr. Digby," she said. "There's no need to worry."

Imogene's father shot Bennie a hard look as he left the room. She made her way to the couch opposite him and took a seat. When their eyes met, he could sense her holding back. She put on a guarded look and crossed her legs.

"I didn't mean to intrude," he said.

"You didn't. What can you tell me about him?"

"He's rattled, but he'll shake it. Did you know he was in hock? Owed big money."

"I gathered as much, even though I didn't know details. I take it that's why you're here, to question me?"

"Something like that." So many questions, he thought.

"Well, like I said, I just worked on the cars," she said. "I didn't bother with the business side of it."

Bennie pulled out his steno and fingered through it. "When I came to the garage, that morning after the break-in, there were three cars in for service." Bennie read them off, one by one. "This morning, there was only one, the Plymouth. What can you tell me about who picked up the other two?"

"Why? You think they're related?"

"It's a long shot, but yes."

"Well, the Ford belonged to an older gentleman. He seemed innocent enough. Was just in a hurry to get his car back."

"Remember his name?"

She searched her mind. "Krueger, I think it was."

Bennie winced. Cops should roust him just for having a Kraut name. "And the Chevy?"

"A man, younger than the Ford owner. Paid cash."

"Remember *his* name?"

She looked up, thinking. "Jack Gentry."

Bennie felt his heart skip a beat. "Say that again."

She eyed him askew, as if he were talking gibberish. "He said his name was Jack Gentry, I'm sure of it."

Bennie felt his spine go wobbly. He felt this lightning bolt sting him. He ruffled through his steno and said, "Do you remember *when* he picked it up?"

She fished for it, remembering. In a low voice, she said, "The evening before our *date*, if I recall correctly."

Bennie felt his skin prickle. It's right there in his notes — two weeks back. They had to be one and the same. *His* tail car. The *same* Chevy.

"Think about this, please," he said. "Do you remember anything about this guy, anything at all? Defining features, strange behavior, the way he talked?"

She searched her mind, her face twisting slightly at the memory. "You know, it's funny. He did have a bruise on his face. Like he'd been in a fight, or taken a fall. And he was in a hurry, too."

"Did he also have a scar on his face?" Bennie ran a finger down his right temple.

She shook her head. "I don't know. Maybe."

"He would have signed something, right? When he picked up the car?"

"Yes, an invoice. It'd be at the office, with Hollis."

Bennie nodded, hopeful. He'd call Niles next, get him looking for it. Run a signature check off Gentry's bar tabs.

She could sense his unease. "What is it?"

"I don't know who picked up that car, but it wasn't Jack Gentry."

"Oh?"

"Jack Gentry was murdered four days before he just happened to pick up his car."

She flinched at *murdered*.

A floorboard creaked in the hallway. Call it Papa McKenna, listening in.

Their eyes met again and held, briefly. He sensed an alarm take hold of her, as if the silence between them was a threat. She rushed to speak first.

"Is that all?"

"Yeah," he said, disappointed. "If I think of anything else, at least I know where to find you."

He scribbled in his steno and ripped out a page. "Here's my extension at the Annex. If, you know, you think of anything else."

She took it from him, looking it over. It *wasn't* his Annex extension. It was his home address and number. "Thanks," she said, pocketing it.

They took the hallway to the foyer and stood facing one another. An awkward silence took hold. Bennie shot a look around, stalling again. *Please, don't let me leave.*

There were photographs everywhere, all shapes and sizes. *A big family*, thought Bennie, jealous. Kids, parents, grandparents. Centered on an adjacent wall was a large photo of young man in Army greens. A proud look on his face, hopeful and determined. Probably taken just before he left home, thought Bennie.

"Is that your brother?" he asked.

She ignored his question with one of her own.

"Can I go and see him?"

"Of course. I'm sure he'd appreciate it and anyways, he could use the company."

She opened the door for him and said thank you in a quiet voice, her eyes to the floor. Frigid air circled the foyer as Bennie pulled his coat lapels up around his neck. He stepped outside and turned back, hoping for another look at her, as her father shut the door in his face.

Barton Heights was close to home, so Bennie made a pit stop. It was almost noon and he was famished. He snarfed a sandwich and downed a glass of milk while he leafed through the rest of his paperwork. He'd been staking out Digby's for near four days. Lots to catch up on.

He perused the blotter a second time. Nothing new stood out. A string of memos from The Cane bore the usual decrees: diligence on the job; duty and honor; buy more war bonds. Blah, blah, blah.

The last page gave Bennie chills. It was from Everett.

Detective — my apologies for the delay, but I dug into your request and have an update.

Freddie Graham — by your word, a cook at Doyle's — does not exist on paper. I ran his name through several city and state records — housing and rental properties, automobiles, business licenses, employment checks. I thought I had found a match, but alas, I was wrong. One <u>Farley</u> Graham, of Petersburg, dead since 1939.

Sorry I couldn't be of more help — Everett.

Bennie balled up the sheet and tossed it across the room, miffed. Another dead end.

He grabbed his phone and rang Digby's service station. Three rings got him through.

"Digby's Garage." Niles, on the line.

"It's me."

"What'd you find out?"

"Our dead vic from the Apollo? Jack Gentry? Imogene says *he* picked up the Chevy from Digby's, four days *after* he was killed."

"Holy mother."

"At the time of Digby's break-in, there were three cars in for service. A Ford, a Chevy, and the Plymouth that's there now. Can you dig up the invoices on all three and call me back?"

"Roger that. Give me five."

They both hung up. Bennie mulled on Imogene. God, she was beautiful, and her cagey attitude only made him want her more. He had to know what happened to her, but how?

The phone rang.

"Yeah?"

Niles said, "Got 'em. What do you want to know?"

"The Ford. Who picked it up?"

Niles shuffled papers. "An F. Krueger, a retiree in his 60s. Says here he paid by check."

Her story, confirmed. "And the Plymouth?"

More papers shuffling. "It belongs to a J. Rodolph, a seamstress from the Fan. She's on her way to get it today."

"She called?"

"Yeah. Sounded peeved, too. Been calling for weeks. I smoothed it over."

"Good. Now, the Chevy. What's the name?"

A pause. Niles went, "Huh."

"What?"

"The invoice is signed Jack Gentry, just like you said. But the car belongs to a Jones Godfrey. There's a carbon of the registration right here."

Something clicked in Bennie's mind. "What's the name again?"

Niles said it slow. "Jones Godfrey."

"Hold on." Bennie set the phone down and walked across the room. He picked up Everett's note and smoothed it out. The two names were Freddie Graham and *Farley* Graham.

Bennie picked up the phone again and said, "You remember what I told you about that cook from Doyle's?"

"Yeah," said Niles. "What of it?"

Bennie told him about Everett's note.

"Yeah, so? What's that got to do with this?"

Bennie almost laughed he was so excited. "I think one of 'em is a dummy name. Jack Gentry. Jones Godfrey. They're both JG, they're both easy to remember."

Niles caught on. "*Yeah*. And if you're trying to pass yourself off as someone else, better to use an easy name so you don't get tripped up. Holy shit."

Bennie whistled. "You said it."

"What do we do about it?"

Bennie sighed. "Did you call Jack and check in?"

"Yeah. He was none too happy. Says to make progress lickety-split."

"Well, he's not gonna like this. I've gotta see that Apollo file."

"*He* wants to solve it, doesn't he?"

Bennie thought of The Reeds' standing order on Jedidiah King: keep quiet and stay off him. "Jack's protective about his work, that's for sure. I'll have to push."

"Do it. If it clears the case, it's worth it."

Yes, but at what cost, thought Bennie. He felt his mind jolt. "The scar."

"What about it?"

"Ask Hollis if he remembers whether the man who dropped off the Chevy had a scar like Gentry's."

"Hold on." Silence on the line, followed by muffled conversation. A few moments and Niles was back. "No, he doesn't."

Bennie huffed. "Fine. I'll run the names by Everett, see if we can eliminate one. And I'll see what Jack's file has for us."

"What can I do?"

"For now, nothing. We'll need the Cane's ok to do anything else, so we'll just have to see. I'll let you know what I find out."

"And Rivers?"

"We've got to tie him to the blackout. Jesus, I almost forgot."

"What?"

"A few weeks ago, I talked up Mayor Ambler at Murphy's. You know what he told me?"

"What?"

"That the investigation into the OCD unit responsible for air raid sirens was on *our* plate, not his."

"Who said otherwise?"

Bennie suddenly thought it odd. "Jack."

Niles said, "Well, I did a few loan outs to civil defense when I was on patrol. I can ask around."

"Do that. If we can route it back to Rivers, we could go to The Cane with it."

"Yeah," said Niles, yawning. "Look, I'm gonna knock

off. We've been at this for a few days. I need Cheryl Lee to see that I'm still alive."

"Yeah, sure. Go home." Bennie heard laughter in the background. "Did Cyrus show?"

"Did he ever. *These* two, let me tell you, cut from the same cloth. Telling me *son, you don't know this* and *son, you don't know that.* Christ, get me out of here."

They said goodbye and hung up. Bennie thought of dummy names and dead men. He rang the Annex. Two rings got him through.

"Police Department." A sweet voice, a new volunteer.

Bennie said, "Records room, please."

"Connecting."

Two beats ticked off and the line went live. Everett's gruff voice sounded. "Records. Brown."

"Everett, it's Bennie Sherwood."

"Yeah? You get my note?"

"I did. And listen, I think we're onto something."

"How's that?"

"I've got two different names for our dead man at the Apollo."

"That's Jack's case."

"Yeah, but *one* of the two names came up in *my* gas theft rundown."

Everett perked up. "Yeah?"

Bennie said, "*Yeah.* And so I thought about our pal Freddie Graham."

"Right."

"Look, maybe these guys are using dummy names to dodge. Right now, that's someone else's problem. I just need to know who's real and who's not."

Everett hemmed. "Kid, it's the weekend. And it took me two weeks for Graham's ID."

Bennie pushed. "Off the record?"

A beat. "Alright."

"If I can connect the dots on this — Jack's case, my case — it could blow the Apollo wide open."

Everett hawed. "Is that supposed to impress me?"

"No, it's supposed to *motivate* you."

"Alright, kid, alright. Give me the names."

"Jack Gentry's the name we have for our male Apollo vic. But a car, registered to one Jones Godfrey, was picked up by Gentry four days *after* we found him dead."

Scribbling sounds over the line. "I'll make some calls, kid. But it'll be Monday, at the earliest."

"Thanks Everett."

Everett just grunted and hung up.

CHAPTER EIGHTEEN

JACK ROSE FROM behind his desk and looked as if he might flip it over. His face grew flush, a visible tension spread through his jaw. In a forceful tone, he said, "No."

Bennie stood before him, pleading. "I'm telling you, something is *off*. This guy shows up dead, right? Then how could he —"

"Gentry's a dead end. No background, no KAs. It's like he never existed."

"That's my point! What if that's not even his real name?"

Jack ground his teeth. "What?"

"A mechanic at Digby's said Jack Gentry came to pick up his car four days *after* he was found dead at the Apollo. Niles confirmed it. Gentry's signature is on the invoice, but the car is registered to a Jones Godfrey. I think one of 'em is a dummy name."

Jack suddenly looked as if he were out of breath. Bennie clocked fear in his eyes.

"That's quite a connection," said Jack, composing himself. "I suppose some congratulations are in order."

"Whatever gets us a solved, right? Look, maybe your angle is off. Maybe it's not —"

Jack went livid. "My what?"

"Your angle. On King. Maybe it's off. Maybe the key to the Apollo is whoever Jack Gentry *really* is."

Jack slapped his desk. "Jedidiah King is behind the Apollo, behind the gas theft, behind all of it! Any idea to the contrary will be seen as a deliberate attempt to derail our investigation and land you a disciplinary assignment!" Jack threw a pen against the wall. He turned away from Bennie, fuming.

Bennie stood at ease as it came to him, clear as day. Jack was embarrassed. Here he was, the big cheese, the next in line, and it was Bennie who had broken the case, not him.

Familiar sounds took up in the hall. Foot drags and floor smacks, on the double. The Cane tore into Jack's office like a hunted boar.

"The hell are you two shouting about in here?"

Jack turned to face them, calm now. "Sherwood's made a sizable connection between the gasoline theft and the Apollo murders. And while I commend his efforts, he suggests our pursuit of King may be in error."

"Hold on now," said Bennie. I don't mean to abandon it altogether —"

The Cane pointed his stick at Bennie. "You were told to stay out of that!"

"I am out of it! Jesus, will you listen to me?" Bennie ran it down for the elder Reed. When he finished, The Cane looked at Jack.

"So? Give him the file."

Jack held his composure and reached into a desk drawer. "As you wish." He brought out his file on the Apollo and handed it to Bennie. "Add your findings and return it to me when you've finished."

Bennie saw ice in Jack's eyes as he took the file.

The Cane said, "You two better find a way to work together or I'll hogtie you to one another and parade you down the middle of Broad Street. I've got enough on my plate without all this infighting, so cut it the hell out." He looked at Bennie. "You, work *your* case, not his. And see me when you're done looking that over. And you," he said, turning to Jack. "Fucking cooperate, alright?"

The Cane vamoosed.

Bennie said, "Jack, I can do this right h —"

"Get the hell out of my office. Now."

The lair was empty. Bennie was relieved, no one to peek over his shoulder. He took a seat at his desk and set Jack's file before him. Deep breaths prepped him. He opened it and felt queasy. Front and center: site pics from the scene, all angles covered. That night came rushing back to him. He felt the blood under his feet again, saw the two limp bodies on the bed. He fought off memories of dead men in the jungle.

He fingered through the snaps. He came to close-ups of Gentry and took his time. Gentry's twisted neck exposed the left side of his face. Bruising covered his cheek. Small gashes peppered the underside of his chin, as if he'd been choked from behind. *There*, just under the ear, something faint. Bennie looked closer. Is that… a hickey?

Bennie studied close-ups of the Negro woman. No similar marks on her neck.

He put the photos aside and found examples of Gentry's handwriting. A torn page from the Apollo's check-in ledger and an unpaid bar tab from the Westwood Supper Club.

An electric current ran through him. He reached into his pocket and pulled out the matchbook that Skipper had given him, the one he'd found in his pants pocket a few weeks back. It, too, was from The Westwood. The inscription read JH M10 10P. Bennie had carried it with him ever since but kept it to himself. For one, he'd been unable to crack the code. And two, he didn't want to raise suspicion that he'd deliberately withheld evidence.

He returned the matchbook to his pocket and looked over Jack's report. It was virtually empty. Gentry had no known relatives, no KAs, and no employment history. Cue Jack's voice: it's like he never existed. Bennie felt it more and more. Gentry's a fake. Godfrey's the real deal.

He turned the report over and detailed his own findings. He made carbons of the handwriting samples and returned the originals to the file. He slipped the carbons into his steno and left the lair.

Jack had vacated his office, so Bennie slipped the file under the door. He walked across the hall and rapped on the Cane's door.

A brute command echoed. "Enter!"

Bennie took timid steps into the office. A seat beckoned. Bennie sat his ass down.

The Cane chomped a cigar and held up a newspaper. "Seen the latest headlines?" He sounded pissed.

Bennie shook his head and tensed up. Here comes a pop quiz.

The Cane futzed with the paper and read aloud. " 'Local Ration Rackets On The Rise! Police Have No Answer!' That's one. 'Slain Police Lieutenant's Killer Still At Large.' That's another. 'Did Cops Bungle Gas Theft Investigation?' Another. Need I go on?"

Bennie didn't know what to say.

The Cane tossed the paper across the room. "Someone is feeding this shit to the newspapers. Someone from *inside* the department. I want you to find out who."

"Sir, with all due respect, I've got my hands —"

"I care shit about your respect! If you've got time to harass Jack about his cases, you've got to time for this."

"I wasn't —"

"Enough. *This* is hurting us, hurting our chances to make the best of it here at home. You see that, don't you?"

Bennie nodded, peeved.

"Good. You're our glory boy, our war hero. It shouldn't be hard for you to bend someone's ear at the papers."

"But the Digby case — "

"Is going nowhere. And slower than molasses, I might add. You can make the time."

Bennie saw an in. He said, "I do for you, you do for me?"

The Cane laughed. "That's not how this works, son."

"Humor me."

The Cane leaned back and puffed on his cigar. "What is it?"

"A few weeks back, I stopped in at Murphy's for some chow. Ran into the Mayor, we made chit-chat."

Alarm flashed across The Cane's face. "I don't think I like where this is going."

"I asked him about his inquiry into the air raid siren. You know what he said?"

The Cane just looked at Bennie, stewing.

"He said it was on *us*, that it was *our* investigation. What gives?"

The Cane smiled, puffing on his cigar. "Funny you should ask."

"And why's that?"

"Because we just locked up the responsible party. The Mayor's office got nowhere, so they kicked it back to us. Someone out of First nabbed him. Some lowlife with civil defense. Said he'd had a few too many that night and set the thing off by accident."

Bennie almost laughed. "You believe that?"

"Hell, you can ask him yourself! He's all nice and cozy, down at the jail. And he sure ain't going anywhere. He's looking at three to six, easy."

Bennie didn't know if it was bull or truth. He yawned big. It'd been a long day.

The Cane said, "Find me whoever's feeding the press, son. And find me that gasoline while you're at it. Whatever you do, get the hell out of my office, 'cause it's my quitting time."

Bennie left the Annex thinking of a tall whiskey and a warm bed. He was halfway down the front steps when he heard his name. A patrolman was calling to him from a second floor window.

"Just took a message for you, Detective. Thought I'd try and catch you before you went home."

"Yeah? What is it?"

"Walter MacKaye says you're due for a trim."

Bennie felt a second wind coming on.

"Thanks," he said, making for his wheels. The whiskey can wait, he thought. Get me to Dougie Swyers so I can put him to bed for good.

Chapter Nineteen

THE BARBERSHOP WAS closed for the night, so Bennie walked around back. The rear was outfitted with two entrances: one for deliveries, one for runners. Bennie recalled the knock pattern and rapped his knuckles along the leftmost door: one-two/pause/one-two-three. Seconds later, the eye grill slid open and gave way to a set of menacing browns.

Bennie held up his badge and said, "Tell Walter it's Bennie."

The grill went shut. An icy chill filled the alley. Bennie pulled his coat in tight and got warm.

The door jutted open. One of Walter's goons stuck his head out and ushered Bennie inside.

A short hallway led them to a spacious and busy room. The latest Artie Shaw blared from a corner radio. A couple of gals sorted slips near the door while a few runners worked a table along the far wall, counting bills and shuffling them into stacks. If Bennie didn't know better, he'd say it was a well run war factory.

"Bennie!" A buoyant and jolly Walter approached.

"What gives, honcho?"

Bennie held his excitement in check. "I got your message. You tell me."

Walter said, "Ah, yes." He craned his neck toward the far wall and shouted, "Hey, Linus!"

Linus looked up from his stack of bills. He had a thin, crooked nose, a square jawline, and frayed, shaggy hair that hung down around his eyes.

Walter waved him over. "I want you to meet someone. Bring a few of the mags with you."

Linus picked up what looked like a couple of thin newspapers and walked their way. He stood before them, sheepish, holding the rags behind him as if he were ashamed of them.

"Bennie, this is Linus. Linus, this is Detective Sherwood."

Linus nodded at Bennie, hiding his eyes.

"Tell Bennie your story, Linus."

Linus was all nerves. He coughed and bit at his lower lip, stalling.

"*Now.*"

Linus said, "So, yeah, we did like Walter said, we asked around about that guy Swyers."

Bennie was lost. "We?"

"My runners," said Walter. "I told 'em to ask around, keep an eye out."

"And well," said Linus, "we didn't get anywhere with it. Nobody'd seen him, much less heard of him."

Bennie was still lost. "Okay."

"But then," Linus continued, "a few days ago, this guy approached me, said he had something I might like for sale and would I be interested."

Bennie flashed a *what?* look.

Linus pulled the magazines from behind him and handed them to Bennie. They were girly mags. Bennie flipped through them, wide-eyed. The photos inside were so-so: tasteful poses, shoddy lighting. Bennie recognized a few of the models from recent prostie busts.

"This might interest vice," said Bennie," but it's not really my beat." He massaged the paper stock. It was cheap and coarse. Some of the ink rubbed off on his fingers.

Walter nudged Linus. "*And?*"

"And I'm standing there, talking to this guy, thinking about it. Like maybe I'll buy one, you know. And damn if he don't look like this cop you're after."

Bennie looked right at Linus and felt a rush. "*Ex* cop. Small eyes, kinda pudgy, hair parted to the left?"

"Yeah," said Linus. "That's him."

Bennie made a fist and stymied his nerves. "Go on."

Linus started to blush. "Well, I get to thinking. If it is the guy, I don't want to just let him go, on account of Walter said he'd up our take if we put eyes on him. So I said, let me have a look at these rags, see what we're talking about. And, well…"

"*Yeah?*"

"I got to thinking again, I should make *sure* this is the guy. So I ask him a few questions, just to see what I can find out, you know? I said I got pals who might want in on these skin rags and how could I reach you, that sort of thing. And he laughed and said that nobody could reach him, it was a now or never kind of thing. So I pumped him a little more and said why couldn't nobody reach him. And boy, did he get serious then. He got up real close to me and asked if *I* was a cop."

Bennie felt his rage bubbling up. "*And?*"

"I said hells no, I ain't no cop!" Linus stopped and found a more courteous tone. "No offense."

Bennie shrugged it off, anxious. "Like I care. What else?"

"Then he got all wild and spooked, as if maybe somebody was after him. Then he rushed the deal, said he had to split. I thought he might not come back for another go, so I bought the rags and that was that."

"Where was this?" asked Bennie.

"Off Canal Street, down near the docks," said Walter. "We got a little spot there where folks can find us if they want to make a bet."

Bennie took a step toward Linus. "I want you to think real good on this. You say he looks like my guy. Did you notice anything else about him?"

Linus bit his lip, desperate to please. "*Yeah*," he said. "Come to think of it, he *was* pretty dirty. And he smelled bad, too. If I didn't know any better, I'd say he took a nap in the dirt somewhere."

Walter howled. Bennie pictured Dougie Swyers on the fritz: peddling smut to get by, spooked on cops, hiding out in the woods. He almost smiled.

"You want us to keep an eye out for him?" asked Linus, smiling. Fishing for reward money, thought Bennie.

"You did good and I thank you, but I've got it from here."

Linus slinked off, deflated. Bennie looked at Walter and said, "Thank you."

"Sure," said Walter, winking. "Anything for the RPD."

A measured smile passed between them.

"You really think he had something to do with your old man?" asked Walter.

"I don't know. When I find him, I'll be sure and ask

him." Bennie turned to leave and stopped. He pulled the Westwood Club matchbook from his jacket and handed it to Walter. "Check the inside flap. See what's written?"

Walter flipped open the matchbook and read the inscription.

"That mean anything to you?" asked Bennie.

Walter studied it for a few beats. Bennie clocked the concern that flashed across his face for a split second. Walter looked up and handed the matchbook back to Bennie.

"No," said Walter, working a smug grin. Years of getting away with it had given him a cocky smile. "Doesn't mean a thing to me."

CHAPTER TWENTY

NIGHT TERRORS WOKE him early, so Bennie took his coffee on a predawn stroll down East Grace Street. Just west of 22nd, the street dead-ended, spilling into a steep-sloped hillside that, to Bennie, offered an unmatched view of Richmond to the west. He took a seat on dewey grass and watched as the sun, now rising slowly behind him, bathed Tobacco Row, the financial district, and Court End with soft rays of light.

Many a time, he and his father would sit on this very hill, rehashing Bennie's latest baseball win and the old man's recent arrests. Later, when their conversation had died down, the old man would take to riffing on his favorite subject — the city in which they lived.

"It's diseased," he would say, his voice tainted with disgust. "Just look at it."

Bennie *would* look at it, often in delight. Before the war, Bennie saw a *different* city — one of adventure, romance, possibility. Nowadays, he thought, it looks like the old man was right all along.

"There's blood seeped into the streets," his father would

say. "It's in the cobblestones. It's in the river, too. It's in the very hill we sit on now," he said once, patting the ground with a fist. "Ours is a city born of violence, son. Slavery, the Civil War. *Industry*," he'd say, gesturing toward the Row. "You smell it, don't you?"

Bennie breathed deep into his lungs, just as he had so many times before, the sweet scent of tobacco just touching his nose.

"That's the unmistakeable smell of greed," his father said one night. "It's all around us, every day. It poisons the air and breeds toxic desires." He drifted off then, his eyes toward the horizon. Thinking of his work, Bennie suspected, of the ceaseless ways in which men and women hurt one another in the name of love and best intentions.

"Well, if nothing else, it's a helluva good reason not to smoke," Bennie had replied, trying on some wit. He'd never forget how his father had laughed, thrown his head back, and howled at the moon.

Walking back to the house, Bennie caught wind of some newsboys out on Broad hawking the early edition. Sitting at the kitchen table over breakfast, Bennie scanned headlines. The Cane would be pleased — no cop scandals today. Just a beaucoup writeup on Jack's big get at the War Price and Rationing Board. Check the accompanying photo — a rare snap of Jack smiling. The copy gave top billing to Jack's cunning and detective expertise. It went on to suggest that Jack himself was next in line for the Cane's job, linking the idea to a kind of benign nepotism and citing praise for Jack's police work from the mayor and other high ranking city officials.

Detective expertise, thought Bennie, raising an eyebrow.

A host of minor infractions were detailed beneath Jack's story. Juvenile delinquency is spreading like the plague;

beware the pickpockets and purse snatchers that linger on the north side of Broad. Nothing on Pearl's, Digby, or the ration rackets.

Bennie crumpled the paper, miffed He thought a byline on a story critical of the police would lead him to whoever was leaking damaging information to the press. He needed *something* to feed The Cane, and with no press contacts —

Bennie's memory pinged with the image of an eager young man sporting a bow tie and an ear-to-ear grin.

Right — Archie Smith, that up and comer, fishing for police scoops.

Bennie smiled and grabbed the phone.

The white working class district of Oregon Hill boasted close proximity to the Albemarle Paper Company, employer to many of the neighborhood's residents. "Move out there, you might as well be moving west, to Oregon," went the saying. Bennie shared in the sentiment as he wound through narrow streets past low-rent two-story pads. A few wrong turns detoured him, but he righted course and found the intersection of China and Laurel.

A short walk brought him to the address. Since it was the weekend, Bennie figured the kid would be off. It was a stretch, but he couldn't think of anyone else.

Bennie double-checked the house number and knocked on the door. After a time, he heard shuffling inside and a lock turned. An older woman stuck her head out the door. Stringy brown hair, a faded nightgown closed up tight. A cigarette dangled from her mouth.

"Yeah?" she said.

Bennie held up his badge. "I'm Detective Sherwood, with the city police," he said. 'I'm looking for Archie."

Her eyes went wide. So did the door. "Is he in trouble?"

"No, m'am. I just need to talk to him."

Relieved, she turned and hollered into the hall. "Archibald!" A moment later, the kid came strolling their way, annoyed. "What is it, ma?"

"It's the police!"

Archie caught sight of Bennie and blanched. "Detective," he stammered, "I did what you said, I quit your old man —"

"Kid, it's alright. It's not that."

"What did you do?" said Archie's mother, slapping him on the shoulder.

"Nothing, Ma!"

"Archie's right, he did nothing wrong," said Bennie. "But I need his help with an investigation. If you please, could he and I speak out here on the porch?"

Both Archie and his mother were in awe. "Well, sure," she said, suddenly proud. "You want something to eat, Detective?"

"No, but thank you, m'am."

Archie came onto the porch, pulling the door behind him. His mother held it back. "You sure?" she asked.

"Yes, m'am."

"Ma!" screamed Archie, wrestling the door closed. He walked onto the porch and faced Bennie.

"So, what can I do?" The kid's face: all smiles and hope.

"I got your name from the personnel department at the paper. I don't know anyone else on staff, and I need someone on the inside."

"For what?"

"Someone from the department is feeding the paper information we want kept under wraps."

"What information?"

Bennie rattled off the headlines The Cane had shared with him.

Archie shrugged. "Lots of information running around the office these days. I'll see what I can find out. But, it might be tough for me to get a read on where it's coming from."

"And why's that?"

Archie's energy soured. "*Well...* I couldn't generate enough story leads, so they bounced me from copy and put me on research."

"So you're a...."

"Fact checker."

"Hmm."

"*Yeah.* So, I'll do what I can, but —"

"Are you good at it?"

"What?"

"Doing research?"

Archie got cocky. "I sure like to think so. Why?"

Bennie chewed on an idea. The kid's eyes said *Tell Me.*

Bennie said, "My caseload is spilling over and I need some help. I want you to look up everything you can on two people. Get me some good info and I'll feed you some war stories. Things you can write about. Get you a byline."

Archie's eyes went candy-store wide. "No foolin'?"

"No foolin'."

Archie pulled a notepad from one pocket, a pen from the other. "I'm in. Who do you want to know about?"

Bennie gave him the lowdown on Imogene: her name, her looks, her grease monkey bent, and her part-time cab gig. He summarized it with this: "Kid, something happened to her, something traumatic. I want to know what it was."

"You got it. Who's the other person?"

"Jedidiah King."

Archie quit writing and looked up. "Now, that's gonna be a problem. We're on order to stay off him no matter what. Only the top dogs get the goods on him and even then, it's wrung through red tape something fierce."

"You always do what you're told, kid?"

Archie recoiled, getting hot. "What's that supposed to mean?"

"Off the record?"

Archie cooled off a bit and coughed. "Sure."

"I think King's *dirty*. I think he's moving black market goods around town *and* I think he had something to do with my old man."

Wide-eyed Archie said, "Whoa."

"But I can't get close enough to him to learn anything. I'm on orders to stay away, same as you. I thought maybe you could dig around without anyone noticing. And, listen, someone *does* get wind of it, tries to hang you out to dry? Put it on me. I'll take the heat."

Archie weighed it for a beat. "Okay, sure," he said, smiling at the thought of a big story. "Couple guys I know? They're 4F, like me, pulling nights at King Tobacco. I'll see what they know."

"Thanks kid."

"Sure. Say, how do you want to do this? I mean, if we're keeping this between us, how do I contact you?"

Bennie mulled it over. "Third Street Coffee. Know it?"

"Sure."

"We'll do it there. Have a call service leave me a message at the Annex when you want to meet."

The kid wrote it all down and looked up, excited. "I'll start on this today."

"Thanks, kid. And those headlines — see what you can find out, we need to put a lid on it."

"Sure thing. And you'll keep your word, yeah? You'll really tell me what it was like?"

"Yeah," said Bennie, already afraid of the memories he'd revisit.

Archie coughed. "Boy, I sure wish I could've gone. This asthma, I'm telling you. You've got it *made.*"

Bennie gave him a hard look and said, "No, kid. *You* do."

Bennie grabbed a rail seat at White's for lunch. Soup, a sandwich, and coffee. The food was good and hot. He ate it slow and got a refill on the joe. The afternoon was his. He'd drawn the Victory desk's graveyard shift and wasn't due at the Annex until later that night.

A radio sat on the serving counter across from him. Bennie sipped coffee and listened to a peppy WRVA broadcaster rattle off a string of local ads and news.

"Dance the night away at Tantilla Garden, the South's most beautiful ballroom! Dial 5-9151 for reservations!"

"Live like a King! Smoke River City Royals, from Richmond's own King Tobacco!"

"Bonds or Bondage? Be sure and stock up on war bonds today!"

"And now, in local news, the city's mayoral race is heating up! Who'll get your vote, Perkinson or Herbert? Get the latest on both candidates in today's Richmond News Leader, where you'll find more on that big win for Richmond's finest. Just last week, Lt. Jack Reed of the Richmond Police Department stopped a robbery at the War Price and Rationing Board, foiling theft of valuable ration coupons. Chief Reed, currently under fire for the city's dismal crime stats, had this to say about his son's achievement…"

"It's a great day, indeed," said The Cane, his usual bark toned down for the broadcast. "And not just for Jack, but for the department as a whole. And we're capitalizing on his success, with new leads and active investigations that are getting us closer and closer to the systematic troubles plaguing our city."

Bennie almost laughed. Bull*shit*.

"The message is clear," said the announcer. "Crime does *not* pay. Be sure and salute our men in blue for the fine work they're doing here at home."

Local chatter died off as a war segment came on. Bombing sounds gave Bennie a sudden jolt. He felt a headache coming on and resisted the urge to look up. He paid for his meal and ducked outside, shielding his eyes from the harsh sunlight. He leaned against a wall and breathed fresh air. Inhale, exhale, repeat. Just like they taught him. He looked this way and that, hoping no one noticed.

Next door, a confectionary beckoned. Bennie ducked inside and bought a short dog of whiskey, hiding it inside his coat as he left the store.

A short walk brought him to the Byrd theater. Today's double matinee: a Mickey Rooney and a Betty Grable musical. Bennie was relieved: no war pictures.

Bennie found a seat off in the corner and settled in. The lights dimmed and a newsreel took over the screen.

Goddamnit, he thought, there's no escaping it.

Bennie opened the bottle of whiskey and chugged.

It was going on dusk when Bennie wandered under the massive granite and iron entrance gate that led to

Hollywood Cemetery. So named for the many holly trees nearby, not for any predilection to movie star burials. He nursed a coffee as he walked. It helped to warm him against the cold.

Once inside, Bennie noticed a calming aroma, the scent of freshly mined earth. As he moved along the walkway, he felt himself grow more lucid, felt his whiskey buzz fade away.

He met the watchman just outside the office door. A Negro in his 50s with a lunchpail and a hurried look.

"We're closed up, mista. You'll hafta come back tomorrow."

Bennie held up his badge. "I only need a few minutes."

The black man sighed. Another white man's request. "Alright, then. I can wait."

Bennie fingered a fin from his pocket. "Listen, how about we come to an arrangement? You close up, just like you would any other night, and I'll hop a fence on my way out. What do you say?"

The watchman eyed the fin like it was gold. "You catch heat on this, it's *your* hide, not mine."

"Agreed."

The watchman beamed and took the bill. "I got a memory on me, mista. I find graves dug up, I'm gonna draw a picture of *your* face for the paper."

Bennie angled his head so the left side of his face was clear. "Then be sure and get my good side, ok? Don't want anyone mistaking me for someone else."

The watchman laughed. "You're just a little cracked, ain't ya?"

"Just a little."

"Well, a good night to you. *Behave* yourself."

Bennie nodded and they parted ways. He heard the

gate lock behind him as he wound down the path. Whispers of sunlight were a poor guide along a familiar route. The encroaching darkness threatened to throw him off course, but he was undeterred.

He knew the way.

Bennie took soft steps around a large family plot on his way to the old man's grave. The goal was simple: don't disturb the dead.

Samuel Ethan Sherwood had been laid to rest along a southern edge of the cemetery. Bennie could just make out the contours and pulse of the James River, maybe a hundred yards off. He took a seat right there on the grave.

Damn. The ground was cold.

He thought back to the morning. He felt devious roping Archie into his madness. It was like he'd conscripted a spy, but he had no choice. He was stretched too thin. Sure — some of it was self-imposed — but all of it fit in, all of it was relevant.

He took another swig of his coffee and rattled off his many objectives to the old man.

Find Dougie Swyers. Corner him, *hurt* him. For *you.*

Locate Hollis Digby's gasoline.

Solve the mystery of Jack Gentry. Imposter or dead man?

Smoke out the department's press leak.

Learn Jedidiah King. Finger him, *expose* him.

Reconnect with Imogene. *Help* her, if he could.

It *sounded* like too much. It *felt* like too much. But he had Niles, and now he had the kid.

You survived the 'canal. You can do this.

More coffee. A rush of warmth.

Keep working, keep moving. Don't succumb to the madness.

Bennie laid back and rested his feet on the headstone. Both it and the gravesite had been bought and paid for by the RPD.

Bennie looked up at the stars and said, "What happened, Dad? How'd you end up like this?"

I know it's all connected.

There's so much at stake.

I won't let you die an unanswered death.

CHAPTER TWENTY-ONE

BENNIE TOOK BROAD at a fast pace and headed east. He lit up his siren and flexed cop privilege all the way to the Annex. Lights, people, the home front — all of it whizzed by in a blur.

He had renewed energy. He'd napped at Hollywood Cemetery, sleeping right on top of the old man's grave. His whiskey buzz had come and gone. It was Saturday night in the River City and he wanted to work.

He parked in front of City Hall and zipped across the street. A few flatfoots milled about the Annex steps. They muttered something and laughed as Bennie approached. Dirty looks went both ways.

One of the flatfoots said, "Fuck your mother, soldier boy."

Bennie threw a shoulder into one and a haymaker into the other. They spilled onto the steps, groaning. Bennie said, "Do some real fucking police work or I'll haul you both to the Cane's office, right now."

They lumbered to their feet and limped off. Bennie waited until they were out of sight before he let himself slump onto the steps. A dizziness came over him, along with a tension in his neck. He rolled his head and stretched.

He looked up, relieved.

No Jap planes overhead.

The Annex was buzzing. The Vice desk had its hands full with prosties and johns. Three girls, four guys, all lined up for booking. The Juvie desk juggled curfew violations en masse. Girls, boys, all skin colors. The war stretched River City families thin. Dad went to fight, Mom went to work, the kids ran wild.

Bennie peeked into the squadroom. The Cane had wrangled some AOs into a huddle and was barking orders. Cue his oft repeated directives: stay sharp, buddy up, and respect the military. His hearty bellow was in full swing: "The streets are full of shit and sin and you're all I've got, so make us look good!"

Bennie found the detective's lair humming. Five bulls sat at their desks, scanning notes and lists. The pressure was on: squash the black markets. Bennie was surprised: a few of them nodded his way, semi-friendly.

On his desk — a note from the evidence room. It read: *See us, ASAP. This regards open case #80407.* Bennie knew the number right off: it was Pearl's.

No time to waste. He hoofed it to the first floor. The evidence room was down the hall, around back, tucked in a corner just beyond the interrogation rooms. Bennie walked in a hurry as a wave of nostalgia hit him head on. In high school, he'd filed evidence away during his off-seasons.

Bennie found two women playing darts amidst shelves and boxes. Their target: a page-sized caricature of

Hirohito, done up as a sniveling rat with big buck teeth.

Bennie said, "You wanted to see me?"

One of the women looked his way. They were both young, both brunettes, both done up in sweaters and denim. Make them volunteers, war wives tired of worrying away their Saturday nights. She said, "That depends. Who are you?"

Bennie held up his note. "Detective Sherwood. I found this on my desk."

"Ah, right. One sec."

She turned and disappeared into the stacks. Her partner hit a bullseye, right between the eyes. She raised her arms in Victory and shot Bennie a smile.

"If only that was enough, huh?"

Bennie agreed. "If only."

Her attention stirred him and he thought of Imogene. Was she alone on this Saturday night?

The first woman returned and handed him an evidence bag. "This came in off the street earlier today. We cross-referenced the serial number and tied it to one of your cases."

Bennie reached into the bag and pulled out a ration book. He flipped through it, curious. The signature page had been forged, but the serial numbers had been left untouched. It was a clumsy black market job, at best.

"We pulled a lot of contraband out of Pearl's," he said. "This could belong to anyone."

She checked her notes. "This was tied to a specific person," she said, running her finger along a line of detail.

Bennie felt his gut turn as she read the name.

"Ah, yes. Right here. It belonged to one Stephen Holly…"

Bennie dropped the book and ran.

The morgue hallway was dark and clammy. Bennie cracked the door to the incinerator room and stuck his head inside. It was still and warm and smelled of char and ash.

Muffled voices found his ears. Bennie followed them down a hallway and around a corner. He came to a small room with some shelves and a desk.

War news buzzed from a desktop radio. There really is no escaping it, he thought. In the corner, that morgue attendant from the other day shelved chemicals. Sampson, his name was.

Bennie cleared his throat.

Sampson turned around, startled. "Can I help you?"

"Do you remember me?"

Sampson's face went from confusion to clarity in a flash. He gulped, speechless.

"When I was down here the other day," said Bennie, "I told you to burn some things. *One* of those things ended up on the street, care of the black market."

Sampson stepped down off his stool. "W-w-what?"

Bennie stepped toward him, his rage building up. "It's a ration book that belonged to my dead friend. I told you to burn it."

Combat sounds muddled the radio broadcast. A machine gun went *rat-tat-tat-tat-tat-tat*. Bennie flinched.

Sampson took a few steps back. "Now, look, I don't know anything about that. I burned those things, j-j-just like you said."

The radio broadcaster talked advances for Germany. A bomb went *Kaboom!* Bennie felt his neck tighten.

Bennie said, "I think you're lying to me."

"I swear, honest! Now look, if you'll just…"

"Just what?"

"If you'll just…"

The broadcaster talked up the Pacific. Bennie heard the names of places he recognized: Cape Gloucester and New Britain. He heard the word *Japanese*. He saw a mirage of Jap faces blend together in ghoulish harmony.

Sampson tried to rabbit.

Bennie lurched for him and heard this *scream*.

Time *skipped*.

Quick flashes/blinks — pulling hair/yelps/fingers gouging skin.

Time *warped*.

Sampson's legs kicked and thrashed.

A door pushed open.

This tidal wave of *Heat* rushed them.

Bennie thought, *It's like fire on my skin*.

Something *snapped*.

Bennie came to in a frenzy.

He had Sampson in a full nelson. They were next to the incinerator. Bennie grabbed a door handle and threw it open. Fire scorched the air.

Sampson caught the gist and scrambled for his footing. "No way, you shit!"

Bennie forced him face down and threw jabs into his ribcage. Sampson cried out, his body writhing with pain.

Bennie got dizzy. Sweat pooled in his eyes and his pulse hit overdrive. He thought of that Jap sniper who took out Sammy and Montana Bill, the one they found hiding in a tree.

He *saw* the sniper.

He did *not* see Sampson.

Bennie turned the Jap over and grabbed his left forearm. He jammed it into the oven, stopping just short of the flames.

"Where is your regiment?" screamed Bennie.

The Jap's face twisted in misery. He swatted at Bennie's face with his free hand.

"DOAK-o-nee ee-MA-ska?" Bennie's Japanese phrasebook came alive: *where are they?*

"Jesus, you're crazy!" said the Jap.

"WHERE IS HIROHITO?"

The Jap said, "Oh Christ, you're nuts! Let go, you crazy fuck!"

Bennie rammed the Jap's arm into the flames. The Jap went sheet white and shrieked at an opera singer's pitch.

The squeal brought Bennie out of it.

There was no Jap, only Sampson. Bennie released his arm and recoiled. The room spun and smelled of burnt flesh.

"Oh, Jesus! Oh God!" Sampson sank to the floor, cradling his charred arm, repeating the words again and again.

Bennie felt it coming. He turned as fast as he could and threw up all over the floor. Three heaves emptied him.

His mind ping-ponged, now to *then*. He panicked and felt around for his rifle. All his hands could find were vomit.

Something brushed his leg. He turned and saw Sampson, crawling along the floor like a worm. Bennie lurched for him and grabbed ahold of his legs.

Sampson wailed tears. "Oh, God, please, let me go!"

Bennie crawled alongside him. They were both spent, no fight left.

"Tell me everything," he said, "and I'll get you to the

ER."

"It's a cop thing," said Sampson, finding his breath. "You know Captain Rivers?

Bennie nodded.

"Oh, Christ, *my arm* —"

Bennie threatened with a weak fist.

"Okay, okay! Look, word got around down here. This cop'll pay good money for anything he can use on the street. All this unclaimed shit we got down here? It's a gold mine. Oh, Jesus!"

"How do you get it to him?"

"I call a number. This guy, on the other end. He sets it up. It's the same every time."

Bennie described Arthur Brown for Sampson.

"Hell, I don't know, I never seen the guy. Oh my god — "

"Girly mags, pin-up snaps. Rivers ever have any of that to peddle?"

"What? How the hell should I know? Pal, *you said*, oh geez, please…"

Bennie's mind zoomed, now to *then*. They dragged that Jap sniper out of the tree, lit him on fire, and watched him burn.

Bennie pulled a gurney from the cold room and wheeled Sampson to the ER. He came upon an elderly nurse working the reception desk.

"I'm with the RPD," said Bennie. "I went down to make an ID and found him on the ground. I think he had an accident."

She scrambled from behind the desk. Sampson looked cold and numb. "Oh my goodness, yes," she said. "I'll take him now."

Her nose twitched. Bennie shielded his hands

The nurse started off with the gurney but Bennie gripped a handle and held them back. He leaned down and whispered into Sampson's ear.

"You hold your tongue and I'll hold mine."

Sampson couldn't nod fast enough. The nurse shot Bennie a hostile look as they darted off.

CHAPTER TWENTY-TWO

BENNIE REACHED INTO the back of the liquor
cabinet and gripped one of the mason jars. He brought it
out and braced himself against the kitchen sink. A long
shower had dulled his nerves, but he was still a bit shaky.

He blew the dust from the lid, unscrewed the cap, and
winced. The shine's odor was strong, even a little toxic. He
raised the jar to his lips and drank. It burned his throat
and made his eyes water. Warmth tunneled through his
veins and sent a buzz up his spine.

A glance at the wall clock — it was just after midnight.
Bennie rubbed his temples and saw the morgue
attendant's eyes bulge. He heard his screams and watched
his skin burn. He took another gulp and remembered
more things he'd never forget.

He wanted to sleep.

He needed to work.

He took another drink and ran through his caseload.
Pick one.

Lingering bloodlust steered his thoughts to Dougie
Swyers. He cut into the dining room and leafed through

the pin-up rags. The snaps were from hunger and most of the girls looked bored. A few of them even looked to be laughing, as if it were all a lark, a fun way to pass the time.

One of the snaps caught his eye. A brunette with hard eyes and a beauty mark on her right cheek. Bennie knew her face. He did a tour with vice around Christmas and busted her on a morals charge. She had a room at Cherry Anne's. It was Saturday night — she might be in.

He forced himself from the chair. He was achy and spent. He trekked upstairs and dressed. A sweater, jeans, some old boots.

He donned his coat and started for the door, pausing at a photo on the wall — a portrait of his parents as newlyweds. A rare smile on the old man. His mother, model pretty. He wished he could travel back and meet them, have a drink or two, and share in their hopes and dreams.

He left them smiling and moved into the night. A good buzz had taken hold and he moved easier now. He quickened his pace, afraid of his own hopes and dreams, as the cold stung his face.

Cherry Anne Westerman lived in a spacious two-story rowhouse just off Broad, on the east side of 26th. Hers was one of two police sanctioned cathouses inside the city limits. The other belonged to Doris Potter, off North Adams. Both women operated tidy establishments and made sizable contributions to the department's pension fund. They operated at the sole discretion of The Cane and made a priority of the city's upper echelon. Bennie thought of these things as he cut onto the walkway that led to Cherry's front door.

The parlor was crammed with girls and soldiers on

liberty. A bouncer walked Bennie down a short, cramped hallway to a room just off the kitchen. Bennie stood inside the doorway and felt himself stir. Revealing pictures of women adorned the walls. High quality stuff, not like the pin-up rags.

Against the far wall, seated square in the middle of a lavish couch, sat Cherry herself, sipping a cocktail. She was prim and erect, her legs crossed firmly in front of her. Her dyed black hair was cropped short, her manicured eyebrows trimmed thin. A tight fitting robe hugged her svelte figure and showed but scant cleavage. She reminded Bennie of a French courtesan he'd once seen in a matinee at the Colonial.

Cherry spoke in a voice both seasoned and delicate and said, "You asked to see me?"

Bennie cleared his throat. "I'm doing follow up on a lead. I need to speak with one of your girls. And since I'm here, maybe I could run a few things by you, too."

Cherry took a slow sip of her drink. "You're Sam Sherwood's kid, yes?"

"Yes, m'am. Been on since October."

She rolled her eyes at *m'am*. "And you truck for Wyatt, around this area?"

Wyatt, as in Captain Wyatt Rivers. Word was, he hated the name. "No, m'am. I'm out of HQ, working the Victory Squad."

"Ahhh," she said, her interest piqued. "And does working for the Cane agree with you?"

Bennie smiled. "It has its challenges. But we go back, he and I, so I'm used to it."

Cherry peered at him for a moment. "Your old man spent some time here."

"I should hope he did. I've been here a few times

myself, so let's not make a thing of it, alright?"

She sipped her drink and grinned, appreciative of his candor. "Kid, I'm not a canary."

"And I'm not asking you to sing. I've just got a few questions." Push her, thought Bennie. "Consider it a favor to my old man."

She met his eyes with a solemn look. She reached for a pack of cigarettes and shook one out. Bennie caught the make: River City Royals. He recalled an ad he'd seen in the newspaper: a sleeker, more feminine smoke. Cherry took a long drag. When she exhaled, she blew rings for show.

"Shoot," she said.

"You mentioned Captain Rivers before. You two close?"

"No."

"But you know him?"

"Yes."

"Has he ever tried to sell you anything?"

"Like what?"

"Like maybe something you can't find much of right now."

"Something rationed, is that what you mean?"

"Yes."

She paused for a beat. "Ask me something else."

"What about Arthur Brown? He's a cop. He and Rivers are thick as thieves."

She shrugged. "So? Lots of cops come in here."

"But the name, do you know it?"

"No."

Bennie pulled the picture of Dougie Swyers from his pocket and took a few steps toward Cherry. "How about this one?" he said, holding it up. "He *used* to be a cop."

She gave it a good look. "Yeah, he's been in. But the

girls don't care for him much."

Bennie felt his back tighten. "And why's that?"

"He's unkempt. And he can't afford much, if you know what I mean."

"When was he in last?"

"A week ago, maybe two. But lots of people move through here. After awhile, their faces just sort of run together, you know what I mean?"

Bennie saw a dozen Jap faces come together as one. Their eyes rolled back, their noses bled, their mouths stretched open.

He shook it off and described the brunette from the pin-up rag, the one with the beauty mark. "Is she here?"

"That depends."

"On what?"

"On whether or not she's in any kind of trouble.'"

"Not real trouble, no. I just want to talk to her."

"In that case, then yes, she's here. Upstairs, number 3. Might not be *available*, but she's here."

"Thanks."

"You're welcome," she said, flashing an inviting smile. "Is there anything else I can do for you?"

"You know, I am curious about one thing."

"And what's that?"

"Those cigarettes you have. Do you like them?"

She gestured to the Royal in her hand, amused. "These?"

"Yes."

"Why, would you like one? I have more."

"No, I just… wonder about the man who makes them. Do you know him?"

"Jedidiah?"

"Yes."

She took a long drag. "Does The Cane know you're here, asking me questions about Jedidiah King?"

Bennie felt himself freeze up. "No, he does not."

"Then I suppose," she said, offering him a wink, "that you best go on about your business, don't you think?"

Bennie said, "Have a good night, Ms. Westerman."

"And the same to you, Detective."

Bennie felt her leer at him as he turned and left the room.

Bennie took the stairs slowly, one at a time, with a look in all directions. Annex men were frequent habitues of Cherry's. An unplanned run-in could land him on The Cane's shit list for good.

He came to the second floor and took in the hall. Five doors, all closed. A myriad of sounds spilled into the hallway: laughter, grunts, music.

A door in the corner sent shockwaves through his memory. That summer, after high school: he and Skipper popped their cherries in that very room. The two women were more amused than excited. It was all forced machismo and awkward coupling. He and Skipper lasted thirty seconds a piece, tops. The four of them laughed about it afterwards over a bottle of cheap wine.

A door opened. Room no. 3. A sheepish man walked out. Mid-40s, unshaven, half-drunk. He buttoned up his pants and stumbled for the stairs. Bennie gave him a hard look and sent him running.

He stepped into the open doorway and rapped his knuckles on the jamb.

A weary voice said, "I'm due for a break. See me in twenty."

Bennie said, "I'm not looking for anything physical. I

just want to talk."

She stepped into view and wrapped a nightgown about herself. As advertised: brunette, beauty mark, hard eyes. She ran a hand through her tousled hair, smoothing it. "You being straight with me?"

"Like an arrow."

"You still gotta pay, you know."

"Not a problem."

She considered it for a beat. "Shut the door."

Bennie stepped into the room and did just that. He turned and stood before her, studying her face. Pretty, in a worn out kind of way. Before Imogene, he might have made a pass at her. But now, the thought of anyone else just cooled him off.

"I don't have to take anything off, nothing like that?" she said.

"No."

Convinced he was for real, she relaxed and said, "Fine by me. Mind if I smoke?"

Bennie found a seat opposite the bed. "Go right ahead. What do they call you?"

"Barbara." She propped her pillows up and sat on the bed.

"Is that —"

"No, it's not," she said, lighting up. Bennie caught the make: River City Sovereigns, again.

"That your favorite brand of smoke?"

"Nah-ah, not yet. You gotta pay first, remember?"

Bennie smiled at her business acumen and pulled two sawbucks from his wallet. He leaned over and laid them on her dresser. "We good now?"

She reclined, pleased with herself. "Talk away, pretty boy."

"Your smokes, you like those the best?"

"Why, you want one?"

"Nah, I'm just interested in the fella who makes 'em."

She shot him a puzzled look. "Well, I don't know about all *that*, but you can have one if you want. They don't cost me a thing."

"You get 'em on the house?"

"Sort of. This guy Jonesy, he drops by with cartons of 'em, just leaves 'em for us to have around."

Bennie almost froze. Get more out of her first, he thought. "Sounds like a nice guy."

"I suppose, if you like that kind of thing. He and Cherry have business, I think."

"This Jonesy. How often does he come around?"

"You know, it's funny you should ask. He used to come by once a week, but he ain't been around in awhile." She took a drag and shot Bennie a curious look. "You sure this is what you want to talk about?"

"For now."

She raised her eyebrows, concerned. "You sure you're in the right place?"

Bennie missed her point.

She smiled. "Honey, let's just say Jonesy isn't interested in what I have to offer."

Bennie didn't know what to say. He didn't care, but he was surprised nonetheless.

Barbara let out a nervous laugh. "That's, uh, *news* to you, it would seem."

"Jonesy got a last name?"

"Boy, you aren't interested either," she said, a dejected tone in her voice. "If he does, I don't know it. You might could ask Cherry. Say, you got anything else you want to talk about? Because this — "

"Look, I'm a cop. I need some info."

Her eyes went ice cold. "You're a cop?"

"That I am." Bennie held up his badge.

"Well, why didn't you say so?" she said, folding her arms in a huff. "I ain't done nothing wrong."

Bennie pulled the pinup rag from the crook of his back and unfolded it. The color drained from Barbara's face. Bennie flipped to a middle page and held it up for her to see.

"That's you, right?"

Her eyes began to water. "Look, I —"

"Listen, I'm not with vice," said Bennie. "So you're not in any kind of trouble. At least, not with me. I'm just looking for answers to a few questions. Help me out, I'll leave you alone."

She dried her eyes with a handful of blanket. In an unsteady voice, she said, "Alright."

Bennie folded the rag and laid it in his lap. "Now, let's go back a second. This Jonesy character. Describe him for me."

Her voice quivered. "He's about your height, a little shorter. Skinny, with brown hair that's thick and curly."

Bennie tingled at *curly*.

"And he's got a scar," she continued, "right down the side of his face."

Bennie almost stood up. "Where on his face? Show me."

Slowly, she raised her right hand and touched that side of her face, drawing a finger down along the temple.

Kaboom. Bennie felt a bomb go off inside him. Jones Godfrey/Jack Gentry — peddler of King Tobacco cigarettes.

He said, "Your pal Jonesy. You ever hear anyone call

him Jack?"

She shook her head right off.

"What about the cigarettes? You ever get the idea that maybe Jonesy worked for King Tobacco?"

She shook her head again. No idea.

Bennie leaned forward and gave her a hard look. "Tell me about the photos."

She sighed, hiding her eyes. "What's there to tell? I needed the money."

"Where they taken here?"

"Yeah, downstairs."

"The camera man. He go by Dougie?"

She nodded. "He comes around, but we're not... together." She looked repulsed by the idea. "It was just a one time thing."

Bennie said it slow. "Do you know where Dougie *lives*?"

She shook her head.

"Does Cherry?"

She shrugged. No clue.

Bennie slapped the pin-up rag against his leg and began to crumple it into a ball.

A quiver took up in her voice. "You sure I'm not in any kind of trouble?"

Bennie stood, shaking his head. "No, you've been a big help." He scribbled into his steno and ripped the page out. "You see Dougie again, you call me, alright? And don't let on that I asked about him."

She took the page from him, nodding.

He looked around the room. It looked... lived in.

Without thinking, he said, "You got someone overseas?"

She toughened up and said, "Not anymore."

Bennie left the room as she burst into tears.

CHAPTER TWENTY-THREE

BENNIE LUMBERED FROM the floor, his joints slow to wake. He'd slept the last 24 hours straight through. He felt both utterly rested and wholly immobile. He stood slowly, stretching his neck, his back, his legs. He glared daggers at his unruffled bed. You're like an absent friend, he thought. Never there when I need you.

He donned sweats and made for the kitchen. Kicked up the boiler, made a pot of coffee. More stretches, a round of push-ups. Two cups of joe and he was alive.

He checked the wall clock. It was 8am, Monday morning. Eight hours until roll call. Work beckoned. He started for the dining room when the phone rang.

Bennie nearly jumped out of his skin. He grabbed it on the first ring.

"Sherwood."

"Kid, it's Everett."

Skin prickles. "Yeah?"

"Got you some info on your two names. A clerk at City Hall ran 'em through the birth and death records. It's not exhaustive, but it oughta do for now."

"Shoot."

"Jack Gentry. That's the name on the Apollo vic, right? The one we got off that bartender?"

"Yeah."

"That's a dummy name. Just like that cook, Freddie Graham. Jack Gentry died from pneumonia in 1907. He was a Confederate veteran. Lived in the old soldier's home on Boulevard."

"And the other?"

"Jones Godfrey was born in 1923, right here in Richmond. That one's legit. That's who you're chasing."

Bennie felt vindicated. But something about it eluded him — this ghost of an idea, teasing him. A thread he couldn't chase.

"Thanks, Everett."

"Yeah, well, I had to grease the clerk for a speedy job, so you owe me two sawbucks."

"You got it. Next payday."

Everett grunted. "Yeah, well, don't forget." And then he hung up, just like that.

Bennie dialed Niles.

"Hunter residence." Niles' cocky voice. Laughter in the background. His family, happy as can be.

"It's me."

"Yeah? Whaddya know?"

Bennie told him what he knew — all of it. From Jack's Apollo file to his interview with 'Barbara' to Everett's big get.

Niles whistled at the suggestion of a hickey on Godfrey's neck. "So our boy's a swish, huh? Damn."

"There's more. 'Barbara' said Godfrey used to load Cherry Anne's place up with cigarettes from King Tobacco. Just brought 'em in and gave 'em away."

"Holy shit. That's it, then! That's our way to King."

"Only we can't touch him. Cane's orders."

"Goddamnit! There's gotta be something we can do."

Bennie thought of Archie. No word from him yet. "I've got an idea, someone I can push."

"What about Swyers?"

"That's my thing. I'm not roping you into that."

"The hell you're not. We're partners, see? Your shit is my shit."

"Fine. But I say we go after Rivers first."

"Count me in. How?"

"Tonight, after roll call, I'll say we've got leads on the gasoline. The Cane'll eat it up. We'll stake out Rivers, see where it gets us."

"Fine by me."

"Tonight, then."

"Yeah. Say — "

"What?"

"You went to Cherry's?"

"Not for *that*. Jesus."

Niles laughed. "You're bent on that mechanic broad."

"Yeah, well, that's a long shot and then some."

"Well, hell, then — best go on back. You've got time, ain't you? Or you could just do like our pal Jonesy and switch sides."

Niles barked like a wild dog as Bennie hung up.

He made the Annex with ten minutes to spare. A quick run by his desk for the usual. Carbons, memos, reports — all of it inconsequential. Nothing that played to his casework.

Roll call was brief and succinct. The Cane talked up the local rackets: numbers, gambling, bootlegging. Bennie did *not* take notes. He had enough on his plate already.

Jungle instincts needled him. Someone, watching him. He scanned the room. There, in a corner — Jack, glaring daggers *his* way.

The Cane's rod smacked the lectern.

"Dismissed."

Bennie met him as he lurched from the squadroom.

"Sir?

"What is it, Sherwood?"

"Niles and I caught a break in the gasoline theft."

The Cane lit up. "Oh? Some progress, finally."

"With your permission, we'll pursue it right away."

The Cane hesitated and looked over at Jack, holding court with a throng of patrolmen. "I think we're gonna need to table that for now."

"Sir?"

The Cane turned back to Bennie with a put on smile.

"You're doing excellent work, son. Just excellent. But I've been reminded of more... *pressing* matters."

Bennie was surprised. "More pressing than ten drums of missing gasoline?"

"Oh, it's a concern, yes, but, uh — look, Jack's got some good ideas for us, things that'll help us make a splash over at City Hall. He'll talk with you about them soon."

Bennie felt gutted. "I don't understand."

"You will, " said The Cane, leaning in close. "And what of the other issue I tasked you with?"

Bennie lowered his voice. "I've made a connection at the paper. He's looking into it now."

"Excellent, just excellent." The Cane gave Bennie an *attaboy* touch on the shoulder as he walked off. Bennie watched him go, feeling like he'd just been benched from the biggest game of his life. He turned, looked for Niles, and caught Eugene Mills making for the stairs.

"Eugene! You're back!"

Eugene froze, a startled look on his face.

"Bennie. Yeah, hey."

Bennie looked him up and down. His right arm rested in a sling. Light bruises mapped his face. Strange — Eugene could hardly meet his eyes.

"It's great to see you on your feet. What's your desk?"

"Don't have one yet. I'm on light duty right now, just this and that. Until I'm a hundred percent."

"Yeah? Well, it's great having you back in any capacity. We need all the help we can get."

Eugene nodded and looked away. Bennie caught sight of some deeper bruising around his neck.

"Say, are those from Pearl's?"

Eugene met his eyes and blanched, as if he'd suddenly been found out. *For what?*

"These? Oh, yes, they're from Pearl's," said Eugene. "Yeah, we fought those Negroes, and it… it got ugly. Look, I need to run. Cane's got me on some errands, you know how he is. Good seeing you, Bennie. I'll see you around."

And just like that, he was off. Down the stairs and away.

Bennie watched him go, wondering what Eugene had to hide. Bruises, those Negroes —

Something *clicked*.

Negroes.

At the jail.

Those *notes* —

Bennie scrambled for the lair. Made his desk, spilled open his steno. Flipped back a few pages — *there*.

That day at the jail — digging into Skipper's time in

stir.

Three arrests, three sets of roommates.

Skipper's second arrest — August, '42. He did two nights for burglary — busted for filching booze. His cellmates were J. Godfrey and E. Moore.

A *louder* click.

That afternoon with Skipper's mother.

He heard her say *'I think it was during one of those spells in jail that a fella offered him a job working for Mr. King.'*

Bennie steadied himself against the desk. If Godfrey *did* work for King, they could go to Jack and the Cane with it.

But King Tobacco employment records — how?

Everett? Iffy. Everett was a Cane loyalist.

City Hall? Maybe. Play up his veteran status, garner a favor with one of the clerks.

And then he remembered — Archie said he had pals who worked at King Tobacco.

Bennie grabbed the phone. An operator put him through to the Times Dispatch. A receptionist got him to the right desk.

"Research."

"Archie Smith, please."

"Sure. Can I tell — "

"Just put him on."

A few beats passed. Scrapes and shuffles on the line. The receiver, changing hands. Then, the kid's bright voice.

"This is Archie."

"Kid, it's me."

"Boy, you must have some kind of sixth sense. I was just about to ring you."

"You've got something for me?"

"Do I. But —"

"What?"

Archie talked low in a dour voice. "It's not the kind of thing you want over the phone. Say, I thought you wanted me to call you?"

"Something else came up I need your help with. It's related."

"Something new?"

"Sort of. Look, can you meet?"

"Sure thing. An hour? At that coffee spot?"

"See ya then."

Bennie hung up, buzzing. What did the kid have for him?

Just then, Jack strolled into the lair, cocky as all get out. He had the air of a DI about to administer a surprise inspection.

"Jack, you're not gonna believe this, I —"

"Can it, Sherwood. This concerns everyone, so listen up."

The other bulls snapped to attention. Bennie stifled a groan and followed suit, miffed.

BOHICA — bend over, here it comes again.

Jack cleared his throat. "Our city is overrun with drunks, disorderlies, and charges of assault. One often feeding the other two. Additional crimes, the black market, and an increasingly unmanageable auxillary force only add to our woes, leaving our department scattered and without focus.

"With my father's help, I've gotten City Hall to approve a brief redirection of our efforts. This will involve temporary reassignments for many of you — "

Moans around the room. Jack let it pass.

"With the ultimate goal being a rise in our overall clearance rate. Additionally, this will offer us internal focus, juice with the higher ups, and, most of all, good press. Put your nose to the ground and play ball. You'll be back on your regularly assigned desks in no time."

Bennie was dumbfounded. One of the other bulls said, "When does this take effect?"

"Immediately," said Jack. "Take what time you need to put your open cases to rest and then see me in the squadroom."

Can-you-believe-this-shit looks circled the room.

Jack said, "Cooperation is mandatory. Duty and honor, gentlemen. Remember — there's a war on."

He left the room before anyone could protest. Niles waltzed into the lair a second later, chomping a cruller. He caught the sour mood and paused.

"What'd I miss?"

CHAPTER TWENTY-FOUR

THIRD STREET COFFEE was crowded. Counter stools, booths, tables — all full. The room hummed with chit-chat and laughter. It irked Bennie. He didn't feel like either.

A back booth opened up. A couple of politicos were next in line, but Bennie badged the server and pulled rank. They scowled at him as he walked past.

"Official police business," he said, flashing a put-upon smile. He slid into the booth and ordered a double whiskey. The waitress shot him a icy look and made for the counter.

Bennie stewed on Jack's *coup d'etat*. There was something at play here, something more than just a higher clearance rate and good press. Jack wanted King, sure. But he wanted something else, too. What, Bennie didn't know.

Archie slid in across from him, amazed.

"How'd you snag a booth?"

Bennie held up his badge. "I bear the mark of the afflicted, so they let me pass, for I am damned."

The kid went *huh?*

"Just something my father used to say."

The waitress brought Bennie's whiskey. The kid eyed it like it was poison.

"Something for you, sweetheart?" She batted her eyes at Archie.

"Just a soda pop," he said, blushing. She winked at him and walked off.

Bennie took a long sip of his drink. Archie was surprised.

"Is this, uh, how you normally start your afternoons?"

Bennie's look said it wasn't. "I've just been told I've so many weeks on a shit detail of which I know nothing. Call this my last rites." He downed the rest of his drink in a single gulp. The rush of heat was glorious. A buzz took hold and softened his edge.

"So. What have you got for me?"

Archie leaned forward and fidgeted with his hands. He looked afraid to talk. "You're not gonna like any of it."

"I don't like much of anything these days, kid. Just pile it on."

"I asked one of our crime reporters about your press leak."

"Yeah?"

Archie lowered his voice. "He got tough with me, told me to get lost."

"Shit. What's his name?"

"No. If word gets around, they'll know it was me. I want to help, but I'm not losing my job over this."

Bennie was vexed but impressed. "Fine. What else did you find out?"

Archie's soda appeared. He drank half of it, prepping himself. "Before I say anything else, this woman. She's your… ?"

Bennie let it hang there for a beat. "Does it matter?"

"Well, no. You just… never said."

"She's a friend."

"Okay."

"Why?"

Archie paused. "This is not the kinda stuff you'd want just anyone to know."

"She's a friend I care about. Let's leave it at that."

Archie slurped soda pop. "Okay, then. Here goes."

Imogene Anne McKenna had lived in Richmond for all of three years. Just about the duration of the war, the way Archie had figured it. She lived in Highland Park with her parents and younger brother. Her father was a machinist at Tredegar. Her mother was a seamstress and her brother assisted local grocers — and the war effort — by delivering the milk on his bicycle. Imogene worked at Digby's garage, fixing cars.

"She worked there most of '42," said Archie, "and then she took a hiatus. Came back to work about four, five months ago."

"A hiatus?"

"Yep."

Archie got the skinny on Imogene's 'hiatus' from a couple of mechanics who'd left Digby's garage for higher paying war jobs.

She got pregnant.

Bennie felt a ripple of jealousy run through him. He'd never even considered she had someone else.

"Okay, she was pregnant. Is that it?"

Archie made a face. "No."

"What else, then?"

Archie sipped more soda pop and told him how he'd

combed area hospitals for info on her delivery. Girl/boy/ name? He tracked her to MCV and discovered... something else.

"I ran into a nurse I know from the neighborhood," he said. "I fed her some bull about a story on goodbye babies. She knows I'm trying to get ahead at the paper, so she let me see some maternity records. I saw your friend's name on the list, and well..."

Archie fought with it for a beat.

"She lost the baby, last April."

Bennie's gut twisted into itself. A rush of sadness and horror came over the table all at once. He felt cheap. The kid was right. He shouldn't know this.

"Jesus."

Archie nodded and drained his soda pop. All this chit chat made him parched.

Bennie sat there for a time, speechless, processing it.

Archie said, "You want the rest?"

"There's *more*?"

The kid nodded, a grave look in his eyes.

"My nurse pal, she caught on that I was interested in your friend. She pulled me aside and told me that the father of your friend's baby was killed in action. Right about the time that she... "

Bennie went numb. He heard the Confederate Cab dispatcher say *'They don't give out medals for what she's been through'*.

Archie broke the tension. "I haven't been able to dig into Mr. King yet. Between looking into this and work, I haven't had time. Plus," he said, shooting a look at the wall clock, "I gotta motor. My boss'll have berserks if I'm not back soon. I'll get info on King next week, alright?"

"It won't matter. I'm off the radar for awhile. Just leave

a message and I'll find you." Bennie suddenly felt rigid and stiff, as if the news had impaired him physically. He wondered if he'd be able to leave the booth.

Archie nodded. Bennie remembered —

"Kid. These guys you know at King Tobacco?"

"Yeah?"

Bennie felt crass pushing his case, as if nothing were more important than what he just learned. He wrote the two names — Jack Gentry/Jones Godfrey — on a napkin and handed it to Archie. "Ask them about those two. I need to know if either one worked for Mr. King. Some kind of proof, if they can."

Archie stood, pocketing the napkin.

"Look, I'm sorry about your friend. Not sure if this is what you wanted to know, but… there it is."

Archie walked off and left Bennie alone with his thoughts.

Chapter Twenty-Five

THREE WEEKS FLEW by and suddenly, it was the middle of February. As part of Jack's *coup d'etat*, Bennie and Niles were assigned to three successive details. Each one lasted a week and worked them both to the bone.

Detail #1: Running point on a warrants squad. Bennie and Niles at the head, two grunts for muscle. Quickie arrests to boost the department's crime stats. Their targets were mostly wife beaters and unlawful cohabiters. Jack threw in a few fences for good measure.

It was grueling work. Seven, eight jobs a day, all over town. From Barton Heights to The Fan, out Monument Avenue to the West End, and back downtown to the edges of Tobacco Row. Most of the perps tried to rabbit, so they worked a front-to-back blitz. Bennie and Niles at the door, papers in hand. The grunts in the rear, ready to pounce. All of it in winter's frigid temps. It almost made Bennie wish for that Guadalcanal heat.

Almost.

Detail #2: Rounding up schlubs who avoided the draft because they refused to treat their syphilis. The local war office reported that 700 plus men with the clap were roaming the city limits. Bennie and Niles went door to door, one neighborhood after another. Like the warrants gig, it was an all-over-town job. The easy ones came willingly, resigned to their fate.

The rest — well, they came around.

"And what if I don't wanna?" squawked one afflicted man. Rail thin, shit attitude. Cannon fodder, thought Bennie.

"Then we'll make sure every honeygirl in town knows your name," said Niles.

"We'll even put it in the paper," added Bennie, "along with everyone else who's got it."

"Yeah," said Niles. "You'll have to leave town just to look at another woman."

Bennie and Niles would howl, the men would cave, and they'd all take a trip down to the VD Center on West Cary.

Detail #3: Assisting the traffic bureau in the paint shop. With all the bootblacks and military convoys in town, designated traffic patterns had gone to shit. New signs had to be made, old ones repaired. Bennie and Niles were given a map and a hauling truck. They worked up a route and got to it. They set new sign poles and safety zones. They lugged busted machines to the Police Court at City Hall. They fixed street car doors and made over bus stops. If nothing else, it was good exercise.

The last job of the third detail was a new bus stop marker on Main Street, out near the Jefferson Hotel. Niles had bowed out early — he and Cheryl Lee were due for a night out — so Bennie flew solo. He detached the old sign, tossed it into the truck, and set the new one with fresh screws. Tidied up the stop with some fresh paint. Easy and done.

It was over. Three weeks of shit work that actually made for real progress. Hundreds of arrests, fresh blood for the war machine, and look — some pretty new signs to make it all look nice.

Bennie packed up his tools and got ready to leave. Down the block, he caught sight of the Jefferson Hotel. A real swanky place. Not that he would know — he'd never actually stayed there, just been inside a few times. A few dinners with the old man, the occasional police ceremony.

Month-old whispers bugged him — January summary sheets mentioned mob sightings and suspicious characters at the Jefferson.

Bennie was starved for real police work. He tucked in his shirt, wiped smudges of dirt from his face, and grabbed his jacket from the truck.

He strolled in through the main entrance off Franklin, looking more like a hired hand than someone in for an overnight stay. A haughty bellhop caught sight of him and strolled over.

"Can I help you?" The bellhop spoke as if Bennie were lost.

Bennie flashed his badge. "Police inquiry," he said.

The bellhop's eyes went wide. "Oh, my. I'll get the manager."

"As a matter of fact, it's you I want to see."

"Me?" The bellhop feigned a guilty look. A real showman.

"You see most everyone that comes through here, don't you?"

"Why, of course."

"In the last month, have you noticed anyone, say,

suspicious?"

The bellhop took offense. "The Jefferson is one of the finest hotels in all of the South. We don't cater — "

"Oh, come off it. If they pay, they stay."

The bellhop cooled and brought his voice down to a whisper. "Can you be more specific?"

"Mob types. Hoods."

The bellhop shook his head. "Oh, *them*. They don't make a fuss, mind you, but they *are* noticed."

"Well-heeled?"

"Oh yes, and wary of attention. What's the word you used, suspicious? Yes. *That*."

"You ever see them hobnobbing with in-town folk?"

"Can't say I have, but there is talk among the elevator operators about late night gatherings and certain... visitors."

"Like who?"

Two cars hit the drop off line. Ritzy folk and luggage flooded the scene.

"Try the service area. Downstairs, behind the dining room."

"Thanks."

The bellhop put on a smile and went to greet the guests.

Bennie snaked through the foyer and ducked the crowd. Politicos and bigwigs, done up in ball gowns and tuxedos, ready to do the town.

He took the Grand Staircase to the lower lobby and checked the scene: rowdy soldiers everywhere, living it up. Beer bottles in hand, female companions by the dozen. Bennie thought of boot camp furloughs and illicit nights on Parris Island.

He took a side door to a service hallway and found it empty. He heard a noise around the way — *jackpot*.

Someone he could brace.

Bennie turned the corner and stopped dead in his tracks.

An *alligator*, right there.

Fat and bloated, the beast hissed at him and snapped its jaws. Bennie took a step back and froze.

A Negro kid stepped into the hallway. A boy, all of sixteen.

"Go on an git now, Pompey. Just git."

The kid nipped at Pompey with a broom handle. The gator hissed and split the other way. Bennie breathed a sigh of relief and steadied himself against the wall. Guadalcanal memories surged: a crocodile on the beach, gnawing a dead man's leg.

"Jesus," said Bennie. "They just roam the halls like that?" Rumor was there were near half a dozen of them at the hotel. Bennie's father had told him the story of vacationing Northerners, returning home from Florida by way of the East Coast, who just up and abandoned the creatures as a lark.

"Back here they do," said the Negro kid. "Sometimes they get out all over. 'Specially with all these soldiers around."

"You been working here long?"

"Couple of months here, but almost four years in hotels. Murphy's, the John Marshall. I been around. Why?"

Bennie showed him his badge and ran down what he was after. The kid was silent for a time, thinking. Finally, he said, "Why?"

"What do you mean, 'why'?"

"I mean, why's you asking?"

"We've got a mess of trouble on our hands already. Last

thing we need is organized crime in the mix. If they're around, we need to know."

"I don't know nothing about organized crime."

"But you *do* know who I'm talking about, yes?"

The Negro kid took his time. "Yeah."

"What about late night gatherings?"

The kid said nothing.

"You ever see these guys party?"

The kid just shrugged and looked at the floor. He could have said he didn't know and walked away. Be he didn't.

Bennie caught on. He pulled some cash from his pocket. Three fins, a few singles. He peeled off one of the fins and handed it to the kid.

"What's your name?"

"Wesley."

"Wesley, I'm Detective Sherwood. Now, have you ever seen these guys throw a party?"

"Yeah, I help some of the kitchen staff deliver food to their rooms sometimes."

"And what do they do at these parties?"

"They drink, mostly. And entertain girls. Top shelf, all around."

"They entertain anyone else?"

Wesley pulled a face. "Like who?"

"Anyone you can describe. People of note, like the Mayor, perhaps."

Wesley shook his head. No dice.

"What about big names around town. Someone like Jedidiah King?"

Wesley lit up. "You know Mr. King?"

Bennie got tingles. "I do."

"I like Mr. King, we all do. He's a regular, stays here all the time. And now that you mention it, I do believe I've seen him with these folks you're asking about."

"Is that so? You're friendly with him?"

"Well, sure," said Wesley. "He tips big and gives out cigarettes to everyone. See?" Wesley pulled a pack of River City Sovereigns from his back pocket. "He leaves cartons of these, everywhere. Something for everyone, he says. Say, you want one?"

"No, thanks."

"Mind if I do?"

Bennie shook his head. "Look, Wesley. You think of anything else about these 'folks' in the hotel, you let me know, ok? Just ring the City Hall Annex, ask for me."

Wesley nodded and lipped a cigarette, indifferent. He felt about his various pockets, lost.

"Boy, all ready for a smoke and I got no fire. You got any matches?"

Bennie reached into the inside pocket of his jacket and pulled out the Westwood Club matchbook that Skipper had given him. He'd been carrying it around for weeks, trying to crack the code. He handed it to Wesley.

"Here. You can keep 'em."

Wesley nodded thanks and lit his cigarette. He took a long drag, his eyes lingering on the inscription inside the flap.

"You got a room here?" asked Wesley.

Bennie almost laughed. "No."

"Says here you do. Next month."

Bennie was lost.

"Here," said Wesley, turning toward Bennie, pointing at the inscription. "This here is hotel code," he continued, spelling it out. "J H, M ten, ten P. In our local hotel speak, that's Jefferson Hotel, March 10, 10PM."

Bennie just stared at it, speechless.

Wesley howled. "You got a room here next month, mister, and you don't even know it!"

Chapter Twenty-Six

THE SQUADROOM WAS SRO. Too many people, too little room. Bulls from every desk, patrolmen from every unit. Bennie and Niles stood in the back, ready to get to it.

The Cane took up at the lectern. "Gentlemen," he said, holding up the morning paper, "I am in your debt. Thanks to your hard work, recent crime's taken a nosedive and we're back in City Hall's good graces." He opened the paper and showcased a headline. It read POLICE TIGHTEN UP, CRIME RATE HEADS SOUTH.

"Now," he continued, "I can't take all the credit. Jack had the foresight to set us on this path, so let's give credit where credit's due."

Everyone clapped and nodded Jack's way. He just nodded back, a dutiful look on his face. *Just doing my job.*

"As of today," The Cane continued, "you're to return to your regular desk and resume your active in — "

Whoops and hollers circled the room. The Cane walloped the lectern with his rod and silenced 'em quick.

"Celebrate all you want," he said, glaring daggers around the room, "but if you make me look bad again,

207

you'll find yourself permanently reassigned. Is that understood?"

Curt nods and yessirs made the rounds.

"Good. Now get out of my sight."

The room scrambled for the exit. Bennie and Niles exchanged wide-eyed looks and did the same. They were almost out of the room when they heard The Cane's bark.

"Sherwood. Hunter. My office."

Jack said, "We're suspending the investigation into Digby's gasoline theft. We've got more pressing matters to attend to, and it's taken too long to net any valuable leads."

Bennie almost went through the roof. "Are you kidding me?"

It was a familiar setting. The Cane sat at his desk. Jack stood behind him, pacing. Bennie and Niles sat across from them, like schoolboys about to be scolded by the principal. The air in the room was near toxic. Don't strike a match, thought Bennie. The whole place'll blow.

The Cane said, "You've had close to six weeks, son. Give it up."

"Give it up? How could I get anywhere? One minute, I'm tracking it down, the next I'm putting up a damn bus stop. You two have us doing rookie work when we should be out there running this shit down!"

"Watch yourself, son. That rookie work got us the best press we've had in months and put me in the right with the higher ups. You know I've got more than just stolen gasoline on my hands. That shit could be anywhere by now! It's time to move on and focus on other things."

Bennie and Niles looked at one another. Niles' eyes said *tell them.*

Bennie said, "Rivers."

Jack said, "Excuse me?"

"Captain Rivers. He stole the gasoline."

Jack laughed, but The Cane did not.

"Explain that," he said.

Bennie and Niles ran it down for them, all the way back to Hollis Digby's gambling debt.

Jack was furious. "Why is this the first we're hearing of this?"

"We didn't have enough to go on," said Niles, "and with all the press headaches, we didn't want to add to your troubles without something solid."

Bennie thought of what he learned from the morgue attendant. "I've also learned from a trusted source that Captain Rivers and Arthur Brown run a back channel of stolen goods from the morgue. He's a significant part of our black market problem, sir. We just can't prove it."

"This is ridiculous," said Jack, turning to his father. "You don't actually buy any of this, do you?"

But The Cane *did* buy it. "Wyatt's as crooked as they come," he said. "The previous occupant of this chair gave him the First, not I. He's got tenure with City Hall and I can't touch him."

Niles said, "So you've known about him."

"For some time. I just couldn't get anyone across the street to listen."

Jack huffed and addressed his father. "This is *not* what we decided on. You and I, we — "

The Cane turned to his son and looked as if he might throw him across the room. "The last I checked, *I* am the Chief of this police department, not you. *You* had your play. This is my call, not yours. Now shut up and listen."

Jack took a step back and found composure. Bennie and

Niles were too afraid to breathe.

The Cane looked at them both and said, "Five days."

Bennie said, "For what?"

"The two of you have five days to get me something on Rivers. Something strong, something I can use."

"Why five days?"

The Cane looked grave. "Because in five days, I have to dissolve the Victory desk. City Hall's orders. Ineffective police resources, they said. If you can get me something good, I just might be able to keep it alive."

Bennie and Niles stepped into the lair, relieved.

"It was like a sweatbox in there," said Niles.

Bennie agreed. "Looks like we're on."

"Are we ever. If we don't bring this in, I'm gonna be hoofing a beat."

A secretary made the room. A pretty blonde with glasses and a red dress. Every bull in the room looked her way.

"Detective Sherwood?"

Bennie walked over to her. "That's me."

"A message for you."

She handed him a note and left the room. When she'd gone, a vice bull pretended to take her from behind. The room yukked.

Bennie unfolded the note. It read *Call Me ASAP —* *Archie.*

Niles gnawed a toothpick. "What?"

"My guy at the paper. He's got something."

Niles lowered his voice. "King?"

Bennie nodded. "You start in on Rivers. I'll see what the kid found out. We'll meet later."

"Aye aye, captain. And hey, if you do see King, get me

some smokes, will ya? Cheryl Lee just loves those Royals."

Bennie hightailed it to Third Street and seized that same back booth. He was jazzed, ready for a hot tip. Archie was spooked and talked low.

"Look," he said, "I feel threatened just knowing this stuff, so promise me — you won't mention where you got it?"

"It's just me, kid. Don't fret."

A nervous laugh escaped Archie. "Easy for you to say. You don't know what I know."

"Then let's have it, huh?"

Archie spilled *all*.

His pals at King Tobacco had delivered. As a matter of fact, they'd been more than willing to talk. Goings-on at King Tobacco were *odd*, to say the least.

The man himself was quite the enigma. Archie's pals had Jedidiah King pegged as a night owl who partied hard with liquor and dope. He rarely made an appearance at the warehouse before noon and, despite his scandalous reputation, was in fact a great boss, often pitching in when things got busy, working side by side the lowliest of employees.

Archie brought his voice down to a whisper.

"His *preferences*, though —"

Bennie missed it. "Preferences?"

Archie clarified. King swung both ways — he dug on women *and* men. *This* was no real secret — talk around the Annex had long pegged King as a swish. But, according to Archie's chums, it went even further.

Archie looked around the room before he spoke.

"Whites *and* Negroes."

Bennie could care less. White, black, straight, homo —

he'd seen it all in the barracks during boot camp. But *this* could be their tie-in to the Apollo murders. Those two bodies — one white, one black...

"Your pals say anything else?"

"They say it's just *weird* around there — people coming and going at all hours of the night. Delivery trucks with *strange* schedules."

"What kind of trucks?"

"All kinds. Tobacco, of course, but supplies for the warehouse, too. Machinery, containers, heck — whatever it needs. Sometimes at 2, 3 in the morning. That's, uh, what you wanted to know, yeah?"

Bennie nodded. "Yeah, kid, you did great. Say — what about those two names I fed you?"

"Oh, right," said Archie. "I almost forgot. One of 'em *did* work for King, after all."

Bennie felt pinpricks on his skin. "Which one?"

"Jones Godfrey. Not the other. I just memorized the one name. Didn't want to write it down and have someone find it on me."

Bennie's mind was racing, processing it all.

"Detective?"

Bennie looked up and met Archie's strained gaze. Earlier, the kid looked spooked on what he knew. Now, he looked spooked on *Bennie*.

"Sorry, kid. It's just a lot to take in."

"Yeah, well. You seem like the type that goes looking for trouble. Figure you can handle it."

"Comes with the job."

"Then it's a better job for you than me, that's for sure. Listen, I gotta get back."

"You really came through, kid. Thanks."

"Yeah, well, next time, it's your turn to talk,

remember?"

CHAPTER TWENTY-SEVEN

NIGHT'S CURTAIN FELL across the River City as Bennie steered the old man's wheels toward the Row. A 2-door Ford sedan in jet black with faired-in headlights. No unmarked wheels tonight. Bennie had to stay *off* RPD radar.

King was off limits — that, he knew. But Archie's intel — King's *preferences*, his warehouse goings-on — it was just too strong. And with the dissolution of the Victory desk looming, Bennie had to move on it *now*. Niles was off tailing Rivers and Brown. Bennie had King all to himself.

He coasted to a stop behind some furniture delivery trucks. The spot offered Bennie a clear view of King's warehouse. It was just across the intersection, not a hundred yards off. The company's namesake was painted in large white letters above the front door.

Bennie killed the engine and looked around. A few tobacco workers were milling about, just off their shift. They hailed a cab and were gone.

He was all alone.

Until an RPD prowler hit the intersection and stopped

for the light. Bennie tensed up and sank into the driver's seat quick. He peered over the dash and made two mugs — an old dog out of First and, by the looks of it, his AO lackey. They yawned and sped off when the light changed. Bennie counted off five beats before he sat up. He shot a quick look around — all clear.

Darkness settled in around him like an old friend. Bennie found comfort in an even darker thought. He felt as if he were back in the jungle on a night raid, hot on a blood trail, in it until the end.

He reached for his knapsack, pulled it open, and reviewed his stakeout vitals: a flashlight, binoculars, a thermos of coffee, two roast beef sandwiches, his steno, his badge, and his .38 special.

Bennie grabbed the thermos, twisted it open, and poured a cup. He leaned back, sipped hot coffee, and waited.

Bennie yawned and rubbed his eyes. Two hours had passed. He was sleepy and restless. Coffee jitters stretched him thin. Sitting for that long made his legs ache. Call it the stakeout blahs.

Movement across the way. Someone exiting the warehouse.

Bennie grabbed the nocs.

Bingo.

Jedidiah King himself marched out of his warehouse and beelined for a '39 Packard. He fired it up and sped off on Main, due west.

Bennie dropped the nocs and counted off three long beats before following suit, pulling after him just in time. He leadfooted it and closed the gap to four car lengths.

They took Main all the way to Belvidere, cutting north

at Monroe Park, and doubled back down Franklin, heading east now. Only two blocks, though, and King slowed, parking his wheels just outside The Commonwealth Club. *The* place for fat cats and bigwigs. Bennie kept a steady pace and drove past him. He found a spot a few blocks up, just east of the club.

He grabbed the nocs and ducked from his wheels in a crouch. He eased the front door shut and padded the sidewalk back the other way. He had good cover — a line of fancy automobiles, parked all in a row.

Bennie crawled across the street like a rat, staying low on all fours. He found a good spy spot on the next block. He was on his knees now, peeking around the hood of a nice sedan.

The front steps and side patio of the club were unoccupied. No surprise there — it was cold as all hell outside. The building itself was magnificent. Even at night, Bennie could make out the deep red brick and brownstone trim. Inside was ritzy charm to the nines, or so he remembered. He'd been only once, as a boy, with his father. A police function of some kind. Typical Dad — the old man drank a few too many and got thrown out for arguing with The Cane.

The cold was too much. Bennie shuffled back to his wheels and slipped inside. He turned in his seat, facing the club, and rested against the steering wheel. He gnashed a sandwich and sipped coffee. Thank the stars for the thermos — the joe was still hot.

Time passed. Ten, fifteen minutes.

Bennie found a sightline and looked up the street — King's ride, still there.

Nature called. Too much coffee in too short a time. Bennie snuck outside and found a tree to water, looking

over his shoulder the whole time. It was fear instinct —
too many men from his battalion had bought the farm this
way.

Raised voices hit the air. Bennie finished up quick and
stayed low, right back to that same spot. He made himself
still and just listened.

The talk was heated. Two men, one of them King. The
other — *familiar.* Bennie caught just pieces of what was
said.

King: '...corral those slimeballs...'

The *other* voice: '...we had an agreement...'

King again: '...Josephine Scott...'

The other voice, Bennie *knew* it —

He turned and looked through car windows across the
street.

No, no, holy shit, no.

There, on the steps of The Commonwealth Club, were
two men.

One of them was Jedidiah King.

The other was Stolmy Reed, The Cane himself.

Bennie's knees buckled and he sank to the ground, short
of breath.

Holy shit, no no no.

A car door slammed. An engine fired up.

Bennie saw Jedidiah King tear onto Franklin and speed
off. He shot eyes across the street. The Cane was *gone,* like
a ghost in the wind.

Bennie up and ran to his wheels. No point in hiding
now.

King cut left off Franklin and Bennie just *knew.*

They were headed for Jackson Ward.

King drove wildly — zipping across lanes, honking his

horn. Bennie kept to a three-car distance and eased on the gas. If King suspected a tail, he might lose him for good.

Jedidiah King and The Cane, working together, holy shit…

They made The Deuce in no time. Bennie felt his nerves hit overdrive — the Apollo was just up ahead. *Please — don't go there.*

King drove just past and parked. Bennie curbed his wheels a few blocks away. He watched with relief as King sprinted across the street and ducked into The Eggleston Hotel. Its restaurant, Neverett's Place, was a popular Deuce spot.

Bennie felt himself shake. It was all too much. Deep breaths brought his heart rate down and calmed his mind. Inhale, exhale, repeat. Just like they taught him.

An odd feeling took hold — someone watching *him.*

He pulled his .38 from the knapsack and eyeballed his perimeter. Just a few people hustling from spot to spot, dodging the winter air.

He looked back at the Eggleston. He had to risk it.

Bennie holstered his gun, grabbed his badge, and stepped from the car. He jetted to the hotel and rapped on the front door. A black man opened up. His smile deflated as he registered Bennie's shield. He stood aside and held the door open as Bennie stepped into a beehive of music, joy, and smoke.

The atmosphere in the room was vivid. Affectionate couples of all pairings kissed in plain sight. There was laughter and spirits at every table. Cigarettes and dancing, too. A sea of smiles and freedom. The entire room generated its own heat — no furnace necessary.

Up on the stage, a tight band played the blues behind a woman's sad song. The words poured out of her thin, raspy voice like a sermon exits a preacher, all feeling and conviction. Shouts came her way from the crowd. Bennie thought he heard someone call her Billy.

There — across the room.

King and bandleader Duke Ellington, chatting it up. Bennie's jungle vision kicked in and he saw details. Duke was consoling a most distraught King. Bennie replayed those fragments from the steps of The Commonwealth Club —

'... corral those slimeballs...'

'... Josephine Scott...'

Bennie felt a jolt hit hard, he remembered now — Josephine Scott was the dead woman from the Apollo.

He felt a tap on his shoulder.

Bennie turned and found three Negro men, right there. Hard eyes, hard faces. Men you want to fight with, not against.

One of them spoke up. A direct man, built tough. Tired of taking another man's shit.

"What'cha want here?"

Bennie held up his badge. Before he could speak —

"Yeah, we know. You're a policeman. So what?"

Bennie grasped for something quick.

"I'm doing follow up on something that happened awhile back. Across the street, at the Apollo?"

"Oh yeah? So you're finally coming 'round about that, huh?"

"Well, I was first on the scene, but another detective worked the investigation. I'm just doing some follow up."

"What's that mean?"

Bennie was puzzled. "It wasn't my case, is what I mean."

One of the other men piped up. Taller, deep voice.

"Ya'll just full of it. Wasn't nobody's case."

Bennie was lost now. "You don't understand. It wasn't my —"

Mr. Direct got hot. "We don't understand? We don't understand? We understand just fine. Bodies in The Deuce ain't your problem, they're ours."

Bennie looked around. A crowd had formed around him. The music slowed to a halt, the lights came up. He shielded his eyes and shot a look across the room — *shit.*

King was *gone.*

Bennie felt himself start to sweat. All eyes were on *him*, just like in the jungle. He steadied himself against the wall. Oh boy — a dizzy spell, coming on quick.

"Listen, I —"

"Listen to what? We ain't had no one to listen *to*! And here you are, doing *follow up*? On what?"

Someone from the crowd: "Look at him, he can't hardly stand up."

Another: "That's 'cause he ain't been around this many Negroes at once. He about to be sick."

A round of laughter made the room. It was a real hoot.

Bennie felt his legs start to give. He fell against the wall and started for his gun, but a hand reached out and stopped him.

It belonged to Jedidiah King.

"Ladies and gentlemen, please, please, don't you know who this is?"

Jedidiah was suddenly right next to him, holding him up. Bennie looked at him aghast.

"Why this here is Detective Bennie Thomas Sherwood," said King, a grand smile on his face.

"Not only," continued King, "does he work for our *esteemed* police department..." — letting it just hang there a moment as a round of laughter made the room — "but his father, the late Samuel Sherwood, was knifed to death not five blocks from where we now stand. Bennie here served our country, as well, just as many of your fathers, brothers, and sons have done, and continue to do. So we'll dispense with the ridicule and offer this man the respect he deserves."

King commanded the room with the ease of a seasoned politician. Clearly, he was not only welcome here, but revered. Bennie was both in awe and in conflict. Here was a man he wanted to throw to the ground and thrash and yet had saved him from embarrassment, maybe worse.

The house lights came down, the music took up again, and Mr. Direct handed Bennie a drink. A double whiskey on the rocks.

"Sorry for the roughhouse," he said. "If you're with him, you're alright."

The crowd dispersed, leaving Bennie alone with King.

Bennie had to force it out. "Thank you."

"Yes, well, let's put it behind us, shall we?"

Bennie found his legs again and drank. The whiskey was smooth, beaucoup stuff. It relaxed him.

"I... I don't know what came over me," he said.

"Well, I *do*, Detective. You've fought in a war, have you not? Surely, the threat of physical violence makes you uneasy. I do believe you'd have found yourself in the midst of some had I not stepped in when I did."

Bennie felt resentful and got cocky. "I can handle myself, if that's what you mean."

King smiled at his embarrassment. "Yes, Detective, there's no doubt about that. But, I ask you, at what cost?" he said, his eyes gesturing at Bennie's gun.

Bennie drained the rest of his drink and handed the glass to King. "I wouldn't have hurt anyone. I just... Look,

I said thank you, alright? I need to be on my way."

Bennie started off, but King grabbed his arm and held him back.

"Tell me, Detective. What *are* you doing here?"

They were so close now. Bennie could just reach out and muscle him to the ground. Get it out of him, right here and now.

"Just like I said. Follow up on the Apollo. There were two murders there awhile back."

"Yes, I know."

"Do you?" Bennie felt bold, teasing him. "What's it to you?"

King chewed on it a moment, forming his words. "I'm a wealthy man, Detective, as I'm sure you know. I have investments all over town. I happen to help support many of the hotels in this area, including the Apollo. Let's just say I have a *vested* interest in the outcome of that murder investigation." King's voice quivered at the word *murder*, as if it had some special significance for him.

Bennie shook his arm free of King's grasp. "Well, it's like I told your friend. It's not my case."

King stood erect and put on a face. Smoothed his jacket and tie. "If you don't mind my asking, just whose case is it? I'm no stranger to the department. Perhaps I know the individual."

"Detective Lieutenant Jack Reed, the chief's son."

"Is that so?" said King, a hint of fear in his voice.

"Do you know him?"

"As a matter of fact, I do," said King, offering his hand. "I do hope our paths cross again soon. Although, I should say, not in such a way as this."

Bennie stumbled out of the Eggleston into the cold. He

wobbled and swayed. The whiskey warmed his blood, but it was no match for the frigid air.

He felt damaged and weak. The stakeout, The Cane on the steps of the Commonwealth Club, King The Savior. All those eyes — looking at *him*.

He hit the alleyway just in time. He wretched, spilling roast beef and whiskey all over the ground. He steadied himself against the brick of the hotel, thankful for its existence.

There's that feeling again: someone watching *him*. He was too fuzzy to care. He could see the old man's car. *Just get there and rest.*

He started to walk and wished he hadn't. He fell fast and hard. It was as if the concrete had suddenly risen from the earth and slapped his face. He wished for the jungle then. At least the ground was soft and the air was warm.

Then — hands on him.

Soft hands, like his mother's.

Lifting him, pulling him up.

Please, don't let it be a Jap.

CHAPTER TWENTY-EIGHT

BENNIE WOKE IN a peaceful daze. He felt more rested than he had in years. He sat up and looked around his room. Surprisingly, he was still in his bed. Yesterday's clothes were piled on the floor.

He took stock of himself. He was in nothing but an undershirt and skivvies. The left side of his face hurt. A reigning thought offered him pause.

How did I get here?

He left his bed and rifled through his dresser for new clothes. He changed into denims and a sweatshirt, stepped into the hall, and froze.

Someone was in the house.

Bennie heard sounds coming from the kitchen. The clatter of pans, the someone whistling. He smelled coffee and eggs.

He skipped back into his room and ruffled through his clothes. *There* — his shoulder holster and .38, undisturbed. He pulled the gun and stepped softly down the stairs. He moved slowly through the foyer, two-handed his .38, and tiptoed into the kitchen.

No one in the room. Coffee on the stove, eggs in a pan. Two place settings at the table — plates, forks, cups. It was like he'd been invited to breakfast in his own home.

Footsteps came from the dining room. Bennie moved that way on quiet feet. *Quickly now, 1, 2, 3* —

He broke through the doorway and drew a bead on Imogene McKenna.

She was leaning against the dining room table, sipping coffee from a mug and looking over the casework hanging from the walls. She turned and regarded his aggressive state with the all the alarm of a still pond. A fall of light from the window bathed her face in sun rays. Bennie released his grip and let the gun fall to his side, stunned at the angel come to save him.

"All I did was make breakfast," she said. "Are you going to arrest me for stealing your coffee?"

Bennie just looked at her, speechless. In awe of her, yes, but puzzled and slightly unnerved.

"What are you doing here?"

"What do you think I'm doing here? I'm taking care of you. You collapsed outside that hotel last night. Or don't you remember?"

Bennie *did* remember and touched the left side of his face.

"You were following me?"

Imogene's face went a bit sour then, and she was about to speak when a smell from the kitchen alarmed them both.

"The eggs," he said.

Bennie moved for the stove and killed the heat. He plated the eggs and motioned for her to join him at the table, pulling the chair for her.

"Thank you," she said.

He refreshed their coffee and took a seat. He was ravenous, but made sure not to wolf his food. She finished first and sat back in her chair, taking little sips of coffee to pass the time while he ate.

When he was done, she took their plates to the sink and brought the coffee pot to the table. She topped them both off and returned it to the stove. It was then, as she sat back down, that she started to cry.

Bennie knew why, of course. He had to know she'd find out eventually.

"It's just that I *cared*, you see? The dispatcher at Confederate Cab, he said — "

"You had no right," she said, wiping tears from her eyes. "No right at all."

She set her mug on the table and covered her face with her hands.

"I'm sorry," he said. "I didn't mean to hurt you."

Bennie moved for the sink as she wept, in search of something to wipe away her tears. He found a handkerchief in a drawer and laid it at her place. He sat back down and said nothing.

When she could cry no more, she said, "It was not for you to know. It's private, you understand? *Private*."

Bennie nodded that he understood. Bravely, he reached over and took her left hand in his right and held it. He was surprised when she didn't pull it away.

Bennie said, "You first."

"Why me?"

"Because you're in *my* house, uninvited. You're an intruder. Explain yourself."

They were in the living room now, sitting across from one another on the floor. The couch and chairs were still all tore up from the break-in. There was a fire in the fireplace and a bottle of whiskey on the coffee table. It was noon, or thereabouts.

"Well, now," she said, a tone of indignation in her voice. "Perhaps I should just leave."

"Go ahead then."

She tsk'd. "I hardly believe you want me to go."

"How do you know what I want?"

"I know a great many things, Bennie Thomas Sherwood. I know where you live, of course. I know where you work, where you went to high school, what kind of car you drive, wh —"

"Now, that right there. How do you know that?"

"Because I know cars and how to get information about cars. Like whose father owned what kind."

Bennie was impressed. "You still have to go first."

"Why?"

"My house, my rules."

"Well, now. Aren't *you* a gentlemen."

Bennie winked and reached for the bottle. She guffawed.

"You really must be joking. At this hour?"

Bennie poured a finger's worth each into two glasses and held one out for her.

"Drink," he said. "It'll make it easier."

She thought it over and, knowing he was right, took the glass in her hand. She considered it for a moment, as if it were some affront to decency, and downed it in one gulp.

Imogene took Bennie back a year and filled in the gaps to her tale of woe. Her late husband's name was Johnny, they lived in the same neighborhood, they both loved cars. When they met, Johnny was a mechanic at Digby's. He got her a job there and soon after, they were inseparable. Grease monkeys in love.

Then, his papers arrived. He'd been drafted into the US Army.

They had three weeks.

With their parents' blessing, Johnny and Imogene exchanged vows at City Hall and honeymooned over a weekend at Buckroe Beach.

The day he shipped out, Imogene knew she was pregnant. She put his hands on her stomach during their last moments together. That was the closest he ever came to knowing his child.

The pregnancy was not an easy one. Morning sickness and exhaustion took their toll on Imogene. Letters from Johnny were a comfort — they came nearly every day.

In July '43, Johnny joined the front lines in Sicily. His letters all but stopped then and, either by proxy or circumstance, her pregnancy grew tougher. She took leave from Digby's and spent most of her days in bed.

A month later, she lost the baby.

A week after that, she lost Johnny.

She was near catatonic for days. She didn't speak or eat for a week. She hardly left her room for months.

Both Johnny's parents and her own pleaded with her to venture out and find life again. She could think of only one thing that made her happy.

"Cars," said Bennie.

Imogene nodded.

Digby hired her back on the spot.

It was his turn then and Bennie told her everything. The jungle, the old man, The Cane. Jack, The Apollo, King.

"So what are you gonna do?" she asked. They were closer now, sitting up. Face to face.

"Go back. Start over. See what I missed. It's there, I just can't see it."

"I'm scared for you."

"Don't be."

"It sounds messy, not to mention dangerous."

Bennie almost laughed. "I know messy. *And* dangerous. This is just what I do."

"I mean it. I can't lose anyone else."

"Who says I'm yours to lose?"

"I do," she said, pulling him towards her and locking him in a kiss.

CHAPTER TWENTY-NINE

SECONDS LATER, NILES rapped on the front door.

"Bennie!" he hollered from out on the porch. "You in there?"

Bennie and Imogene were slow to break their embrace.

"I can ask him to come back later," he said.

"No," she said, touching his face. "I need to go."

Bennie stood and helped her to her feet, their hands lingering. She went for her coat, he went for the door. Niles just walked right in.

"What happened to you last night, honcho?" You'll never believe what all I — " Niles froze as he caught sight of Imogene.

"Niles," said Bennie, "this is Imogene McKenna, from Digby's garage."

Niles shot him a dumbstruck look before he turned to her and said, "Ever so pleased to meet you, Ms. McKenna." He took her hand and kissed it like some English dandy.

"Thank you," she said, charmed.

Bennie held the front door for her and said, "Thanks

for looking out for me."

"You're welcome," she said, buttoning her coat.

"Can I call you tomorrow?"

She nodded with a smile and left. Bennie watched as she walked away.

"I can see why you skipped out on me," said Niles. "She's a sizzler."

Bennie shut the door and looked at his partner.

"We've got a problem."

A good hour passed. Bennie nearly went hoarse telling Niles all about his night. From tailing King to seeing him with The Cane to this morning, with Imogene.

"Holy mother," said Niles. "She just picked you right up, brought you home?"

Bennie nodded, tingling at the thought of her embrace. All this crazy shit going down and he just wanted to be with her.

"Something's not right," said Bennie.

Niles laughed. "You think?"

"With King, I mean. It's not him."

Niles was surprised. "You've talked, what, twice with the man and suddenly you're convinced he's innocent?"

"It's just a feeling I have. When he was with the Cane, he said the name of the woman we found at the Apollo. Said it like she meant something to him."

"The Negro woman?"

Bennie nodded. "Josephine Scott. And yesterday, Archie said that King doesn't discriminate as an employer. He's got both whites and Negroes on his staff. Hell, at The Eggleston, he was damn near royalty. Fit right in. I don't know, he just doesn't seem like the kind of man who would stick a knife in someone."

"Well, I hate to put the kibosh on your love affair with him, but we've got less than four days to put something together on Rivers or we're both hoofing a beat."

"What'd you find out?"

"You ever hear the name Sykes Caldwell?"

Bennie searched his mind. "He's one of our canaries, yeah?"

Niles nodded and told him the rest. Sykes Caldwell was a part-time crook and a full-time drunk who stooled for the department in exchange for an expunged record. Sad Sack Sykes: before the war, Sykes' old man caught him boosting from the liquor cabinet and took after him with a hot iron. The old man burned his left ear into a cauliflower nub and jacked his hearing.

A 4F stamp kept Sykes stateside and, to pass the time, he played errand boy to a couple of black market big shots. When his spotty hearing gave them grief, they gave *him* a discipline beating. One too many sent Sykes to the hospital. A nurse administered pain killers and called the police. Sykes' heavy bruising had raised eyebrows. The pain meds loosened him up so much he started to tell these *wild* stories. The Cane arrived just in time to hear Sykes tell all about this illegal hooch.

Bennie was intrigued but lost. "What's he got to do — "

"Hold up there, lover boy, let me finish. Sykes and Rivers are in on something, together. Last night, I watched Rivers until clear past midnight. Sometime after eleven, he saw the last shift out of First and then just waited. Sykes showed up not too long after that. They pow-wowed and split. I wanted to know more, so I tailed Sykes to an after-hours club and got his name off a bartender."

"Think he's in with Rivers?"

"That's my guess," said Niles, "but who knows, right? So

I went to the police gym this morning and did a few rounds, tossing around Sykes' name. Remember Lewis, my sparring partner? He knows Sykes. Says they worked a civil defense beat just last year and that Sykes is *always* on the sauce."

Bennie felt a rush. "A civil defense beat?"

"Yeah."

"Digby hinted that Rivers knew all about that air raid siren."

"*Yeah*. So maybe this is our guy."

Bennie could hardly stand it. "The Cane told me that someone out of First locked up a lowlife from civil defense over the siren. Said the guy had a few too many and set the thing off by accident."

"Locked up? Well, shit — if this is our guy, then what's he doing out?"

Bennie stewed on it all. "Maybe Rivers locked him up for show."

"Holy mother."

"Your sparring partner. Think he knows where Sykes likes to spend his time?"

Niles smiled. "I'm one step ahead of you, partner. Caldwell's a daytime juicer with a yen for the Murphy's Hotel bar."

The lunch crowd at Murphy's was full of politicos and businessmen downing liquor lunches and trading barbs. The dining room reeked of overcooked liverwurst and old men's ways.

Bennie found Sykes Caldwell at the bar. He was snapping his fingers and humming along with Tommy Dorsey. He looked to be a drink shy of face-down drunk. Bennie grabbed a stool two seats down and ordered coffee.

Sykes swayed in his seat like he was on cloud nine. He noticed Bennie and leaned over.

"Say, pal, what are you doing here?"

Bennie felt a rush of panic. Had Sykes made him already? He played it cool. "What do you mean?"

"You, here. In this place. You look of fighting age. You oughta be, I don't know, in uniform somewhere."

"Oh, *that*. I tried that. They said I'd done enough and sent me home. What about you?"

Sykes leaned toward him. "See this?" he said, jutting his knobby ear toward Bennie. "Uncle Sam didn't care for it."

Bennie tipped his coffee. "Their loss."

Sykes beamed — such truth! "Yes, *their* loss. I'll drink to that!" And drink he did, pulling off a brown bagged bottle he had with him.

Bennie saw his way in. "Say, uh, whatcha got there?"

Sykes slurred his words like they were made of wet glass. "Just the finest moonshine you're likely to find south of the Mason-Dixon line."

"Yeah?"

Sykes pulled the bottle from the bag for Bennie to see. Sure enough — white mule.

"Want a taste?"

Bennie nodded. Sykes passed him the bottle.

"You've never had anything finer," said Sykes, a proud look on his face.

Bennie took a sip and almost gagged. It was rotgut, pure and simple.

Sykes pulled a face. "Say, haven't I seen you somewhere before?"

"I don't know. Have you?"

"I know I have. Let me see now..." Sykes searched his mind and came up empty. "You're familiar to me, I just know it — " It came to him all at once. He went sour and sat up straight.

Bennie smiled, having fun with it. "Do you know me?"

"You know, sir," said Sykes, coming off his stool, "I do believe I'm mistaken in that regard. Do forgive me." Sykes steadied himself against the bar. "I've just remembered a prior engagement that requires my presence and ask that you excuse me." Sykes bowed like some country gentlemen and backed away from Bennie. Then he turned and left Murphy's as quickly as he could.

Bennie took his time and finished his coffee. Then he paid for it and left the hotel.

When he came to the street, he found Niles leaning against the hood of his car, cracking his knuckles. Sykes was in the backseat, bloodied and tearful.

Niles said, "Where to next, partner?"

The safe house was clear. No one drying out, no one grabbing a nooner with the mistress.

They holed up in the kitchen, forcing Sykes into a chair and binding his hands to the slats. Bennie rummaged the cabinets. He found crackers and soda pop.

Sykes sobbed and drooled. Bennie shook his head — nothing worse than a drunk man in tears. He kicked Sykes' chair and passed the crackers to Niles.

"You better talk, pal, or it's back to jail you go."

"Talk about what?"

"You know what. The air raid siren. And, while we're at it — " Bennie pulled the half-empty bottle of rotgut from the bag. "This shit, whatever it is."

Niles rubbed his belly. "These crackers taste *good*. You want one, pal?" He stuck one in Sykes' face, only to jerk it away at the last second, laughing. "No dice, jackass. Talk or you won't even get the crumbs."

"Okay, okay. What do you want to know?"

"The air raid siren. All of it."

"So I broke in and set the thing off. What about it?"

"What about it?" said Niles. "*Why*, you jackass?"

Sykes took his time with it. "Because I was paid to."

"By who?"

"Wyatt."

"For what purpose?"

"He had this black market setup going. Said the siren would get him the biggest score he'd ever had. Set him up for good. That's it, that's all I know. I don't know what he took. I just… I just did what I was told."

Bennie took the bottle of rotgut and smelled it, wincing. He held it over the sink and slowly began to pour it down the drain.

Sykes broke into a rage, thrashing in his chair. "No, no, no!"

Niles said, "What is that shit?"

Sykes protested. "This isn't right! This isn't right at all. I give you guys street talk, I tell you who's who, who's doing what. I get a pass, that's what I get. Not this shit. Not tied up like some animal!"

Bennie kicked his chair. Hard. "*What is it?*"

"Okay, okay. It's this cheap shit I sell on the street. Soldiers, seabees, they go for it cause it gets 'em drunk fast. But if I don't sell it, I don't get paid, see? Look, that's it, yeah? That's everything? Come on, now. Let's be friends. Untie me."

Bennie let it stew and thought back. That day at the jail — looking up Skipper's arrests. The whole place smelled of vomit. The intake officer said a bunch of army grunts got sick off some back alley liquor. And every week, it was the same — blotters at the Annex reported drunks all over the city.

Everyone liquored up makes for *bad* crime stats.

Bennie said, "Wyatt gives it to you sell?"

Sykes nodded, holding back sobs. "That's it, ok? I just sell it and get paid. We're good here, right?"

Bennie said, "What about the murders?"

Sykes looked at them aghast. "What murders? The hell you talking about?"

Niles said, "You're full of it, right?"

"No, no, I swear! I don't know anything about a murder. What murder? Wyatt and Arthur said the siren was just for this one thing, that's it. They didn't say nothing about a murder!"

Bennie said, "Arthur Brown was involved?"

"Well, yeah. He and Rivers are always into something. But hell, since I pulled the siren, Wyatt ain't been the same."

"What do you mean?"

"I mean he's funny now. He's not like he was. It's like he's… it's like he's not *him*, you know? He's not in charge no more."

"In charge of what?"

"Jesus, heck, don't you guys listen? His black market op! Someone took it, or he sold it, or I don't know — it just ain't like it was. And all's he's got is this liquor for me to peddle, and damn if I don't need the bread. Hell, fellas, ain't we done this enough?"

Bennie looked at Niles and nodded. Niles fed Sykes a few crackers. Bennie felt something pushing him further. He leafed through his steno, desperate for more.

What is it, goddamnit —

There — his notes on Skipper's arrest records.

Bingo.

January, '43. Skipper does three nights for being drunk in public and resisting arrest. His bunkmates are S. Caldwell, J. Gentry, and N. Ray.

Bennie said, "Skipper Holly and Jones Godfrey."

Sykes said, "What about 'em?"

"Skipper was a friend of mine. He died on New Year's Eve. We'd lost touch. What can you tell me about him?"

"Yeah, a real shame about Skipper. He was a good guy. We sure tipped a few from time to time."

"What was he mixed up in?"

"Well, he worked for Mr. King. That outta tell you something right there."

"What did he do for Mr. King?"

"What anybody does. This and that."

Bennie was losing his patience. "What did he do for Mr. King that got him killed?"

Sykes yawned. He'd sobered up some. "Untie me, and I might remember."

Bennie nodded. Niles loosened his restraints. Sykes stretched and folded his arms behind his head. He smiled and reclined into the chair like he was sunbathing on a beach.

Sykes said, "There's a bigger player in town looking to wipe out all the black market competition. A winner take all kind of thing. Word around my kind is that Skipper found out who and took matters into his own hands. But that's all I know. Might be how he got himself killed, but I can't truly say."

Niles said, "What about Jones Godfrey? What do you know about him?"

"Ain't seen old Jonesy in some time. He and I get along well. He's a good drinker, like me." Sykes grinned, as if it were something to be proud of.

Bennie said, "Jones Godfrey is dead."

Sykes went somber fast. "Really?"

Bennie nodded.

"That's a shame. Old Jonesy was a good one. Pretty mixed up, but a good one nonetheless."

"Mixed up?"

"Well, you know how Skipper worked for Mr. King?"

"Yeah."

"Jonesy got him that job. He worked for Mr. King, too."

Bennie was lost. "We know."

"Do you? Well, Jones Godfrey didn't just work for Mr. King. He was in love with him, too."

CHAPTER THIRTY

THE USO CLUB at East Grace and 2nd was a hive of patriotism and goodwill. Soldiers of all kinds ate, drank, and were, on the whole, quite merry. GIs on liberty hobnobbed with sailors on their way to Norfolk. Some World War 1 vets ogled the fetching War Belles spreading cheer around the room. And a few wounded pilots delighted their assembled crowd with tales of high-stakes heroics in the sky.

Bennie downed his beer and felt pangs of guilt. I should be with them, he thought, wherever they are. In truth, he had no idea where the men of the D-1-5 were laying their heads. He'd not had a new letter in weeks and not seen a newspaper for days.

Niles nudged him. Jack Reed strolled through the front entrance, looking wholly out of place and unnerved by all the joy. He caught sight of Bennie and Niles and made for their table. They were seated at a round top in the back, near the bar.

Jack walked up and cast a disapproving look over them both. "You're both on duty, drinking beer. This is grounds for disciplinary action."

Niles said, "You ought to join us. You'll want one, too, once you hear what we have to say."

"I don't drink."

Of course you don't, thought Bennie. "Have a seat. This'll take a minute."

Jack sat down, reluctantly. "You've got five."

"You're so generous with your time."

"I'm here, aren't I? We could have done this in my office and had all the time you need."

Niles said, "No cops, no curious ears. This is out of range, just between us."

Jack perked up. "Fine. What is you have to tell me?"

Twenty minutes and two rounds of beers later, Jack sat back in his seat, flummoxed. He looked both excited and frustrated by everything Bennie and Niles had shared with him. He sat like this for several beats, just staring at the table.

Bennie broke the silence. "Did you have any idea that your old man and King were in this together?"

Jack said, "No." He looked hurt.

Bennie said, "There were some curious things said to me at The Eggleston. It's as if no one's really investigated the Apollo at all."

Jack's look turned sour. "As I told you before, I'm handling that investigation. Not everything is as it seems, Detective."

"What about Josephine Scott?"

"What about her?"

"King seemed awfully concerned about her."

Jack glared at them. "Who Jedidiah King chooses to favor is his business."

Niles said, "Are you gunning for your old man's job?"

Jack grew livid. "Excuse me?"

"It's a fair question."

Jack relaxed and cracked a faint smile. "I fully support my father's efforts as chief of police. We need men with his experience in positions of authority. Especially now. It's a dangerous time to be a policeman, don't you agree?"

Bennie was surprised. "I'd think you'd be more concerned, after everything we've just told you."

Jack grinned. "Every day, gentlemen, I'm treated to some new insight into human weakness and frailty. Very little surprises me these days. Yes, I'm vexed to learn that my father's been keeping secrets. Not just from me, but from the department as a whole. But I still trust that everything will work out fine in the end."

Niles almost laughed. "How can you be so sure?"

Jack rose from his seat. "Call it a hunch."

You cocky shit, thought Bennie. "We're going after Rivers. Tonight."

"Good. Don't pull your punches. And I want to know what you find out. *Before* you tell my father."

Jack turned and left without another word.

Niles said, "Can you believe the stones on that guy?"

Bennie said he could and watched him go, wrestling with it. He was torn. Was he beginning to respect Jack or fear him?

Her voice almost cracked.

"Is it dangerous?"

"Not if we do it right."

She changed subjects.

"Johnny Pepper's at Tantilla on Friday. Want to go?"

"Of course."

"Good. Please be careful."

"I will. And hey — I heard some chatter about taxi drivers getting ripped off. Be safe out there."

"Thanks, I will. You'll call me and let me know that you're alright?"

"Yes."

She hung up.

Bennie felt thunder in his chest when the line broke.

CHAPTER THIRTY-ONE

NILES BURROWED INTO his coat and blew on his hands. Bennie did the same and rolled his neck. He was tense with anticipation. Niles shook out his arms and flexed his hands. He felt it, too.

It was Pearl's redux. They were hiding out in the old man's Ford, parked behind a storage building off 17th, just north of Broad. From their vantage point, they could just make out First Station across the way. It was a two-story building with five windows and a two-door entrance flanked by ornate columns. It was an old building, full of secrets and lies, that looked eerie in the darkness.

Bennie said, "You ready for this?"

Niles let out a deep breath, steeling himself. "I don't know. After what I went through with him, I might not hold back."

"I'll make sure it doesn't get out of hand."

Niles said, "Look."

Four night duty cops filed out of First and disappeared into the night. A few beats ticked off. Then, a light switched on upstairs. Bodies, movement, shadows. Bennie staved off nerves with deep breaths.

"Let's do it, he said.

Niles nodded, hesitant. Bennie pulled the two masks he'd fashioned out of blackout curtain from his knapsack and handed one to Niles. Save for the eyeholes, they gave full face cover from head to neck. Niles shagged their weapons of choice from the back seat — the old man's sawed-off for Bennie, a slapjack they'd boosted off a street gang for himself. No cop heaters tonight. They couldn't risk ID.

They stepped out of the car and into the night. Niles ran point and padded across Broad, signaling to Bennie when the coast was clear. Bennie made the double doors on light feet while Niles stood watch. He pulled a key ring from his pocket and unlocked the front door. Kudos to the old man: he had a master key to all three stations made years ago, just in case.

They slipped inside and moved through the intake area in silence. They ducked around the desk sergeant's perch and spilled into the large hallway that led to the jails. There were two — one for whites, one for Negroes. Bennie tiptoed their way and peeked inside — two bums apiece, sleeping it off.

They hit the stairwell and made the second floor. There — a room to the right. Voices inside, light under the door.

They moved in closer, side by side.

A shared look between them meant *NOW.*

Niles kicked the door in. Bennie followed him inside and they caught the show.

Captain Rivers and a buxom blonde, going at it on a corner cot. The Captain on top, Blondie on her back. She saw the masks and screamed. Rivers thought it was all for *him.* He howled and let out his own wild bray. "Oh, baby, yes! Me, too! Me, too!"

Bennie nudged him with the sawed-off and spoke in a hoarse voice to hide his own.

"Get off her, *now*."

Rivers jumped up and screamed for real, scrambling for something to cover himself. Bennie leveled the gun at Blondie.

"Get out."

She lit out of bed like a fox on the run. Grabbed her clothes and powdered. Her wig fell off on her way out the door. She was really a brunette.

Rivers cowered on the floor, hiding under a sheet. "Oh, Jesus! What in God's —"

"Shut up," said Bennie, aiming the sawed-off at his head. "Tell us what we want to know and you won't get hurt."

Niles shut the door to the room and went to the windows. He shot looks in all directions and nodded at Bennie. All clear.

Rivers started to cry.

"You better quit that," said Bennie. "My friend here can't stand it when men cry."

Rivers just lay there, sobbing. Niles gave him a good kick to the ribs. Rivers crouched and yelped. "Okay, okay."

"What did you do with Hollis Digby's gasoline?" barked Niles.

Rivers blanched. "What? Who are you?"

Niles threatened with another kick. "*Where is it?*"

"Okay, okay. I sold it!"

"To who?"

"It was a blind sale, I never met the buyer."

"Who brokered the deal?"

"That cop barber, Walter MacKeye."

Bennie felt a thunderbolt run through him.

"On New Year's Eve, Jack Reed put together a raid on Pearl's. Why weren't you involved?"

"Jesus, what the fuck is this? Who are you two?"

"Answer me!"

"You little twerp, don't you know who I am?"

This time, Bennie kicked him good in the chest. Rivers fought for air. Bennie checked himself. He set a voice inside his head on repeat: *Don't kill him. He's not a Jap.*

"*Spill!*"

"Okay, okay! I got left out of Pearl's on account of I got my own thing going. Or did, anyways. I figure Jack knew all about that, so he kept me in the dark. He was right to. I would have boosted every last bit. That's what you two want, yeah? A piece of my action?"

Bennie played along. "Yes."

"Well, you're too damn late. I'm out of it. All's I got to peddle now is this cheap back alley moonshine and hell, I wouldn't serve it to my worst enemy. Believe me, I got plenty of those."

"Who's the girl?"

Rivers started to sob. "She's everything."

Niles walloped him. "*Who is she?*"

Rivers screamed. "Jesus!"

Bennie made the signal — tone it back — and motioned for Niles to look around. Niles got hold of himself and started in on a closet.

Bennie knelt down. "Who is she?"

Rivers choked on his own snot. "She's true love, that's what she is. She cost me everything, but she's worth it."

"How?"

"Somebody put the squeeze on me is how."

"With what?"

Rivers boohooed. "Pictures."

"*Of?*"

"Me and her! Somebody put 'em right on my desk, just left 'em for me. Said if I didn't shut down my op, they'd send 'em to my wife."

"When was this?"

"Before."

"Before what?"

"Before the siren, before that welcher's gas, before all of it."

Bennie felt something *click*.

"The siren. Who's idea was it?"

"Who are you?"

"*Who's?*"

"Jesus! Whoever put the squeeze on me! Said to make it happen or else. Christ, I could have gotten the gas without it, but whoever's onto me said it had to go off. That night, that way. Lucky for me I got this bum I know working civil defense."

Bennie let it sink in. Someone working Rivers, someone behind it all. Jack's words, from before: "*… somebody with juice pulled this off.*"

"Your stash — where is it?"

"Gone. I don't know where."

"Does Walter?"

"Hell, I don't know. Probably. That guy knows everything."

Niles whistled from across the room. Bennie looked over at him holding a gas mask in each hand.

Bennie turned back to Rivers. "You stole the sugar."

"Yeah, I stole the goddamn sugar. Would have made a pretty penny off it, too."

"What do you know about Jedidiah King and The

Cane working together?"

Rivers roared. "Not a damn thing, but that'd be a very *valuable* something to know. Wouldn't that be a pair?" He rolled onto his back and pushed sweaty bangs from his eyes, smiling.

It needled Bennie. "What are you smiling about?"

"I'm smiling 'cause I know you two aren't gonna pop me. You're probably some low level street thugs with more information than you know what to do with. And now you're pumping me for shit I don't know. So I'm clean, you're through, and we're done."

Rivers started to sit up, but Bennie forced him down hard with his foot. Rivers' head hit the floor with a thud.

"Jesus!"

Bennie wanted to ask about the old man, but he knew it'd give him away. He thought of one last question.

"After the raid on Pearl's, you beat two Negro men for information they didn't have. Why?"

Rivers got serious. "Who the fuck are you?"

Bennie pumped a round into the sawed-off and buried the muzzle into Rivers' chest.

"*Why?*"

"Because I wanted to know why I'd been left out of the raid! I had a vested interest in being there. *Big plans* that went kablooey when Jack decided to play lone gunman. What does it matter now? I'm out of it."

"Big plans?"

Rivers started to laugh. "No, no more. You're not getting anything more out of me. You'll just have to fucking kill me. But I know you won't, 'cause you two are chickenshit to the bone."

Bennie caught sight of Niles. He was fuming, his hands twisting around the slapjack.

Bennie knelt down and leaned in close. "Your name is Wyatt Rivers. You live south of the James in a cheap bungalow with your wife and two kids. Jane, Michael, and Susie. If you tell anyone about this, we'll terrorize your family."

Rivers' face went plum red. "You little shit, who are —"

Niles hit him with the slapjack and knocked him out cold.

Chapter Thirty-Two

BENNIE AND NILES cased the alleyway behind the barbershop just to be sure. Nothing but a few stray cats, hunting for scraps.

They flanked the runners' door and readied themselves. Rivers was a cakewalk compared to this. Walter's crew was a mixed bag of ruffians and street trash. All that feral energy could put a wild scenario into play.

Bennie checked the barrel of his .38. Niles loaded his shotgun with shells. They'd raided the Annex armory on their way here. No masks, no slapjack, no kid stuff. This was going to get ugly.

Bennie slipped his gun into the crook of his back and knocked on the door: one-two/pause/one-two-three. A few beats later, the eye grill slid open.

A coarse voice from inside said, "Yeah?"

"Tell Walter it's Bennie."

The eye grill slid shut. Footsteps tapered off beyond the door. Bennie and Niles could do nothing but wait.

The chill of the alley made them both shudder as they threw sideways glances over their shoulders. A sudden noise made them jump — two cats going at it over a chicken bone.

Footsteps inside — just behind the door.

Bennie and Niles shared a measured look.

Get ready.

A lock turned, the hinge creaked. Bennie pulled his .38 and jammed it through the doorway. Niles grabbed the door and pulled it all the way open, leveling his shotgun at the goon before them. Bennie mouthed the word 'hush'.

They turned him around and forced him to the common room with guns at his back. It was such a hive of activity that, at first, no one noticed them. There was chit-chat and laughter, phone calls and dancing. People counted money and stuffed it into paper bags. Walter chomped a cigar and passed around a wine jug.

One by one, his crew took notice. They dropped the money and drew their own guns. Walter just soured at the intrusion.

"For chrissakes, Bennie, what the hell is this?"

"Tell your people to lower their weapons."

"Or what?"

"Or your friend here won't walk so good."

"His name's Donny."

"Fine. *Donny* won't walk so good."

Reluctantly, Walter motioned to his crew. Their guns disappeared.

"Happy?"

Bennie jammed his gun against Donny's ribs.

"Captain Rivers is a shit policeman," he said, "and a player on the black market. Word is, you brokered a deal with him and took some very valuable material off his hands. We want to know where it is."

"Whose word?"

"His."

"Wyatt's no friend of mine."

"I didn't say he was."

"What kind of 'material' are we talking about?"

"The liquid kind," said Niles. "Like you put in cars to make 'em go."

"Ah, *that* kind of material."

"Where is it?" said Bennie. Donny let out a whimper.

Walter cracked a smile. "A few weeks back, I did you a real solid, Bennie. Gave you what you wanted. You ever find that pudgy ex-cop?"

"That can wait. This is *now*. Where is the gasoline you bought off Rivers? And who did you sell it to?"

"I'm just the middle man, kid. I don't deal."

"But you know people who do."

Walter shrugged, a smug look on his face.

Niles had had enough. He raised his shotgun, stepped toward a numbers board, and shot it to hell with a round of buckshot.

Walter's crew cowered behind a table and drew their guns back up. Walter put his hands up, livid.

"Jesus!" he said. "Now you're just pissing me off. This is *not* how this works!"

"Where and who," said Bennie. "Now."

"You little shit."

Niles shot the legs off a table. Phones, slips, and money hit the floor.

"Alright, alright! I'll tell you where, but not who."

Bennie raised his .38 to Donny's temple. He trembled at the thought of pulling the trigger.

"All of it, now!"

Walter lowered his hands. "You really want to shoot him, fine. You'll both be dead inside of a minute."

Donny shed tears. Bennie pointed the gun at Walter. His hand quivered with a visible tremor. "Last chance."

Walter almost laughed. "Or what? You'll shoot me? You don't have it in you, kid."

Niles pumped another round into his shotgun. "I do."

Walter blanched. "Fine. Schmitt Chemical. It's down near the Row, off Franklin, near 17th. I moved the drums there."

"When?"

"A few weeks back. I really don't remember."

"For who?"

"I told you, kid. No. That you'll have to get another way. And if you don't like it, well. We can settle that right here and now."

Bennie looked over at Walter's crew. They might be huddled behind a table, but they didn't waver. They looked ready to do any and all for their leader. It was the kind of devotion Bennie knew well. He'd felt the same way about a few of his COs.

Bennie lowered his gun and gave Donny a shove. He and Niles started to back away, their eyes forward.

"You're done, Walter. No more free reign."

Walter laughed. "Says who?"

"Says me."

"You don't have that kind of pull, kid. You might have been a hotshot Marine, but around here, you're just another cop in the way. Just like your old man."

A surge of rage forced Bennie's hand. He raised his gun and fired at Walter, but nerves botched his aim. His bullet caught Donny in the arm and sent him to the floor, wailing.

Walter's crew fumbled for their guns. He snarled, beet red. "You don't know who you're wrestling with, kid.

You're dead!"

Bennie and Niles slipped out the back with seconds to spare. A litter of bullets pummeled the door and filled the alleyway with a thunderous echo.

CHAPTER THIRTY-THREE

SCHMITT CHEMICAL WAS a stone's throw from King Tobacco. They had to search for it with flashlights. There was a small, unassuming sign and a mail drop next to the front door. Bennie and Niles walked the perimeter, curious. No windows, no side doors. Around back, they found another entrance and a loading bay.

It was eerie and cold. They heard police sirens in the distance. Call it a response to the scuffle at Walter's.

The loading bay was locked. Ditto the back door. Only one way in. Niles leveled his shotgun at the door handle and blew it wide open. Bennie followed his gun just inside. It was pitch black, no sounds. He and Niles futzed with their flashlights to no avail — dead bulbs.

Niles whispered, "Light switch."

Bennie moved one way, Niles the other. They felt along the walls, hoping. Bennie hit pay dirt and flipped a switch. Light flooded the room.

The room was maybe twenty by twenty, about the size of a double garage. Collected on one side, in various piles and stacks, was a goldmine of rationed goods.

Tires piled ceiling high.

Bags of shoes and women's nylons.

Boxes of processed foods.

And large sacks of sugar, piled five high over two rows.

"Partner."

Bennie looked over at Niles. He was standing on the other side of the stash, next to a large, covered *something*. Niles yanked the cover off like it was an act in some magic show.

Presto.

Five metal drums of Hollis Digby's gasoline, right there.

Niles said, "Holy mother."

Next to the drums sat a covered car. Bennie peeled back the cloak and almost froze. It was the dark green Chevy convertible from Digby's garage. Confirmed — his tail car from early January.

Sounds outside pinged their antennae.

They both got it in an instant — an ambush.

They hugged the floor as a bullet impaled the wall just above the stash.

"Holy mother!" screamed Niles.

Bennie motioned for the wall switch. "Cover me!"

Niles knelt behind the sacks of sugar and fired blindly through the doorway. Bennie scrambled along the floor. Another shot missed him by inches. Nerves shook his bones, but he staved them off.

No time for island juju.

More shots came through the doorway, more shotgun blasts from Niles. No chance for Bennie to make a break for it.

A split second idea came to him. He ripped open one of the bags and grabbed a shoe. He ducked more gunfire and launched it at the wall.

The lights extinguished.

The rain of gunfire from outside did not.

Bennie sank to the floor and huddled up next to the sugar. He felt his breathing go short, felt his back tense up. Sweat everywhere — in his eyes, on his hands. It made his gun slippery.

Niles got in close and whispered in his ear.

"You OK?"

Bennie lied and nodded. He held up three fingers.

Then two.

Then one.

They turned and unleashed their own salvos through the doorway.

A voice outside wailed "Ahhh!"

No more shots through the door. Shuffling sounds came next, like footsteps hurrying off. Then, a man crying.

They waited, too afraid to move. Bennie calmed his breathing and wiped the sweat from his face. Christ, he thought. I'm as hot as the sun.

Slowly, Bennie and Niles crawled along the floor, rising to their feet with caution. They followed their guns out of the room and came to a man on the loading dock, whimpering and holding his side. The man's pistol lay within reach, glistening in the moonlight. Bennie kicked it away.

Their eyes adjusted to the night and they began to read the man's features.

Niles said, "Holy mother!"

"What?"

"Remember that night we all got sent out to nightclubs and hash joints?"

"Yeah."

"This guy was with me. He's an AO."

Bennie knelt down for a better look.

"Who are you?"

"Ah, geez! Come on, I'm dying here!"

Bennie threatened with a fist.

"Alright, alright — it's true," he said, straining. "Name's Ernie. I'm with the auxillary crew."

"And the other guy?"

"Christ, I never seen him before. Mi... Mill... Miller. Yeah, that's it. Said his name was Miller."

Niles was incensed. "The fuck you doing here, shooting at cops?"

"I couldn't see, I swear! I didn't know you were cops. The other guy offered me a few bucks just to come and put a scare on. Oh, God, my gut!"

Police sirens in the air again, getting closer.

Niles said, "Help's on the way."

Bennie stood up, alarmed. "We gotta go."

Niles was confused. "What? Why?"

"Something's off. An AO, sent to kill us?"

Ernie grabbed Bennie's leg. "I wasn't trying to kill anyone, honest! You gotta believe me..."

Bennie kicked him in the ribs. "Shut up."

"Bennie, this is *it*," said Niles. "We found it all. It's over."

Bennie's jungle instincts were in the red. "Maybe, ok? But listen — something feels off to me. Please just trust me, Niles — we need to leave. *Now*."

The sirens pierced the air. Five, maybe six blocks out.

Niles relented. A partners' bond — stronger than blood. "Let's go, then."

Ernie pleaded and vise-gripped their legs. "Please, take me with you! I didn't know you were cops, honest!"

Bennie wanted so much to kick Ernie in the balls and leave him to chance. But he'd never left anyone behind and wasn't about to start now. Plus, once upon a time, hadn't he taken money to put a scare on?

Bennie sighed and looked at Niles.

"Let's get him up."

CHAPTER THIRTY-FOUR

THEY DROPPED ERNIE at MCV — literally, dropped him at the curb — and leadfooted it to Church Hill. Bennie figured the safe house was their best bet.

Niles was unconvinced. "But you're spooked on cops?"

"Exactly. It's the last place they'll look."

They parked on Broad a few blocks east of 28th and set out on separate paths. They took the back entrance in stealth, padding through the door locked and loaded. Then, a cautious peek into every room. Niles cased the downstairs while Bennie took the top floor.

Nobody home.

They kept the lights low and fished through the kitchen cabinets. They found a loaf of bread and slices of cheese in the icebox. Bennie allowed himself a smile. The old man's grilled cheese was second to none.

They gnashed on sandwiches and peeked out the windows. They lifted a bottle of gin from the poker room and passed it between them. Their pulse rates came down and they relaxed.

They settled in the front room with eyes out a bay

window. Two plush chairs — comfy lookout spots. They started to talk it out.

"You said it yourself," said Niles. "The Cane and King, working together."

"I know. I just can't believe it."

"Maybe you don't have to — the shit was right there, in a building just around from King Tobacco. You're overthinking it, partner."

Bennie chewed on it. Maybe he *was* wrong. Too many angles crisscrossing had his instincts on overload. For once, he didn't know what to do.

"What next, then?"

Niles yawned, stretched, and closed his eyes. He cradled the shotgun for solace.

"We sleep it off. Wake up fresh and report in. Jesus — they're gonna grill us something fierce. And hey," he said with a smile, "it's your ass if I get demoted for this."

Niles drifted off to sleep. Bennie's mind zigzagged, from King to The Cane, to Jack, caught in the middle. From crooked cops to shady AOs. Hell, he thought — he'd traded one jungle for another.

Somewhere nearby, a dog howled at the moon.

Bennie let himself ride on this dark thought.

Did The Cane have something to do with the old man?

Phone rings woke them both.

They blinked their eyes open from a dead sleep. They'd both nodded off in their chairs.

At first, it seemed natural. The phone's ringing — answer it. But then, they remembered where they were.

Niles shot up and peeled back a curtain. Damn — that sun is *bright*. A look in all directions — nothing suspicious.

They looked at one another. Do we answer it?

The ringing stopped. A weighted silence fell over the safe house and stopped them dead in their tracks.

You could almost hear time ticking away.

One.

Two.

Three.

Four.

Fi —

The phone rang again. Bennie and Niles almost hit the roof.

They tracked the hallway to the back rooms. The phone was in the kitchen. They stood on either side of it, spooked. It was like some contaminated gizmo — touch it and you're dead.

Bennie grabbed the receiver. The final ring ricocheted through the air. He held it against his ear and just listened.

Nothing at first. Breathing, maybe. Then — Jack Reed's voice.

"Bennie?"

Bennie looked at Niles and mouthed, "It's Jack."

Niles' eyes went wide.

Bennie said, "Jack."

"Good. You're there, we've found you. Are you and Niles alright?" Real worry in his voice.

Bennie looked at Niles. Niles just shrugged.

"Yeah, we're alright."

"Good. Listen — you're not at fault for any of it. At least, not yet."

"Not yet?"

"It's messy. Walter, everything found at Schmitt Chemical — we need your side of things. Come in and talk. We'll straighten this out."

"Come in? Where?"

A pause. "You're worried about my father."

"I know what I saw."

"And I believe you. Look — there's a motel out Route 5. Lenny's Lodge. The department keeps a few rooms on hand there for witnesses and loudmouth CIs. Let's meet there. I'll take your statements and go right to City Hall. My father won't know what hit him."

Bennie chewed on it. "Thirty minutes."

"Good. There's an unnumbered room at the far end of the motel. Knock twice and I'll know it's you."

Bennie hung up. Niles could hardly stand it. "What?"

"Jack wants to meet with us in private. Get our side of things and go after the Cane with it."

Niles was pumped. "Let's do it. I want this over with."

Bennie was still unsure. "What if it's not enough."

Niles laughed. "You're a head case, partner. We're gonna wrap this up and get you to a psych ward."

Bennie relaxed. "Alright. Let's go."

Niles went to take a piss. Bennie hit the front room for their coats and guns. He peeked out the bay window one last time. You can never be too careful.

Outside, in the street, some neighborhood kids were playing army. Maybe seven total, a mix of boys and girls. Bennie felt this great urge to join in and coach them through an offensive maneuver. The boys flank right, the girls flank left, he and Niles storm forward, straight up the middle.

Something tugged at him.

One of the girls wore a bright red coat. She blew a whistle and ordered her troops to attack. The kids scattered this way and that. It went from an orderly military exercise to this big game of tag.

Bennie's memory surged. He saw a frightened Negro

girl with big, chestnut eyes in a rose colored smock. That night at the Apollo, before he went into room 211, she stuck her head out the door and screamed.

Niles, right behind him. "Partner?"

Bennie turned around with this look on his face.

"I know who to ask about the bodies at the Apollo."

CHAPTER THIRTY-FIVE

JACKSON WARD, ON this particular morning, was a ghost town. Cold and vacant, absent a human presence. Bennie curbed his wheels ahead of the Apollo and just sat there. Would the girl even talk? Could this be it? The missing piece, there all along, just now discovered?

He forced himself from the car and took measured steps toward the Apollo. It took several knocks to get Mr. Johnson to the door, each one louder than the last. Bennie was afraid he'd wake the entire block.

The door opened in protest. Mr. Johnson craned his head around it, shielding his eyes from the daylight, scratching his head.

Bennie held up his badge and said, "Mr. Johnson, I'm Detective Sherwood. We spoke at police headquarters several weeks ago. Do you remember me?"

Mr. Johnson opened the door a bit wider for a better look. He nodded slightly, unimpressed. He yawned and said nothing.

"Mr. Johnson, the night I came here and found those two bodies, a little girl saw me and screamed." Bennie read from his steno. "Della, the woman who works for you. That's her daughter, yes?"

Mr. Johnson raised his head, intrigued, and nodded.

Bennie said it slow. "Do they still live with you? In that room?"

Mr. Johnson said, "Not in that room, no."

Bennie's gut twisted into itself. He thought he might collapse.

"But," Mr. Johnson continued, "they're still here. After that whole mess, ain't nobody want to stay up there. I moved 'em to another room, in the back. Near me."

Bennie thought he might let out a cry of victory.

"Mr. Johnson, I need to speak with Della's daughter. Right now."

Bennie waited by the front desk while Mr. Johnson went to wake Della and her daughter. He paced and shook the nerves out of his hands. The whole place smelled of sweat and smoke and liquor. It was cold, too. Heating oil, even rationed, was a rare luxury in The Deuce.

Bennie shifted a stack of newspapers off a bench and took a seat to relax. Every headline was either war or crime. It seems they go hand in hand, thought Bennie.

Mr. Johnson escorted Della and her daughter into the room and made introductions.

"This is the policeman I was telling you about," he said, turning to Bennie. "This is Della and her daughter Maggie."

Bennie stood up. "I'm sorry to wake you, but I just have a few important questions I need to ask young Maggie here."

Maggie burrowed into her mother's legs for protection. They both looked at him with fear in their eyes. Bennie felt terrible for scaring them. Here it comes again — some white man accusing us of something we didn't do.

Bennie took a knee and said to Maggie, "Do you remember me?"

Maggie looked at her mother. Della nodded at her, gently. Maggie looked at Bennie and did the same.

"Good. Do you remember *why* you saw me? Why I was in the hallway?"

Maggie nodded.

"That's good. Now, here's where I need you to think real hard. Did you see anyone go into the room I went into *before* I did? You know the room I mean, don't you?"

Maggie looked at her mother. Della nodded at her, gently. Maggie looked at Bennie and did the same.

Bennie stood up and did his best to describe Josephine Scott. Her ash brown skin and raven black hair. Her pretty, exotic face.

Maggie shook her head.

Bennie his best to describe Jones Godfrey. His curly hair, the scar down his right temple.

Maggie shook her head.

Bennie took a deep breath and did his best to mimic Chief Reed. He spoke in a gruff voice and limped across the room, balancing on an imaginary cane.

Maggie shook her head.

"Are you sure?"

Maggie nodded.

Reluctantly, Bennie started to describe Jedidiah King. Mr. Johnson, Della, and Maggie just looked at him.

Wait, the newspapers on the floor —

Bennie fished a News Leader from the pile and fingered through it. There, in the back — a full page ad for King Tobacco. He tore it out and let the rest of the paper fall to the ground.

"The man I'm describing makes these cigarettes. Sometimes he gives 'em out for free." Bennie held up the ad and met their faces one by one. Please say no, thought Bennie.

Mr. Johnson spoke up. "I know who you mean. I see him across the street sometimes, at Neverett's. She ain't gonna know who that is," he said, gesturing at Maggie.

Bennie knelt down in front of her. One last time, just to be sure.

"A white man. Nice clothes, handsome face. See anyone like that?"

Maggie shook her head.

"You're sure?"

She was.

Bennie stood up, weightless. He didn't know if he was relieved or disappointed.

"Maggie, can *you* describe the person you saw go into the room?"

Maggie tugged at her mother's nightgown. Della leaned down and let her daughter whisper into her ear. She raised her head and said, "Maggie says it's not any of the people you described, Detective. It's this one, here," she said, gesturing at the floor.

Bennie was lost.

"What?"

"That one," said Della, pointing down at the floor.

Bennie stepped back and followed her gaze. She was pointing at the papers he'd let fall to the floor. He walked over and stood above them. He looked down and felt his gut flutter.

One of the papers had fallen open on a metro page — city news and whatnot. A headline read, POLICE

CHIEF'S JOB IN JEOPARDY. Underneath it, nestled within the copy, were two pictures.

One was of Stolmy Reed.

The other was of Jack.

Bennie knelt down and folded the paper so it framed the story. He held it up for Maggie to see and pointed at The Cane's picture.

"This one?"

Maggie shook her head.

Bennie felt himself go lightheaded. He moved his finger and pointed at Jack's picture.

"This one?"

Maggie nodded.

Bennie dropped the paper and ran.

The world flew by.

Bennie burned through the Row and took Route 5 at a racer's pace. Honks, horn blares, and curse words came at him from all sides. He ignored it all, the world be damned.

His partner was in trouble.

He'd sent Niles on to see Jack while he took the Apollo. It stung his gut — he'd missed it, this whole time.

Jack Reed for the haul at Schmitt Chemical.

Jack Reed for the Apollo murders.

And maybe, just maybe — Jack Reed for the old man.

He'd yet to truly process it, he was nearly in tears. Embarrassment and anger fueled him in equal measure. He death-gripped the steering wheel and hightailed it.

A sign read LENNY'S LODGE — 2 MILES.

Bennie gunned it, almost there.

Go, go, go — just one more mile.

Suddenly, he felt his wheels spit and sputter.

A check on the gas gauge — shit.

Bennie eased the car to the side of the road as it puttered to a stop. He screamed and jumped outside, ditching his coat. Fuck the cold, he needed to lighten his load.

He started down Route 5 in a jog. Boot camp lessons had learned him well. Start slow and work into a sprint. His lungs opened up and he upped his pace.

An Army convoy passed him. GIs catcalled and whistled. Bennie shot 'em the bird with both hands and broke into an all-out run.

He made the motel lot with his gun drawn and slowed, scanning the layout. Two cars — one of them Niles' unmarked. Nobody outside. One long building, maybe fifteen rooms, capped by an office on the westernmost corner. Bennie moved toward the opposite end, his arms locked in a steel grip around his gun handle.

He stood aside the unnumbered door, his back to the wall. Curtains drawn on the window — no way to see inside. He leaned his ear toward the door and listened. An odd sound, like mumbling — he couldn't make it out.

"Jack!" he called out. "Jack, are you in there?"

No answer.

"Niles? Niles, are you inside?"

Mumbled moans through the door.

Bennie reared back and kicked the door in.

There's Niles, crumpled on the floor, groaning.

Bennie scanned the room with frantic eyes — no one else there.

Quick — the bathroom. Shove the door in, smack the light on, check the shower stall.

No one.

Bennie rushed to the floor and turned Niles onto his back.

Jesus, fuck — stab wounds, all across his chest.

"Oh, God. Niles — "

Niles was pale and weak, his fire extinguishing. He fought to speak. "Jack… he's evil, partner. It's been him this whole time."

Niles wretched, coughing up blood. It was Skipper at Pearl's, all over again.

"I'm gonna get you out of here, come on." Bennie moved to lift him. Niles screamed in pain.

Sounds in the doorway.

Bennie grabbed his gun and whipped around, drawing a bead on a man standing just outside. Stout, mustachioed, his hands suddenly up.

"Who are you?"

"I'm Lenny!"

Bennie fumbled for his badge. "Get an ambulance here," he said, holding it up. "Now!"

Lenny took off. Bennie turned back to Niles and cradled him. "Hold on, I got a bus coming, just hang in there." He could see the resignation in his partner's eyes, a look he knew all too well. He started to weep.

Niles coughed through the words. "Don't tell Cheryl Lee I bought it over this sucker play. Please."

Bennie couldn't speak he was crying so hard.

"You gotta get him, Bennie. He did your old man, didn't he? You gotta get him."

Niles reached for Bennie's shoulders and gripped them as if he were about to fall. Then he shuddered and gave out, collapsing into the floor, a final grunt escaping him as he died.

Bennie wept as he never had before. His mother

leaving, his father dying, another boot from his unit, dead and gone — nothing compared to this.

He sank into the floor, sobbing, his body writhing with anguish. He clawed at the carpet and smacked his temples. Shoot me, hit me, anything but this.

He stumbled to his feet and swayed in a circle, dazed. He kicked things, he punched the wall. He let out a war cry and emptied six shots into the bed.

A flash of anger overtook him. It sparked a clarity of vision.

He darted from the room and made Niles' car. Start the engine, check the two-way. Static, hiss, fuzzy sounds — bingo. The dial registered. He was still within range.

He grabbed the receiver, ready to call it in, when he heard someone speaking on the other end.

It was Jack Reed.

"... This is an all points bulletin, direct from the Annex. Code Red. Detective Sergeant Bennie Thomas Sherwood is armed and dangerous. He's wanted in conjunction with covert dealings on the black market and for the murder of his partner, Sergeant Niles Hunter. Apprehend on sight. If necessary, shoot to kill. I repeat, this is an all points bulletin ... "

FUBAR

March 1, 1944 — March 11, 1944

CHAPTER THIRTY-SIX

BAD DREAMS.

IN this one, there's blood everywhere.

And knives. Lots of knives.

The jungle is hot and sticky and smells of fear. Jack is there. The old man, too. They're playing catch right out in the open.

Japs hover above them, watching from the trees. Bennie screams for them to take cover, but they don't hear him. He tries to move himself — he must warn them! — but he cannot. He's pinned against a tree and his arms and legs are lifeless. Bennie looks down at the dozens of stab wounds piercing his chest. Blood is seeping from his body, pooling on the jungle floor.

He looks to his left. Oh God, there's Niles, as dead as he was on that motel floor.

He looks to his right. There's Jones Godfrey and Josephine Scott, as alive as can be, playing cards and smiling.

Panic rushes through Bennie's veins. He tries to scream but makes no sound.

Suddenly, there are soldiers at the clearing's edge. It's his old unit, every last boot, done up in dress blues and nice shoes. They're dancing to the music that suddenly floods the jungle, courtesy of Johnny Pepper and his band. The clearing becomes a dance floor and now it's a full-on jitterbug contest. There's Japs and gyrenes, arm in arm, a sea of joy across their faces.

Which is odd, because they've all got holes in their heads and they're missing limbs. Jones and Josephine cheer them on while Jack and the old man judge the contest from above.

It's a cut and dry system. Thumbs up, you keep dancing. Thumbs down, you pull knives and fight to the death. It's an ocean of blood and body parts and Bennie is screaming, he's sure of it, his throat chafed and dry, and now there's one last duo remaining. Get in there gyrene, get your man! But that filthy Jap pulls a switchblade and slices through his partner's throat.

Japs Win! Japs Win! Japs Win!

Oh look, there's a prize for the winner —

Oh God, it's Imogene. She's in the clearing now, ready to two-step with the enemy. One by one, they take her hands and slow dance like it's the prom, but the formality doesn't last, because they're stripping her down now and Bennie is screaming, screaming as loud as he ever has, but his vocal cords have been ripped out and no one hears a thing.

Something woke him.

Bennie came to slowly, thinking first about just how sweaty he was, and looked up.

Hollis Digby stood over him, nudging his ribs with a foot, a coffee cup in his hand.

"You're, uh… doing it again," said Hollis.

Bennie nodded, embarrassed.

"Look, sun's up and we've got coffee. Just come on when you're ready."

Bennie nodded that he would. Hollis tipped his cup at him before walking off.

With much effort, Bennie propped himself up with his arms, stretching his back. The garage floor was rigid, and the blankets he'd fashioned into a mattress did little to soften it. He'd been sleeping in one of Hollis' empty car bays for the last few nights and it was starting to wear on his back.

Bennie yawned, rolled his neck, and shot a quick look around. His sole remaining possessions were just within reach — his .38, his steno, and his badge, not that it mattered.

He stood, pulled on slacks, and walked through the garage to Digby's office. There he found Hollis, reformed gambler and current owner of an inoperative gas station, chatting with Cyrus Mitchell, world-weary beat cop out of Third. Together, they made quite the trio. We should form a vocal group, thought Bennie, and sing the blues.

"A cop car drove by earlier," said Cyrus, "but it didn't stop, just went on." Cyrus had been keeping watch, checking both Broad and Hamilton at regular intervals.

Bennie looked at Hollis. "Any phone calls? Anyone just call, wait, and hang up?"

Hollis shook his head. "No one knows you're here, son."

Bennie poured himself a cup of coffee and thought of the last ten days. Of how he'd fashioned a second-hand disguise out of an old topcoat-and-hat combo he pulled from a church's donation bin. Of how he'd sprinkled his shirt with moonshine and faked a stumblebum's lean. And of how he'd slept in transient houses on sixty-cents-a-night cots and rummaged garbage bins for scraps of food. He'd avoided eye contact and stuck to the shadows, waiting out Jack Reed's citywide dragnet for reputed cop killer and black market mastermind Bennie Thomas Sherwood.

That is, until a few nights ago, when a few Second Station cops poured through the downtown room house Bennie was staying in. Exhausted and penniless, Bennie snuck out a back window and trekked it to Hollis' service station, collapsing at his back door.

"What are you gonna do?" asked Cyrus.

"I've got one play," said Bennie. "It's a hunch, but there's a cop I know, another detective. I think *he* knows."

"Knows what?"

"Enough to go to City Hall with, maybe the FBI. Hell, I don't know. Whoever I can find to tell. I just have to get to him first."

"And she's helping you with this?" asked Hollis.

"Yes. We've got a friend at the paper. As soon as she knows something…"

Sounds behind him. He turned and she was there, an angel in the doorway.

"Hollis," said Imogene, "I still have my key, so I just let myself in. Hope that's alright."

Hollis beamed. "You're welcome anytime, sweetheart. Come on Cyrus, let's go see about that 'ole pickup you were talking about."

Cyrus was lost. "What pickup?"

"Just come on."

Hollis and Cyrus left the room. Bennie hardly knew what to say, he was so nervous. He leaned against the desk for something to do.

"You saw Archie?" he asked.

Imogene nodded. "He's pretty wrecked over all this. Doesn't know what to think. I think he feels partly responsible for it all."

"Think he'll give me up?"

"No, I don't think you have to worry about him. I actually believe he's rather devoted to you. He was rather cautious around me, I have to say."

"Well, he was the one who — "

"Yes, I gathered that."

A moment passed.

"Did he get it?"

"Yes. And he made me memorize it so there'd be no paper trail."

Good on Archie, thought Bennie, as Imogene gave him Eugene Mills' home address. An apartment off Marshall, near Second. That night at Schmitt Chemical, that AO gunman, Ernie — he'd said a man named Miller had paid him to put a scare on. But there was no Miller on the active RPD roster.

Not Miller.

Mills.

It made sense, thought Bennie, thinking back to that day at the Annex, running into Eugene on his way out. Mills had come off cagey. And those bruises on his neck — he'd claimed they were from fighting with those Negroes at Pearl's, but Bennie didn't buy it. Eugene was hiding something, and whatever it was, it might be the only way out of this.

"What are you gonna do?" she asked.

"Get to him any way I can."

"And then?"

"Make him talk."

She flinched, uncomfortable at the idea.

"Look, it's the only play I've got. It's just a matter of time before Jack finds me."

A few beats passed. The air in the room felt heavy.

"I want to help," she said.

Bennie was surprised. "Why?"

She folded her arms and looked out the office window at the car bays. Nostalgic, maybe, for a time before all this, when she could just do her work and let it all be.

"I used to think," she said, "that if I had been there, with him, that maybe I could have helped him. Shown him the way, or been a guide of some kind."

Bennie stepped toward her. "You've got to know, there were others. Just like him, right there with him. Whatever he went through, Imogene, he wasn't alone."

She turned and faced him.

"Then, please, let me help you. Whatever this is, I don't want it to consume you. And I can't bear just to sit and wonder what might happen."

Bennie chewed on it. After a time, he said, "Can you get your hands on a taxi?"

Mills worked nights on the juvie squad. He'd opted for a lighter desk after Pearl's. Vice was *sin*-tillating, Victory was cutthroat, robbery was a thrill. Juvie was — round up the kids, talk to the parents (if there were any around), and funnel it all to the police court reps. Boring as shit, easy and done.

Imogene parked her cab on Broad just east of 11th, facing west. It was a loaner from Confederate, hers for the entire night. Bennie hid in the back, hunkered down behind the passenger seat with a length of blackout fabric for cover. Peeking over the seat's shoulder, he could just make out the front steps of the Annex. There were cops everywhere — flatfoots, AOs, vice bulls chewing the fat. Shit — there's The Cane, hobbling to his car. Damn, thought Bennie, I had a better chance of survival on the island.

"How do we know if the one we're looking for is out there?" she asked.

"Because he's right there," said Bennie.

Mills was easy to spot. He was on the tall side and walked with a stoop. There he is, coming down the steps now. He cut straight to Broad — no goodbyes — and waited. A dark sedan pulled up alongside him. Mills got in and the car took off, heading west.

"We're on," said Bennie.

Imogene fired up the cab and pulled onto Broad. Bennie crouched low and stayed out of sight as they passed the Annex. He could hardly see anything more than her right profile and for that, he was glad.

"Can you still see them?" he asked.

"Yes."

"How far away are they?"

"Four, maybe five car lengths."

"That's good. You can get closer if you want."

"Okay."

"Just don't lose them, please."

She smiled. "You don't think I can do this."

Bennie caught himself. "No, I do. I'm just... " He trailed off, thinking of Niles. "I'm not used to this."

"Well, you can relax. I tailed you a few times and you never noticed."

"What?"

"He's turning."

"Stay on him."

A right, another right. Coasting now, slowing. Speeding

up again.

"He's parking," she said. "I'm going past. I'll find somewhere to stop."

"What can you see?"

"Hold on," she said. "There's a street light near them."

The cab slowed as she turned to look. "There's two men getting out. The driver — no, it's not Jack. The other — oh my god."

Imogene looked straight ahead and drove past them.

"What?"

She didn't respond.

"What?!"

"Hold on." The cab jerked left and pulled to a curb. Imogene killed the engine and gathered herself. She turned and shot him a look like she'd just seen a ghost.

"Do you remember when you came to my house?" she said. "To ask me about the cars at the service station?"

"Yes."

"I gave you a name for the Chevy. What was it?"

Bennie got tingles. "Jack Gentry."

Imogene was stunned. "That was him."

"Who, the driver?"

"No, the other one. The taller one."

Bennie could hardly believe it. And then he could — yes, it makes sense. Mills has been in it with Jack from the get go.

"Holy mother," he said.

She was almost offended. "What's that?"

"Take a look around," he said. "See anyone?"

She glanced in all directions. Good girl.

"No."

Bennie tossed the blackout fabric and hoisted himself into the back seat. He felt about himself — his .38, holstered; his toad knife, nestled into his right boot. He buttoned his jacket and looked at Imogene.

"Thank you," he said.

She fought with it. "Are you going to hurt him?"

"If I have to."

She bit her lip, resisting the urge to say more. He leaned in, touched her face, and kissed her.

"I won't kill him," he said.

She nodded, more at ease. "I'll be here."

Bennie gave her a long look and then he ducked from the cab, staying low around the back end. He stepped onto Marshall, heading west, and broke into a jog. Mills' apartment was just up ahead.

He thought of his promise to Imogene. He upped his pace, hoping he could keep it.

CHAPTER THIRTY-SEVEN

EUGENE MILLS LIVED on the second floor of a two story walkup, a low rent pad with broken windows and worn-down steps. The lock on the front door was busted, so Bennie walked right in.

There was a light on in the foyer. Bennie turned back and checked the street — all clear. He killed the light and let his eyes adjust to the dark. He took the stairs and found 2B on soft steps. He leaned against the door and held his breath, listening.

Sounds inside — a radio, maybe. He threw quick looks in either direction — nothing.

With steady hands, Bennie picked the lock with the old man's tools and stepped inside. He eased the door shut, locking it again, and drew his gun.

Those sounds — *not* a radio. In the back, to the right. Go *easy*, thought Bennie. Make every step careful and deliberate.

He made his way through the apartment on light feet — ducking the furniture, checking the corners. He followed the sounds to a closed door. Moans inside — not of pain, but of pleasure.

Oh, great.

Bennie readied himself and checked the handle — it was open.

Deep breaths.

1, 2, 3...

Go.

Bennie opened the door and drew a bead on two figures writhing on a bed under the sheets. He stepped closer and closer, until he was right there, next to the bed. He reached a hand out, ready to pull back the cover, when it shifted toward him.

A young man's face, right there.

Not Mills.

The man screamed. Bennie stuck his gun into the body of the other man and said, "Can it, or you both get it."

The young man went silent fast and threw his hands over his mouth, terrified. Bennie held a stare on him and slowly began to peel back the sheet.

Well now, what do we have here...

Eugene Mills, in bed with a man.

A weighted moment took hold. Mills closed his eyes and began to cry. Bennie looked from one man to the next — '*the hell?*

With a quiver in his voice, Mills said, "I'll tell you what you want to know, Bennie. Just please — don't hurt us."

Bennie looked around the room. There — a closet, across from the bed.

The younger man tracked Bennie's line of sight and got the gist. He gripped the sheet like it was some kind of protection.

"No," he said.

"Either you go in there," said Bennie, "or you both go in

there. If you both go in there, neither one of you comes out."

"Charles," said Mills, "please do as he asks. He's not... He just wants to talk to me. If I tell him what I know, I believe he'll let us be."

"*Now*," said Bennie.

Charles sighed and felt around under the covers. He wrangled about and eased himself from the bed in nothing but skivvies, walking to the closet as he might the gallows.

Bennie opened the door — coats, clothes, shoes. A tight space. He shoved everything to one side and motioned for Charles to get in.

"Stay put. And I mean it — not a peep."

Charles stepped inside, forcing himself to fit. He began to sob as Bennie shut the door.

Mills sat up on the bed, covering himself with a blanket. "That's really not necessary, Bennie. He already knows everything."

Bennie pulled a chair over to the bed and took a seat, his gun on Mills.

"Not that I care, Mills, but I never figured you for a homo."

"Well, good, then. At least I'm hiding something right."

"Cute."

"Where do you want me to start, Bennie?"

"What does it start *with*?"

"It starts... with Jedidiah King."

Bennie felt a jolt. "You and him?"

"No. He and Jack."

Bennie felt himself go slack. "So, Jack's..."

"Yes, like me."

Bennie almost laughed. He felt like the last guy in the

room to get the joke.

"Are they together now?"

"No. They never were together. Oh, they may have indulged one another a time or two, but no, never a couple."

Bennie was already lost. "Then just how does that get us to where we are now?"

"Jack wanted more. Jedidiah did not. This was all before you came home. Jack was spurned, rejected. He thought he'd found his one true love. I saw his pain and offered comfort. But his bitterness, his anger... He just used me and threw me away."

"And this was... "

"We shared time in the Fall. He cut it off after Pearl's."

"Why?"

"He met someone else."

Bennie was getting hot. "I still don't see — "

"Does the name Jones Godfrey ring a bell?"

Bennie perked up. "Yes."

"Jones Godfrey was a close associate of Jedidiah's. Worked for him, made his appointments. Pulled strings behind the scenes, as it were. Jones was also like us, and, like Jack, in love with Jeddidiah. But Jedidiah, well... He holds many a flame in his heart. He is not, as they say, altogether true."

Bennie was losing patience. "Get there, Mills."

"As I'm sure you've gathered, Jedidiah has a vested interest in the black market. How much, I can't say, but my guess is its significant."

"Okay."

"Well, Jack and Jones were so put off by their rejected advances that they banded together and cooked up a scheme to hurt Jedidiah. They set up shop in the black market on their own, hoping to drive Jedidiah right out of business."

"The haul at Schmitt Chemical…"

"Yes, that was all them. It was mostly Jack, with his police connections. Rivers and others like him. But Jones played a part, too."

"Rivers said he was strongarmed by someone he never even met."

"That was all Jack."

Bennie was oddly impressed. "Get to the Apollo."

Mills waved him off. "You have to understand Pearl's first. Jack had gotten wind that someone was onto their scheme. Someone from inside Jedidiah's organization."

"Skipper."

"Yes. So, Jack set up a meet at Pearl's to break bread, come to an understanding. Or so he said."

Bennie knew the rest. "But he never intended to have any kind of sit down, did he? You two went in first. To *kill* Skipper." Bennie felt his grip on the gun tighten.

"No, no — not me! I didn't know what he had planned, Bennie. Believe me, I never would have gone along with it if I did. I'm sorry about your friend, truly I am."

"But it *was* premeditated."

"I can't say for sure, but yes, I think so. Jack said nothing to your friend. Just walked right up and shot him. But your friend, he was quick. He got off his own shots and fled."

Skipper always could move fast. "That's how you got hit."

"Yes."

"What about the Negroes there? What was their part?"

"Jack paid them to be there. He thought if anything went wrong…"

"He could pin it on them."

Mills nodded, ashamed.

Bennie stood up and started to pace the room. "The Apollo."

Mills took a deep breath. "After Pearl's, I confronted Jack about what he'd done and threatened to go to his father with it. He flew into a rage and beat me horribly."

"Those bruises on your face..."

"Yes. He said he'd kill *me* if I told anyone. Then he told me that he'd met someone else and that we were through."

"Jones."

Mills nodded. "And while I *was* hurt by it all, I was more frightened for Jack's new flame. So I asked around. Our kind, mind you, is a tight knit. I heard about Jones and went to him myself."

"And?"

"I told him about Pearl's. He was horrified, said he'd end it immediately. But his concern for Jedidiah — spurned or not, he still loved the man. And if he'd told Jedidiah himself, why, Jedidiah might mistake it for a jealous play, something out of spite. So Jones went another way."

"And that was?"

"Josephine Scott."

"Who was she?"

"*She* was Jedidiah's real love. They'd been together for years. In secret, of course. Jones thought if he could reach out to Jedidiah through her, he could prevent something tragic from happening. But, as we both know, that was not to be."

Bennie's heart sank, thinking of her lifeless eyes. "What about Jones' alias? Jack Gentry?"

Mills wiped tears from his face. "Jones was often making

deals for Jedidiah. In the shadows, if you will. And he did work for King Tobacco. He used a fake name to shield the company from any backlash."

"He sure drank a lot."

"Yes, well, when you have to hide your true self, it sure helps to have an outlet."

"Why'd you use Jones' alias to pick up the car?"

Mills looked at him, surprised. "You don't miss a thing. After the Apollo, I was terrified for my life, but I knew I had to tell someone about Jack. I picked up the car with designs on returning it to King myself. I thought with his influence, we could take what I knew to Chief Reed."

"What stopped you?"

"Jack. He'd been following me, sensing what I'd do. He stopped me before I got to King. God, I thought he was going to kill me."

Bennie felt jungle rage simmering in his veins. He turned from the bed and closed his eyes.

"You could have done something. He's just one man."

Mills started to cry. "Yes, well, I don't quite have your confidence, Bennie. I'm clumsy and I'm not quick. He threatened to hurt me if I went to his father. And that if anything should happen to *him*, letters would be sent to my family. My parents, my sister. Exposing me for what I am."

"A coward?"

Mills looked at Bennie with centuries of hurt in his eyes.

"Is that what you really think?"

"If you'd have done something, Niles might still be alive."

Mills started to truly sob. "Yes, well, perhaps you're right."

Bennie got that dizzy feeling and started to sway. He felt weightless. Lies and bullshit were heavy, like an anvil. But the truth — that was lighter than air.

Bennie steadied himself against the chair. Deep breaths. Inhale/exhale/repeat. Just like they'd taught him.

Fuck what they'd taught him.

He picked up the chair and threw it across the room. Mills scurried for a corner. Inside the closet, Charles started to whimper.

Bennie opened the closet door and found Charles cowering against a heap of clothes.

"You can come out now."

Charles stayed where he was.

Bennie looked at Mills and said, "You're done as a policeman. You and your friend here should leave town. Tonight, for good. If I ever see either of you again, I'll expose you both."

Bennie left the room without another word. Get out now, he thought. Another minute and they'd both be dead.

CHAPTER THIRTY-EIGHT

2AM, LATER THAT night.

Post Mills' tell-all.

Bennie and Imogene huddled together under a blanket on the rooftop of Digby's garage, sharing a bottle of mash and looking at the stars. The hooch was high-test stuff from Hollis' personal reserve. It registered at nearly 80 proof and warmed them against the cold.

Tantilla was just across the way. Music from the ballroom carried through the air. They listened as Johnny Pepper and his band did the latest Glenn Miller. Bennie thought of his wacko dream and took a long swig.

"I'm sorry we can't go," he said, nodding at the Garden and passing her the bottle.

"We will," she said, taking a sip. "We're almost through this."

Bennie felt a buzz coming on. "Let's hope."

"What'll you do now?"

"Give it to Archie. Big headlines ought to shake things up. Expose Jack, clear my name. I just have to lay low until the smoke clears."

She snuggled up close. "Well, at least you don't have to go it alone."

Bennie laughed. "You really hit the jackpot. With me, I mean."

"Don't be silly. You'll come out of this and we'll do the town. Until then, well..."

Slowly, they folded into one another and fell into a kiss. He pulled her close and held her tight. Her soft, luscious lips made the world disappear. He ran his hand along the contour of her body and heard her moan. She touched his face and kissed his neck. They both wanted more.

She tugged at his jeans and undid her slacks. She pulled the blanket up over her back as she straddled him. She cried out softly when he entered her and they rocked together slowly, under the stars. She pressed her hands against his chest and set the rhythm with her hips. Slow, at first. Then, more rushed, driven by instinct, her lips never leaving his. He felt the world move as they climaxed together, their cries of passion entwined, rising into the night sky.

She laid against him now, her back to his chest, and brought the blanket up over them. The air was quite cool now, but the warmth of their bodies was enough to keep it at bay.

She reached for her slacks and pulled out a pack of cigarettes. Bennie had to laugh. They were River City Sovereigns.

"What's funny?" she said.

"Those cigarettes. I see 'em everywhere."

"They're quite good. Would you like one?"

"I don't smoke."

She shook the pack and felt about her slacks. "Then I

don't suppose you have a light."

Bennie checked his coat. That matchbook — still with him. He pulled it out and handed it to her. "Here."

"You don't smoke, but you carry matches?"

"Skipper gave 'em to me, the night he died."

She paused. "Is that why you still carry them with you?"

Bennie shrugged. "Maybe. There's an inscription on the inside flap. Look."

She flipped it open. "JH M10 10P. What does it mean?"

He told her about his chance meeting with the bellhop at the Jefferson Hotel. "Guy said it's for something at the hotel on March 10 at 10PM."

She was intrigued. "That's tomorrow night."

"Is it?"

"Yes," she said, in between drags.

"I used to think it had something to do with all this," he said. "King, Jack, and the rest of it. That maybe that's why he slipped it to me, you know? But it's just a matchbook. I suppose I do keep it around, for him."

They were silent for a time. Tantilla had closed up, no more music. Bennie closed his eyes and rolled his neck, smiling. He might be a fugitive from the law, but he'd never felt more free.

Imogene said, "I think you should go."

"Where?"

"To the Jefferson, tomorrow night."

"Are you kidding? I'll be skinned alive."

"But what if you're right? What if he did give it to you for a reason? Maybe there is something there, something he wanted you to know. We'll go together. Stake it out first, stay near the exits. If someone spots you, we'll duck out. I can get a cab, easy. We'll park it on the street, somewhere we can get to quick. What do you say?"

Bennie wrapped his arms around her and kissed the top of her head. She'd make a hell of a Marine, he thought.

"You're crazy," he said.

"I'm serious. You owe it to your friend to see it through. You know I'm right."

Bennie rested his head against hers and closed his eyes. Yes, he thought, let's go to the Jefferson Hotel, you and I, and honor a dead man's last wish.

CHAPTER THIRTY-NINE

IMOGENE CASED THE Jefferson in her cab while Bennie sat in the back. He kept himself low, watching out the window like some kind of creep. The fact of being here, at this very moment, gave him wicked jitters. He half expected the place to explode, or for the tenants and staff to break out in a song and dance number, just for him, like something out of a Busby Berkeley.

She curbed the cab on Main, facing west, a block from the hotel. A quick look around — nothing suspicious. Light traffic, no noise.

"Let's go in," she said.

They took Adams Street to Franklin and slipped in through the front lobby. So far, so good. No cops, nothing strange.

They descended the Grand Staircase, sidestepping soldiers and beer bottles. They spilled into the common area amidst a jovial scene — music, dancing, drinks everywhere. They got swept up in the tide and did the Jitterbug and The Lindy Hop. They took to the fringes and scoured the room. It was all fun and games —

nothing to raise an alarm over.

Imogene left him and skipped back to the lobby. She was back, a few minutes later.

"No," she said. "No reservation for Holly."

"There's nothing here," he said, sighing. "Let's go, before someone sees me."

She hooked her arm in his and winked. "At least we tried."

He kissed her and they started for the exit.

Bennie froze.

There, by the elevator — two mob types.

He pulled Imogene to the side and watched as they got in and disappeared.

"What is it?" she said.

"Can you go back to the lobby and ask for Wesley. He's a bellhop. See if he's on tonight."

"What? Why?"

"Please, just ask."

She held his gaze for a moment and skipped off again. Bennie looked around — his jungle instincts were in the red.

Minutes ticked off. Bennie felt his nerves kick up. Imogene returned, her face flushed with energy.

"Yes," she said. "He's on tonight, but he's on break. Who —"

"Come on," he said, taking her by the hand. They skirted the crowd and took the same service hallway he'd taken before.

"Watch out for alligators," he said.

"What?" she said, more confused than alarmed.

They came upon three Negroes smoking cigarettes. Wesley and two maids. The girls saw them and got spooked — white folk, down here?

Wesley lit up. "Hey, Mr. Detective Man!"

"You remember me," said Bennie.

"Sure, I remember you."

Bennie wasted no time. "You remember what we talked about?"

"Sure! I even called you about it. You get my message?"

"What?"

"Yeah, you said to call you if I saw any more — what'd you say? Suspicious characters. I called and asked for you, but you weren't around. Where you been at?"

"Who did you talk to?"

Wesley churned memory. "Let me see. Somebody Reed."

Bennie felt himself tighten up, hoping. "*Stolmy* Reed? Maybe *Chief* Reed?"

"Nah — "

"Jack."

"Yeah, that's it."

Bennie hung his head. "Shit."

Wesley's spirits sank. "Did I do wrong?"

"No. Say — Mr. King. Have you seen him?"

Wesley lit up again. "Yeah, he's here tonight! Gave us these cigarettes! And if I didn't know any better, I'd say he's got quite the party going on with these people you're so interested in."

Bennie turned to Imogene. "Please, I want you to go."

"What? Why? What's happening?"

"I don't know," said Bennie. But he *did* know. It hit him, right then. He turned to Wesley and said, "Call the police, right now. Tell them you've found Bennie Sherwood."

"But that's you!"

"I know. They'll understand."

Imogene turned him around. "Bennie, what are you

doing?"

"Look, Jack's killed innocent people before. He knows now. His father, King, all this."

"What's *all this*?"

The pieces fell into place like an explosion in reverse, everything glued together all at once.

"It's an organized crime meet. The mob, a retreat. King's used his influence to bring them together, maybe set up a deal. It's possible he's undercutting them, maybe working with Chief Reed. Skipper must have known, or been told. Either way, he wanted me to know.

"Know what?"

"The he *knew* who Jack was, at Pearl's, and what he might do."

"And what's that?"

"I think he's coming here, tonight, to kill Jedidiah."

"What? It's so public."

"Exactly. He knows now, about the meet. For months, we've been seeing it in the dailies — organized crime sightings in town. He gets it now, he'll use it to his advantage. Make it look like *they* did King in."

"Are you sure?"

"Yes," said Bennie, the weight of it coursing through him like poison.

He turned to Wesley. "Go, now, call the police." Wesley took off. He grabbed Imogene by the shoulders. "Please — don't be here for this."

She shook herself from his grip, offended. "Like it or not, Bennie, I'm staying put. And if you think otherwise, you might *need* the police. Now, what are we going to do?"

Bennie started with the second floor, casing the hallways in plain view. No point in hiding now. Wesley had said,

'King's entertaining a crowd on the fourth floor'. Bennie was working his way up.

Imogene was downstairs, waiting for the police. "If you see Jack," he told her, "slip out, get to the cab. If you see The Cane, make an introduction. Tell him who you are and why you're here."

"Won't he arrest me? For helping you?"

"He might. If he does, string him along. Tell him some of what I've told you and that he'll only get the rest from me."

Bennie sidestepped a shirtless Army grunt sleeping it off against the wall. There were soldiers everywhere. Jawing, drinking, wooing War Belles. Many of their hotel rooms were wide open. There's laughter in one, music and dancing in another. No Jack, no mob types.

Bennie took the elevator to the third floor. Same as before — soldiers, parties, Negro busboys carting liquor from room to room. Still — no Jack, no mob types.

There, at the end of the hall — a stairwell. Bennie could hoof it and get to four quick. The elevator was slow.

He ran to the end of the hall, threw open the exit door, and smelled smoke.

Quick — to the railing, a look down — *Holy Mother*.

Wooden steps below, all in flames.

Bennie threw himself back onto the third floor and screamed "Fire!" He pounded doors, darting from one to the other. A sailor in nothing but his cap and skivvies jerked his open.

"What gives, pal?"

"Ring the front desk and get everyone out! The hotel's on fire!"

Bennie left the seabee scrambling and ran back to the stairwell. Another look down — the fire was spreading fast. He took the steps up three at a time and spilled onto the fourth floor, frantic. He was torn inside — if he screamed, he'd blow his cover. Quick — *how* do I find King?

Bennie skipped down the hall, scanning doors. Knock on each one? Ask for him by name?

Around the corner, down to the northern wing —

Fuck — more closed doors.

Wait — 407 —

There's more space between it and another. *Maybe* it's a suite with the space for entertaining.

Bennie ran to it and knocked. He heard hectic noise below — everyone scrambling. Any minute now, the alarm would sound.

Then, a deep voice from the other side of the door. "Yeah?"

Bennie leaned in close. "Tell Mr. King that Bennie Sherwood is here."

Smoke in the air. *Damn it* — any minute now.

Suddenly — the door, wide open. Jedidiah King, right there, a look of awe and horror on his face.

"The hotel's on fire," said Bennie, "and the police are on their way. Jack knows you're here. He's coming for you."

Jedidiah gulped. Mortal terror in his eyes. He started to speak, but the fire alarm cut him off. Doors along the hall opened, one by one. Sheepish guests stuck their heads out, sniffing. Smoke was wafting in around the corner from the south wing.

"Now, Jedidiah!"

King threw himself back into his room while Bennie banged on closed doors.

"Fire! Fire! Get out now!"

Scantily clad men and women flooded the hall, rushing past him. A soldier caught sight of Bennie and ran over.

"There's a fire hose," he said, pointing back the other way. "Help me!"

Together, they charged around the corner. The hose was coiled inside a break in the wall. Bennie grabbed the nozzle, rushed the stairwell, and threw the door open.

Jesus — the flames!

The soldier got the water going. Bennie two-handed the hose and got ready for this great rush of force.

It never came.

Water trickled out the nozzle — no pressure.

"Shit!" screamed the soldier.

Bennie turned to look — he was all wet. The hose had been slashed in several places. Water was running all over the floor.

"Kill it!" said Bennie, a rush of smoke flooding his eyes. "Get everyone you can and get outside!" *Jesus fuck* — tears and coughs and can't see shit.

Bennie heard a woman scream in the north wing. He darted back that way, shielding his face.

He made the hall, staying low. Smoke was everywhere. He coughed and blinked. No sign of King.

The woman screamed again. A room, to the right — its door wide open. Two figures emerged — mob thugs, clutching valuables and jewels.

"Hey!" screamed Bennie.

The goons just smirked and disappeared down the hall.

Bennie let them go, ran to 407, and tried the door — it was locked.

Sounds inside — yelps and screams. A crash of some kind.

Bennie took two steps back and braced himself, hoping

to do Niles proud.

1, 2, 3 —

Bennie kicked a hole through the door and shouldered it off its hinges, crashing to the floor. He scrambled to his feet and saw them.

Jack Reed and Jedidiah King, beaten and bloody, thrashing on the floor. Bennie felt helpless — he had no gun, no weapon. He could hardly see, his eyes bleeding tears.

A blur, a blink, all of it in a flash —

Jedidiah, thrown onto his back —

Jack, his arms raised, holding a knife —

Bennie rushed over, tackling him to the floor. He wrestled Jack down and got both hands around his neck.

Just squeeze, goddamnit, take it all —

Jack put up a fight, but Bennie's arms were iron-locked.

Just a little harder, that's it —

Bennie felt himself go dizzy, his vision blur —

Goddamnit, not now — it's Jack, forchrissakes — cop killer, psychopath — just squeeeeezze!

No, wait — it's a Jap.

Holy shit — it's Jack the Jap!

What the —

A knee to his groin threw Bennie off.

Jack's hands were on *him* now, turning him over. Bennie looked up as Jack straddled him — his arms raised, his knife ready — and let out a devil's cry.

Just then, two gunshots pierced Jack's chest. Bennie watched as he registered the shots, incredulous. The knife fell from his hands — Bennie caught the handle just in time — and Jack fell like a fallen tower onto the floor and died with tears in his eyes.

Bennie scrambled to his feet and looked over at

Jedidiah, cowering against the wall. There's a gun on the floor, just within reach. Bennie could feel its heat and smell the cordite. He stayed low and crawled over to Jedidiah.

"We need to go, now!"

But Jedidiah was shell-shocked, like Niles at Pearl's.

Bennie slapped him and stood up, hauling Jedidiah to his feet. "There'll be time for this later. Come on!"

Jedidiah blinked himself into focus, wiping tears from his eyes. "H.. How? How do we get out?"

Bennie looked around the room. No windows, just furniture. Wait — that tablecloth, those bedsheets —

Bennie Sherwood and Jedidiah King escaped the Jefferson Hotel fire by way of a south-facing fourth-story window, scaling down the building on strung-together hotel linens. They touched down on Main Street, assisted by firemen, and walked unnoticed through the crowd, their faces masked with so much soot it made them unrecognizable.

Red Cross volunteers handed them blankets and cups of water. Bennie and Jedidiah watched as the firemen tried unsuccessfully to hose down the flames. Ladder rescues reached all the way to the sixth floor.

Bennie shot a look down the block. There's Imogene, next to her cab, looking anxious.

"This way," said Bennie, nudging Jedidiah.

The two of them sifted through a most unusual crowd. A jubilant throng of half-naked men and women had taken up dancing in the middle of the street to express their joy at having so narrowly escaped death.

A familiar voice caught Bennie's ear. He turned back just as The Cane spilled from the hotel, barking orders at startled cops. Bennie watched as he shooed them off, his face a mottled mess, and started to cry.

Jedidiah tugged at his arm. "Come on," he whispered.

As they came to the cab, Bennie could see just how tense Imogene was. She was looking right past them, scanning the crowd, the look in her eyes both hopeful and distraught. When they were just three yards off, Bennie whistled quietly for her attention. She caught sight of him and blanched — who are *you*? — before recognition set in. Relief rippled through her as she fought the urge to embrace him.

She got into the cab and fired it up. Bennie and Jedidiah slipped into the back seat, saying nothing, and they pulled away slowly.

Bennie turned and looked out the back window as they drove off. As flames engulfed the east wing of the hotel and smoke rose higher into the sky, Bennie thought of the stories the old man used to tell about the great fire of 1865 and the destruction left in its wake.

Chapter Forty

BENNIE AND JEDIDIAH sat on opposite sides of an auto repair tool cart that doubled as a dining table. They were seated inside one of Digby's empty car bays. Imogene, Hollis, and Cyrus were over in the office, yarning. Every so often, laughter would spill into the garage and lighten the mood.

On the cart was a near empty bottle of Hollis' 80 proof mash, some bread and cheese, and some leftover steak. Hollis had grilled it earlier and set some aside for his fugitive guest.

"You should eat," said Bennie. "An empty stomach will only worsen your nerves."

Jedidiah shifted in his seat and recrossed his legs. He nursed his highball and wiped sweat from his forehead. He and Bennie were both still warm from the fire's heat.

"Thank you, Detective Sherwood. When my appetite returns, I'll surely enjoy a feast. For now, however, just a drink and some quiet will suffice."

"Call me Bennie."

"Alright. Tell me, Bennie, why did you know to come to

the hotel tonight?"

Bennie ran it down for him — the matchbook, his chance meeting with the Jefferson bellhop. "But I didn't put it all together until tonight," he said, "until I was at the hotel and saw some of your pals get into an elevator."

"They are *not* my pals."

"Did The Cane put you up to it?"

"That's one way of putting it."

"You approached him?"

"After the... horrors of the Apollo, I pleaded with Stolmy to double his efforts and find Jones' and Josephine's killer. He said if I did this favor for him, that he'd be sure and put his best people on it."

"I'm guessing you didn't know he meant Jack."

"Correct."

"Did you know that Jack killed my friend — and your former employee — Skipper Holly?"

"I began to suspect as much. You know this for sure?"

Bennie nodded.

"How?"

"Eugene Mills."

"Ah, Jack's fling. And where is Mills now?"

"Far away from here, if he knows what's good for him."

"When did you find out?"

"Last night."

"Then I suppose you know all of it."

"There's still a few things I'm curious about."

"Oh?" Jedidiah took the bottle and topped off his highball. He motioned for Bennie to extend his glass and poured him the rest. He reclined into his chair and sipped his drink.

"Ask away."

"When I met you at Tantilla, you said you didn't know

Skipper."

"At the time, I was conducting my own investigation into his death and reluctant to share what I knew with those I was *not* well acquainted with."

"So you did know him."

"Of course. Jones introduced him to me. Skipper was looking to turn his life around and I gave him an opportunity. One he took to heart and excelled at, I should say."

"What did he do for you?"

"As you may have gathered, Bennie, I traffic in a great many goods. Skipper saw to my receiving and deliveries. Made sure the right people got the right things."

"Do you know why he was at Pearl's?"

Jedidiah sighed. "My own inquiry into the matter has led me to believe that he was trying to protect me. Skipper was… of the street, if you will, and had gotten wind of Jack's plan to hurt me. Oh, I don't think he knew Jack by name, much less that he was a policeman, but he did act independently. I'd given him another chance, you see, and he was trying to repay me."

Bennie breathed a sigh of relief and felt a calm wash over him. Good ole' Skipper, honorable to the end.

"What is it that you do, Jedidiah?"

"Aside from my tobacco business?"

"Yes."

"I help those who cannot help themselves."

"By dealing on the side? Undercutting rationed prices and disrupting a wartime economy?"

"Goodness. I'd no idea you held such righteous ideals about it all."

"You may remember I fought in this war."

"Oh, I'm fully aware of your sacrifice, Bennie. And

judging by your behavior at the hotel earlier, you must have been quite the Marine."

"*Why* do you do it?"

Jedidiah cleared his throat. "Do you know what it is to be hungry, Bennie? So hungry you'll do anything — and I mean anything — to survive?"

Bennie chewed on it. Sure, he'd been hungry in the jungle, but all he'd really known was fear and fury.

"No."

"Well, *I* do. My mother, God rest her, possessed a certain *joie de vivre*, a real passion for living. We had some real adventures, she and I, but she was bad at men and bad at money. Often, there was nothing to eat and no one to provide for us, so she began to sell *herself* for our sustenance. This was the Depression, Bennie. People were desperate.

"This was our way, for a time, but as my mother grew older, her looks... well. Eventually, the burden to provide fell to me. Since my mother's reputation offered me little in the way of opportunity, I... carried *on* the family business."

Bennie just looked at him. He didn't know what to say.

"The men and women who came to me," continued Jedidiah," were often caught up in illegality of some kind or another. Bootleg liquor, numbers, bookmaking, fixed horse races. I learned from them. And then, when I'd learned enough, I exploited them and made my own ways in their world. I do what I do, Bennie, because no one should have to do the things I did or see the things I saw just to make it through the day."

"So you rob from the rich and give to the poor, is that it?"

"If only it was that simple. Even the rich need to eat,

and they're so much more willing to give to your cause when they've been sated by the very best money can buy."

"Your bond drives, your charities — "

"All of it funneled into the right places, I assure you. Do you know that some families in Jackson Ward don't even have a working toilet? Or that elderly couples are often tricked by heating oil companies into paying a higher price? These are dangerous times, Bennie. Someone has to keep the peace."

Bennie had to admit — it *was* admirable, it its own way. "Still," he said, "there is another side to it, isn't there?"

"Vice is a powerful agent, Bennie. I'm a businessman. The more I make, the better I can serve my community. Why just last month, I made enough on booze to improve the living conditions of the boy's home and add beds to Dooley Hospital. That's the one for Negroes, in case you didn't know."

Bennie was ashamed — he didn't. "You certainly don't discriminate."

"Hunger and need are universal, my good friend."

Bennie downed the rest of his drink. No argument there. But Jedidiah, as if to temper his good deeds, added, "If you must know, there *are* aspects of my off hours endeavors that I find quite distasteful. Why late last year, I became an unwilling partner in the distribution of propaganda leaflets and illicit paraphernalia that truly aren't to my liking."

Bennie raised his head and felt his shoulders stiffen.

"Illicit paraphernalia?"

"Yes. It's rather ghastly, to be honest. Imitation pinups and the like. Really, it's quite tasteless."

Bennie sat up. "Unwilling partner?"

Jedidiah sighed, a vacant look in his eyes. "Jack

arranged it, before we parted ways. Said it was a favor to someone he knew. Really, I should cease involvement."

Forcefully, Bennie said, "The person you deal with. Who is it?"

Jedidiah was taken aback. "Why? Are you interested?"

"Not in the material, just the person you deal with."

"Why?"

Bennie told him why. Jedidiah said, "Yes, that's him."

"Where can I find him?"

Jedidiah took his time. "If I tell you, what will you do?"

"That's between me and him."

Jedidiah stood up and walked over to Bennie. He smelled like fire and looked like hell. He wore a sympathetic look and said, "Killing this man won't bring your father back."

"No, but it might feel real good."

"No, it won't. I should know."

Bennie stood up and almost laughed. "You've killed one man. I've killed dozens."

"This isn't a battlefield."

"After what we went through tonight, it sure feels like one."

"Please. Don't do this."

Bennie took a step toward Jedidiah. "My old man? I used to think it was you, you know?"

"If you mean to intimidate me, Bennie, you'll find yourself at cross purposes."

They were almost face to face.

"I came home with one purpose and one purpose only," said Bennie. "To find out what happened to my father. This schlub's been giving me the slip ever since and *this* is my one shot at getting answers. I've had real reservations about you, Jedidiah. And for the last several months, I've been caught up in a shit storm that has an awful lot to do with you. After what went down tonight, I don't think you're in much of a position to bargain."

Jedidiah held Bennie's stare, never wavering. He understood. "Who am I to dissuade a man with such conviction."

"Where?"

"Down off Dock Street. South of Church Hill, east of the Row. There's a boat landing where I anchor a few of my transports and, off to the side, a few shacks. Storage mostly, but occasionally, a few of my loyal stewards will stay overnight. To guard things and keep watch. I believe the man you're looking for resides there."

Bennie grabbed the cab's keys from the tool cart and ran for the door.

Jedidiah called after him. "At least hear him out, Bennie! You don't know what he's had to do to survive!"

Chapter Forty-One

BENNIE LEFT THE cab on Cary, near Lucky Strike, and took the rest of the way on foot. He was operating solely on adrenaline fumes and forced momentum. A rush came over him. He's back in the jungle — no time for rest, just *go*.

It was almost 4AM. Bennie could hear the tobacco warehouses just behind him — they churned 24 hours — and the river to his right. He came to a turnoff and followed it to a boat landing. Moonlight off the water made it easy to see. He navigated piles of coiled rope and small boats turned on their side. He heard *something*.

He pulled his .38 and padded to his left. Just beyond a storage building, twenty feet from the water, was a line of shacks. Derelict wooden buildings with tin roofs and rickety doors.

Bennie edged his way toward them and peeked into the first one. Nobody home. Just some empty bottles and cans on a table.

The second was full of wooden planks and boards resting against the walls. Tools were strewn about a workbench and shelves.

The third was locked from the inside by a simple catch, like you might find on a screen door. There *was* give to the wood. Bennie gave it a tug and peeked inside. There's a man on a bed, facing away, snoring like a pig.

Bennie skipped back to the second shed and felt about the workbench. He found a thin metal nail and used it to slip the catch.

He pocketed the nail and stepped inside, quiet as a mouse. Moonlight through the door slats hit the bed at jagged angles. Bennie stepped closer, his gun at the ready, his eyes adjusting to the dark.

Fuck — it's him.

Bennie thought about shooting him in his sleep. Right through the head, one and done.

No, he had to know. He could hardly bring himself to speak, but he forced it out.

"Swyers."

Swyers kept snoozing. Bennie nudged him with the gun and spoke louder.

"Swyers."

Swyers' snoozing skipped a beat. His eyes blinked open as he registered a presence in the room. He turned, looked up, and started to scream like some wild animal.

Bennie stuck the gun in his face.

"Shut up."

Swyers fell to the floor and started to crawl for the door, whimpering. Bennie reached down and turned Swyers onto his back.

Swyers coughed it out with his eyes closed. "No, no, no…"

Bennie knelt over him, his gun leveled at his face. "Talk."

Swyers crossed his hands over his face. "God, please, no…"

Bennie stuck the gun into Swyers' stomach. "Gut wounds take time, Dougie. You'll bleed out real slow."

Swyers' steadied his breathing. "Ok, ok, ok…"

"You staged the burglary at Sears Roebuck that night, yes?"

Swyers started to cry. "Yes."

"Jack put you up to it?"

"Yes!"

"How?"

"He… he threatened to tell Sears about why I'd been kicked off the force."

"Underage girls?"

"Yes!"

"How did Jack know my father would show?"

"He… he… he set up this big prostie roundup that night. All the cops were in on it, but your old man, he was running Second. Jack figured he'd have to show with no one around."

Bennie leaned in close and said it slow. "*Why*?"

"Your old man, he found out what Jack was up to. Dipping into the black market and all. He threatened to go to The Cane with it. Oh Jesus, Bennie, I didn't know."

Bennie dug the gun further into Swyers' gut. "But you lured him there, you had to know something."

"Jack just said he needed to *talk* with your old man, I swear. Said it was top secret, that the department had been compromised, that your old man would know what to do. Christ, Bennie, your old man *got* me that job. He gave me a second chance!"

Swyers wrapped his hands around the gun and forced it up, against his forehead.

"Do it, Bennie, just do it! Put me out now, just do it!"

Swyers closed his eyes, sobbing, waiting for it. His jaw clenched, *wanting* it...

Bennie felt his entire body fight the urge to pull the trigger. It was as if his entire life had led to this very moment and let him down. Bennie blinked, just to be sure.

He's not Jack and he's not a Jap.

Bennie went slack. All the rage and anger he'd been holding onto for so long just up and evaporated. He forced Swyers' hands off the gun and pulled it back. He stood up and stumbled into the wall. Goddamn, he was lightheaded.

Swyers looked up, incredulous. "What... what are you doing?"

Bennie holstered his gun and said, "Jack's dead."

"What?"

"Tonight, at the Jefferson. He started a fire and tried to kill someone."

"He's really dead?"

"Yes. And I'm not going to kill you, Dougie. I know you didn't mean for my father to die. You don't have to hide anymore." Bennie looked around the room. It was a rat's nest — scraps of food, dirt and grime, a leaky roof. Only Japs deserve worse, he thought, starting for the door, his hands on the wall for support.

Swyers said, "I'm sorry, Bennie."

Bennie said, "I know," and stepped into the night. A cool breeze off the water gave him pause. He closed his eyes and just stood there, letting it wash over him. It reminded him of her — her breath against his neck, whispering sweet things.

He forced himself to move, excited by the real thing, and started for the cab.

CHAPTER FORTY-TWO

BENNIE LEFT THE Annex and started for home on foot. His legs were heavy and he walked slow. It was noon on Sunday, just twelve hours since the Jefferson fire. He thought of the death toll and winced. Officially, there were seven dead — a state senator from Front Royal, four women, an elderly man, and a sailor.

Of course, *un*officially....

Bennie dug his hands into his coat pockets and forced life into his legs. The last time he felt this exhausted, he was on Guadalcanal. He'd spent the morning in interrogation room #2, telling all to The Cane. From seeing him on the steps of The Commonwealth Club with Jedidiah to finding Niles out Route 5. From his visit with Mills to his timely arrival at the Jefferson. All of it, the facts laid bare.

All but one.

"Who killed him?" asked The Cane, fighting tears.

"I did," said Bennie. "It was self-defense, him or me."

"But Jedidiah — "

"Was just a bystander. You put him there, remember?"

319

The Cane sank into his chair, defeated by the weight of it — losing his only son.

"I've been in over my head since your father was killed," he said.

"Murdered."

"Yes, of course… murdered."

Bennie had so many questions. "You really had *no* idea?"

"Not about your father, no. That should tell you something. But Jack, what he was — "

"You knew?"

"Of course I knew. I just refused to believe it. As a boy, he was always different. When he came of age, I tried to change him. This," he said, raising his hands, as if to blame the whole of the department, "I forced it on him. Wouldn't give him a choice. When he resisted, I…" He fingered his cane, lingering on it. "Tried other methods. I had no idea he'd do such things."

"What'll you do with everything I've told you?"

"Resign, of course. City Hall wants my head and they'll surely have it over this. Unless…"

"What?"

"Does anyone really have to know, Bennie? About *him*, I mean?"

Bennie grew irate. "My father deserves justice! Niles deserves justice! Christ, his family. The Apollo, all of it — you can't be serious?"

"Yes, yes, I know, but the *department*. We need to be strong, Bennie, we need to unify if we're going to come out of this."

"I came here voluntarily, told you everything. If you think you're gonna wash over this — "

"Yes, Bennie, I know, but listen — "

Bennie stood up. "You do right by this, Chief, or I walk. The papers will get all of it and you'll fry. Jack's name, what he did — I'll drag him so deep through the mud it'll take years to get clean."

"Please, son, just give me some time!"

"I'm *not* your son. Your son is *dead*. And if you don't expose him for his crimes, I will! And I'll turn this city against you and watch you burn."

Bennie left the Annex without another word, stepping into the day. Bright sunshine, warmer temps. Spring, on the way.

He was almost home when he heard the sound of kids cheering. To the left aways, north of Broad, somewhere close. He followed the sound past a few houses and came to a clearing beyond them where some boys and girls were playing baseball. Maybe two dozen kids of various ages, white *and* Negro. He watched them for a time, relishing their joy, remembering his own long days playing in lots just like this one.

One of the girls caught sight of Bennie. He recognized her from the neighborhood.

"Hey, it's the police!" she screamed.

The kids started to scatter. Bennie got it — they were probably tangled up in the youth gangs causing trouble around town.

Bennie held up his badge and said, "Hold it! Get back here or I'll have a paddy wagon on the way. Juvie bulls don't like to work on Sunday. They can be especially rough on their day off."

The kids froze. Bennie walked into the lot and motioned for them to return. Slowly, they began to form a circle around him. They were a rough and tumble bunch

— ragged faces, hand-me-down threads. They were the untethered youth, abandoned by the war.

One of the boys said, "Are you gonna haul us in?"

"That depends," said Bennie.

"On what?" said an older girl.

"On whether or not you let me play."

The kids exchanged puzzled looks.

"With us?" said a Negro girl.

"Yes."

Shrugs and smirks circled the group. "Fine by us," said one of the boys. He was drinking from a jar. He had a black eye and was missing a few teeth.

Bennie pointed at the jar and said, "What is that?"

The boy blanched, weighing an answer.

"Lemonade?" he said.

Bennie made the gimme sign and the boy forked it over. The kids looked worried. Bennie raised the jar to his lips and drank. It wasn't lemonade. He took a long pull, savoring it. The kids went wide-eyed. *Get a load of this whack-o!*

Bennie wiped his mouth with the back of his hand and returned the jar to Missing Teeth.

"Who's pitching?"

The Negro girl raised her hand. "I am."

"Who's up?"

Missing Teeth handed Bennie a bat and said, "You are."

A comforting rush came over Bennie as he held the bat. It reminded him of his rifle.

The kids scattered about the lot, taking up positions. Bennie took up at the plate — an overturned street sign, ripped from its post — and found his stance. He felt wooden and awkward. The sun hit his face and he allowed himself a smile.

The Negro girl readied her pitch. She gave Bennie a devious look and set her feet. Bennie was intrigued — a curveball, maybe, something to fool him. He tipped his bat across the sign and got ready.

A spark ran up his spine and he saw things that weren't there. The old man, watching from the wings. Skipper at short, ready to toss him out. He blinked and they were gone. He nodded at the Negro girl.

She stepped out, wound up, and let fly the ball.